MARTHA SPEAKS

CANINE COMICS

W9-AMW-340

Adaptation by Jamie White
Based on TV series teleplays written by
Peter K. Hirsch
Ron Holsey
Maria Finn
Raye Lankford
Ken Scarborough
Matt Steinglass

Based on characters created by Susan Meddaugh

Houghton Mifflin Harcourt
Boston • New York

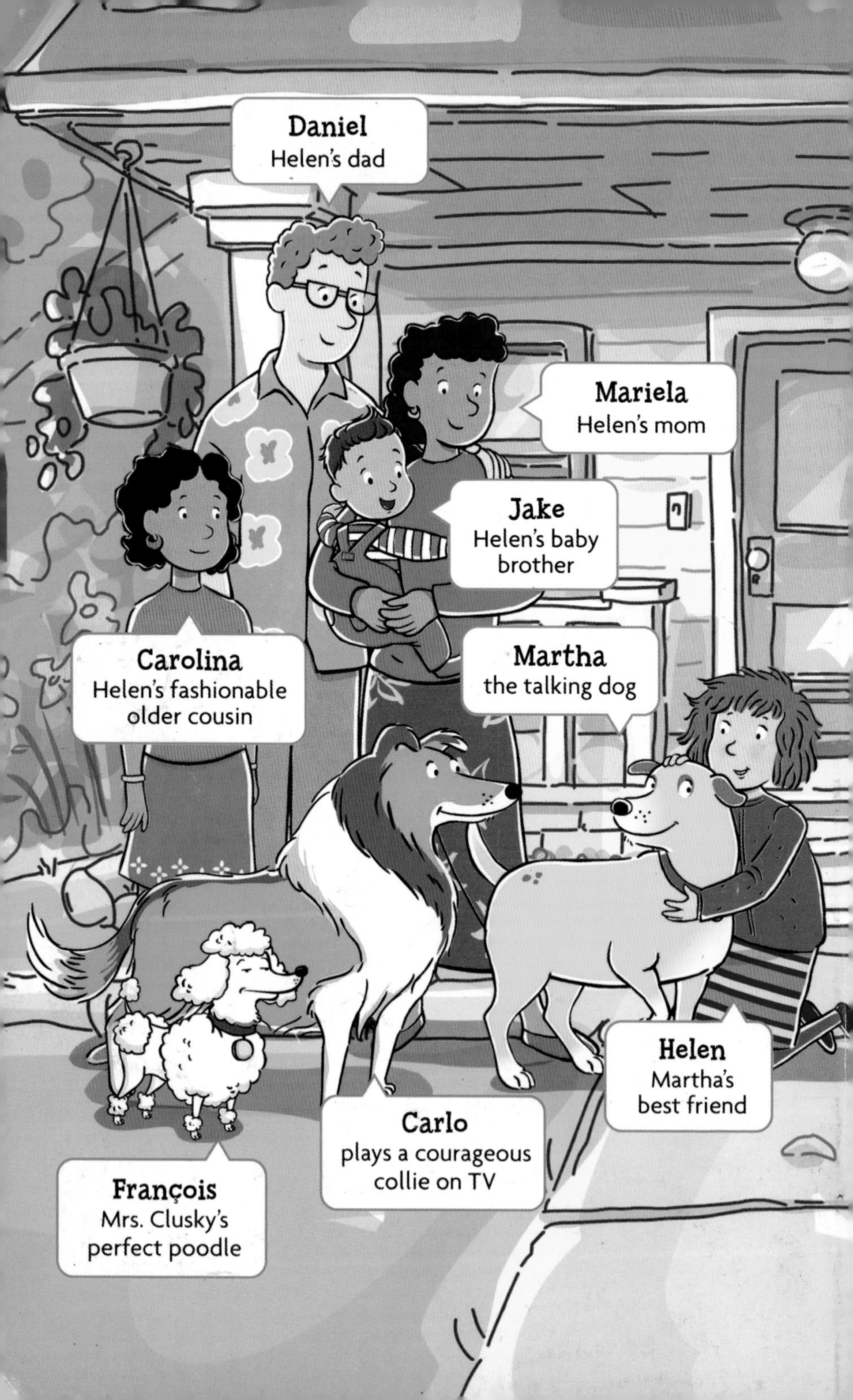

Daniel
Helen's dad
Mariela
Helen's mom
Jake
Helen's baby brother
Carolina
Helen's fashionable older cousin
Martha
the talking dog
Helen
Martha's best friend
Carlo
plays a courageous collie on TV
François
Mrs. Clusky's perfect poodle

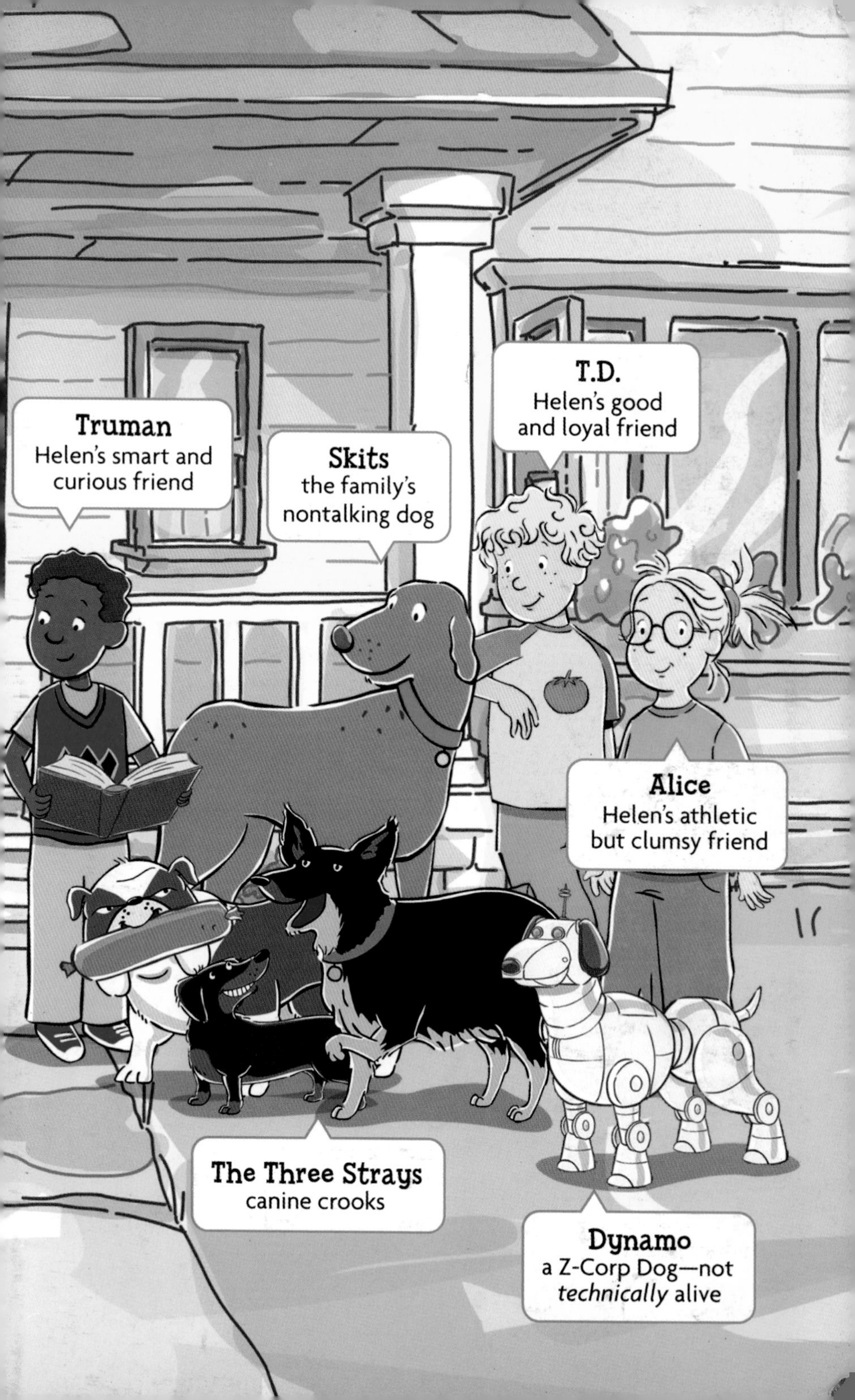
Truman
Helen's smart and curious friend
Skits
the family's nontalking dog
T.D.
Helen's good and loyal friend
Alice
Helen's athletic but clumsy friend
The Three Strays
canine crooks
Dynamo
a Z-Corp Dog—not *technically* alive

For information about permission to reproduce selections from this book,
write to Permissions, Houghton Mifflin Harcourt Publishing Company,
215 Park Avenue South, New York, New York 10003.

ISBN: 978-0-547-86784-7 POB
ISBN: 978-0-544-22056-0 PA

Cover design by Rachel Newborn
Book design by Bill Smith Studio

www.hmhbooks.com
www.marthathetalkingdog.com

Manufactured in China
SCP 10 9 8 7 6 5 4 3 2 1
4500456549

SIX UNBELIEVABLE COMICS!

YIKES!

YUM!

VROOM!

WOOF!

WOW!

GRRR...

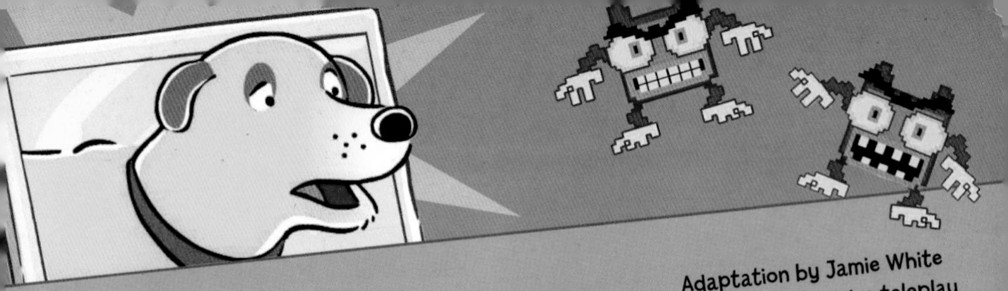

1 Download Dog

Adaptation by Jamie White
Based on a TV series teleplay
written by Ken Scarborough

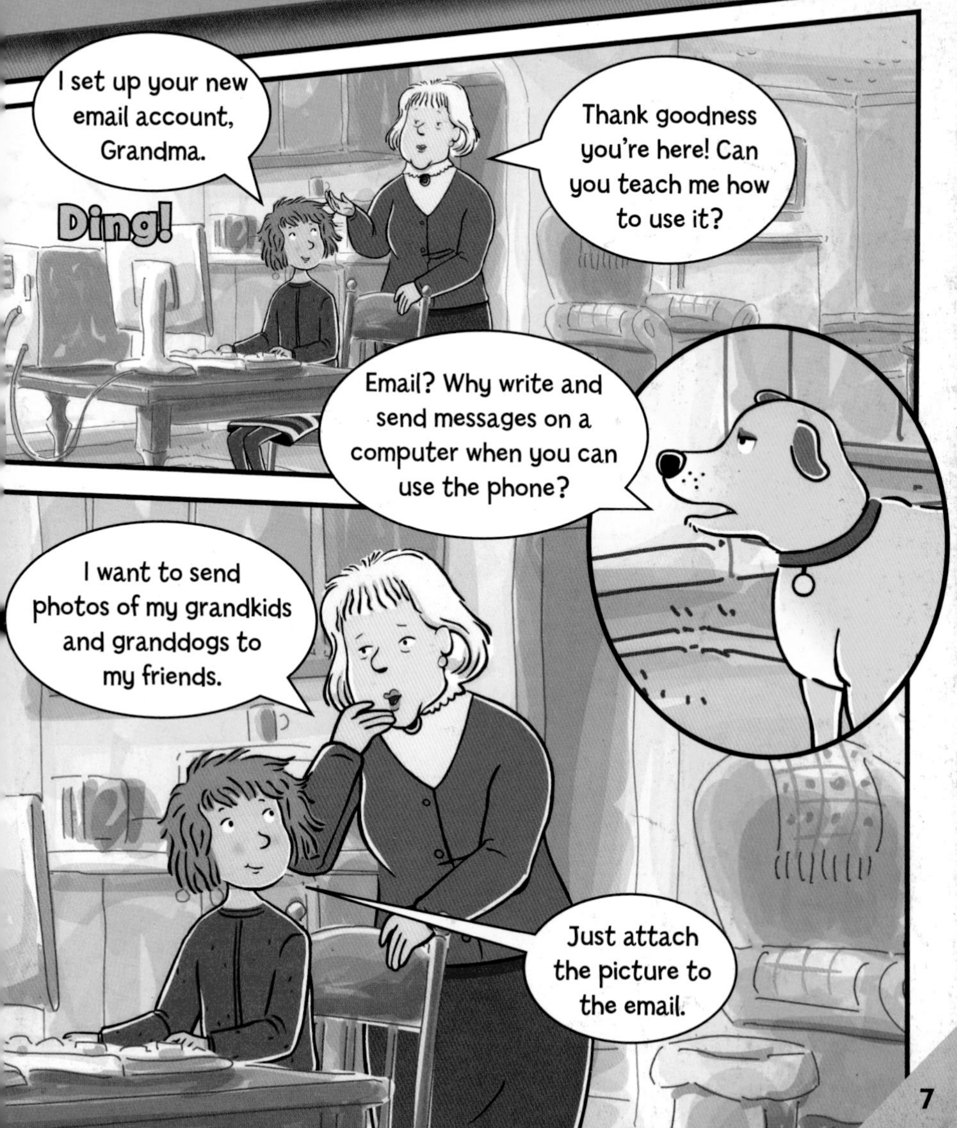
I set up your new email account, Grandma.
Thank goodness you're here! Can you teach me how to use it?
Ding!
Email? Why write and send messages on a computer when you can use the phone?
I want to send photos of my grandkids and granddogs to my friends.
Just attach the picture to the email.

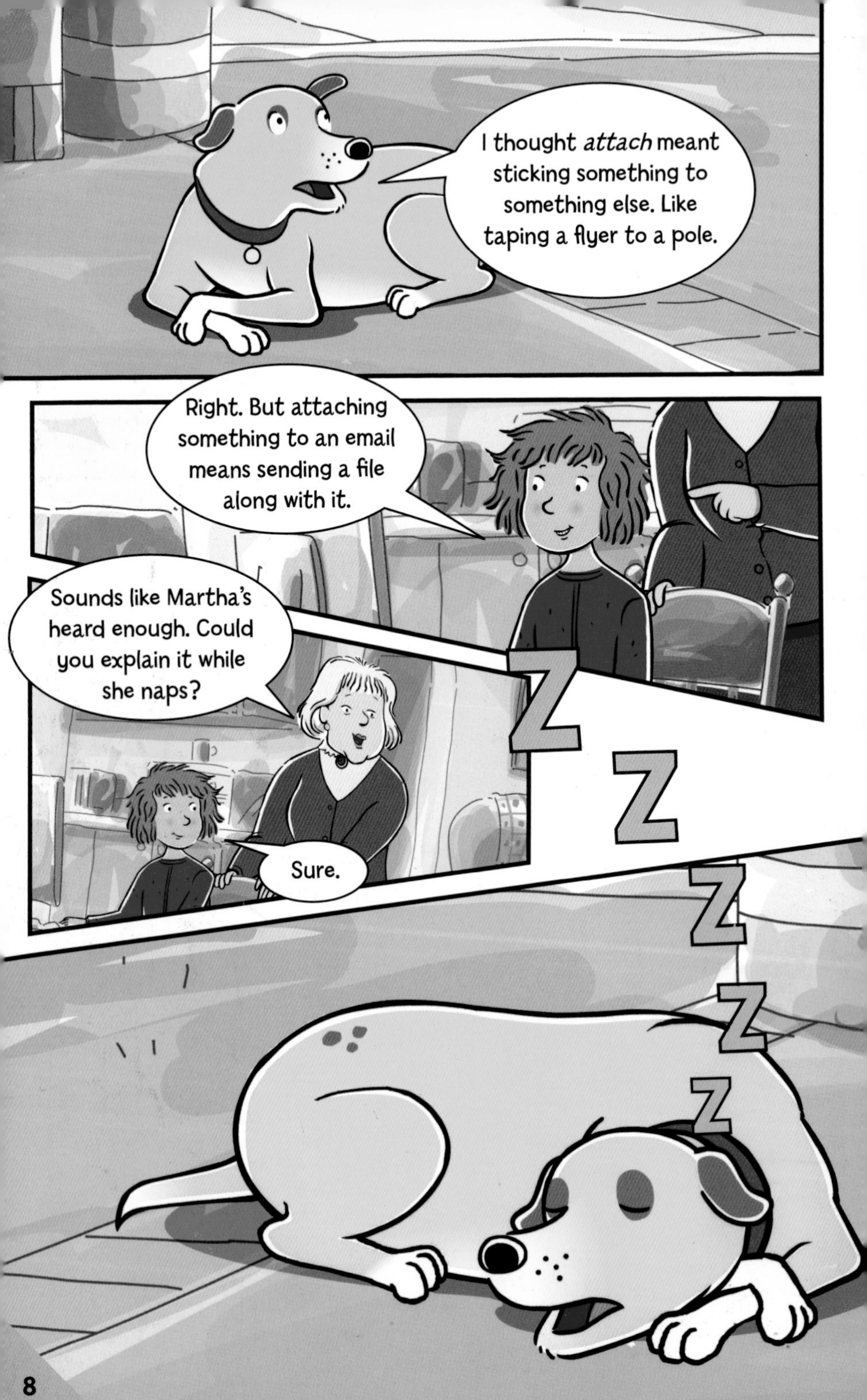

I thought *attach* meant sticking something to something else. Like taping a flyer to a pole.
Right. But attaching something to an email means sending a file along with it.
Sounds like Martha's heard enough. Could you explain it while she naps?
Sure.
Z
Z
Z
Z
Z

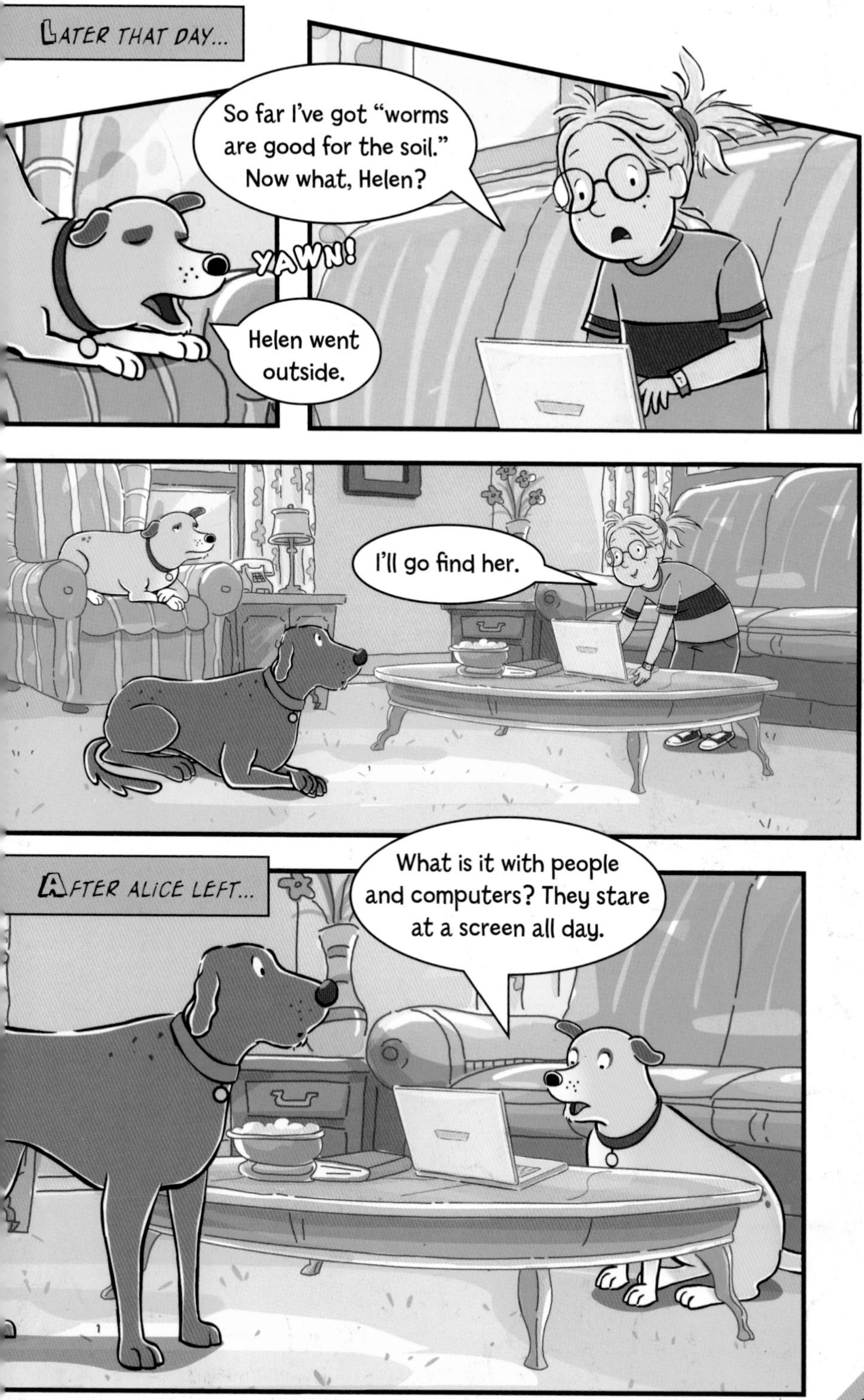
LATER THAT DAY...
So far I've got "worms are good for the soil." Now what, Helen?
YAWN!
Helen went outside.
I'll go find her.
AFTER ALICE LEFT...
What is it with people and computers? They stare at a screen all day.

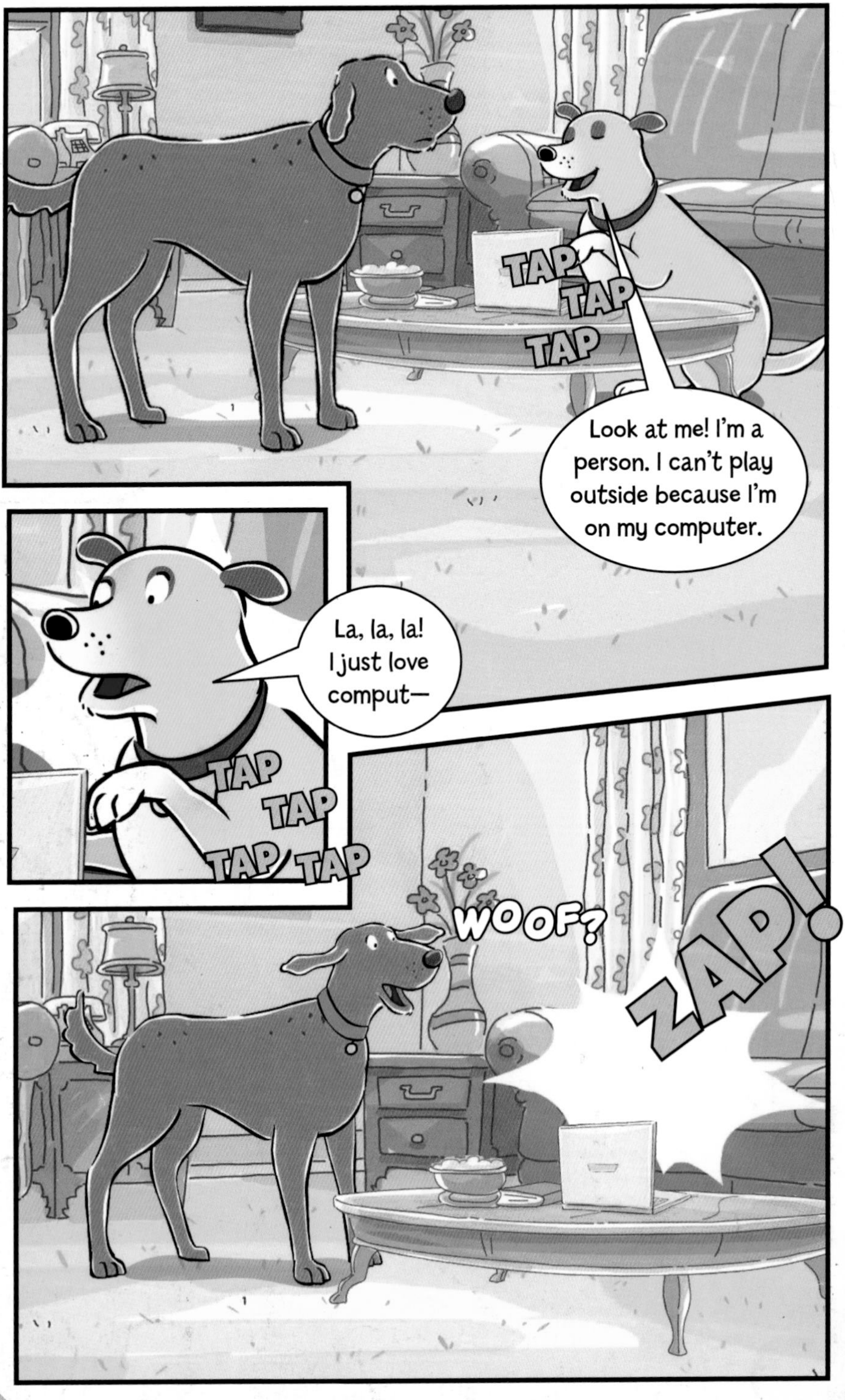
TAP TAP TAP
Look at me! I'm a person. I can't play outside because I'm on my computer.
La, la, la! I just love comput—
TAP TAP TAP TAP
WOOF?
ZAP!

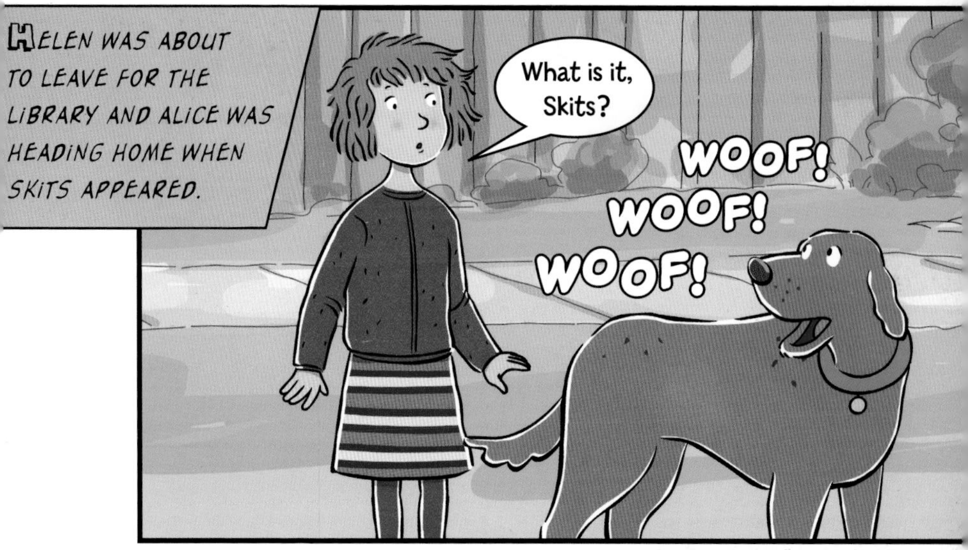
HELEN WAS ABOUT TO LEAVE FOR THE LIBRARY AND ALICE WAS HEADING HOME WHEN SKITS APPEARED.
What is it, Skits?
WOOF!
WOOF!
WOOF!

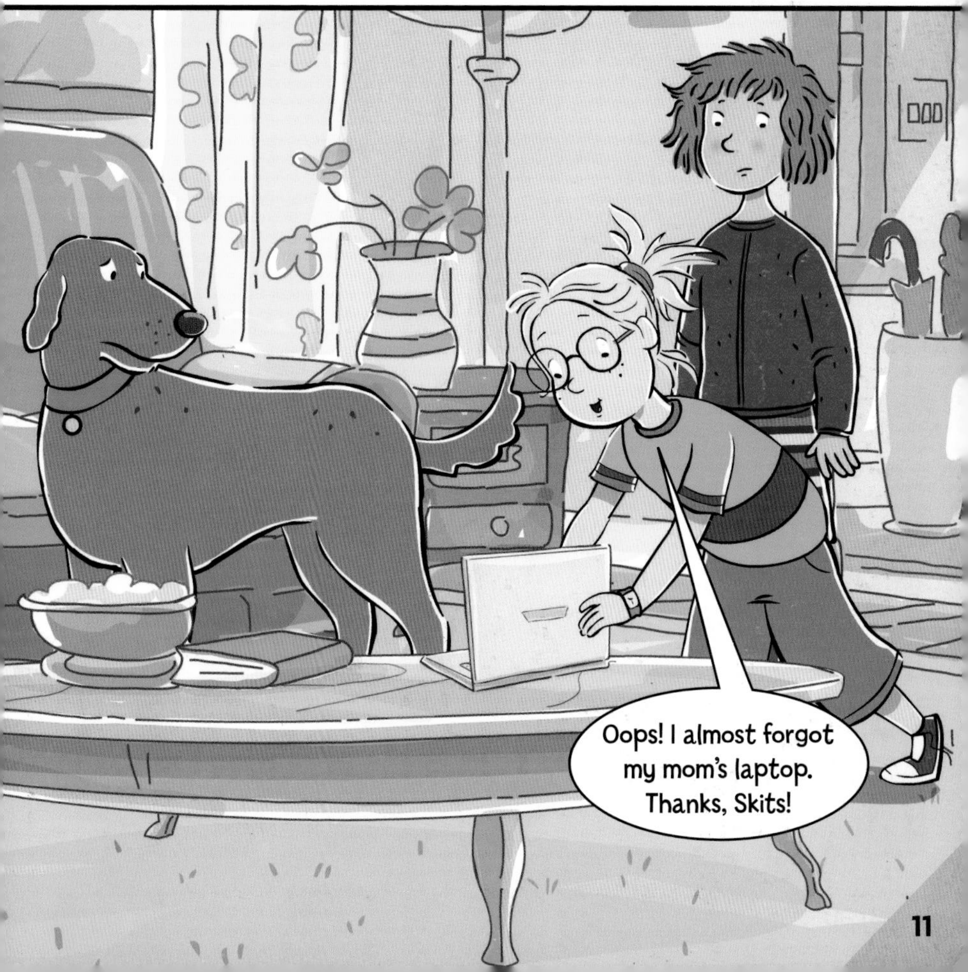
Oops! I almost forgot my mom's laptop. Thanks, Skits!

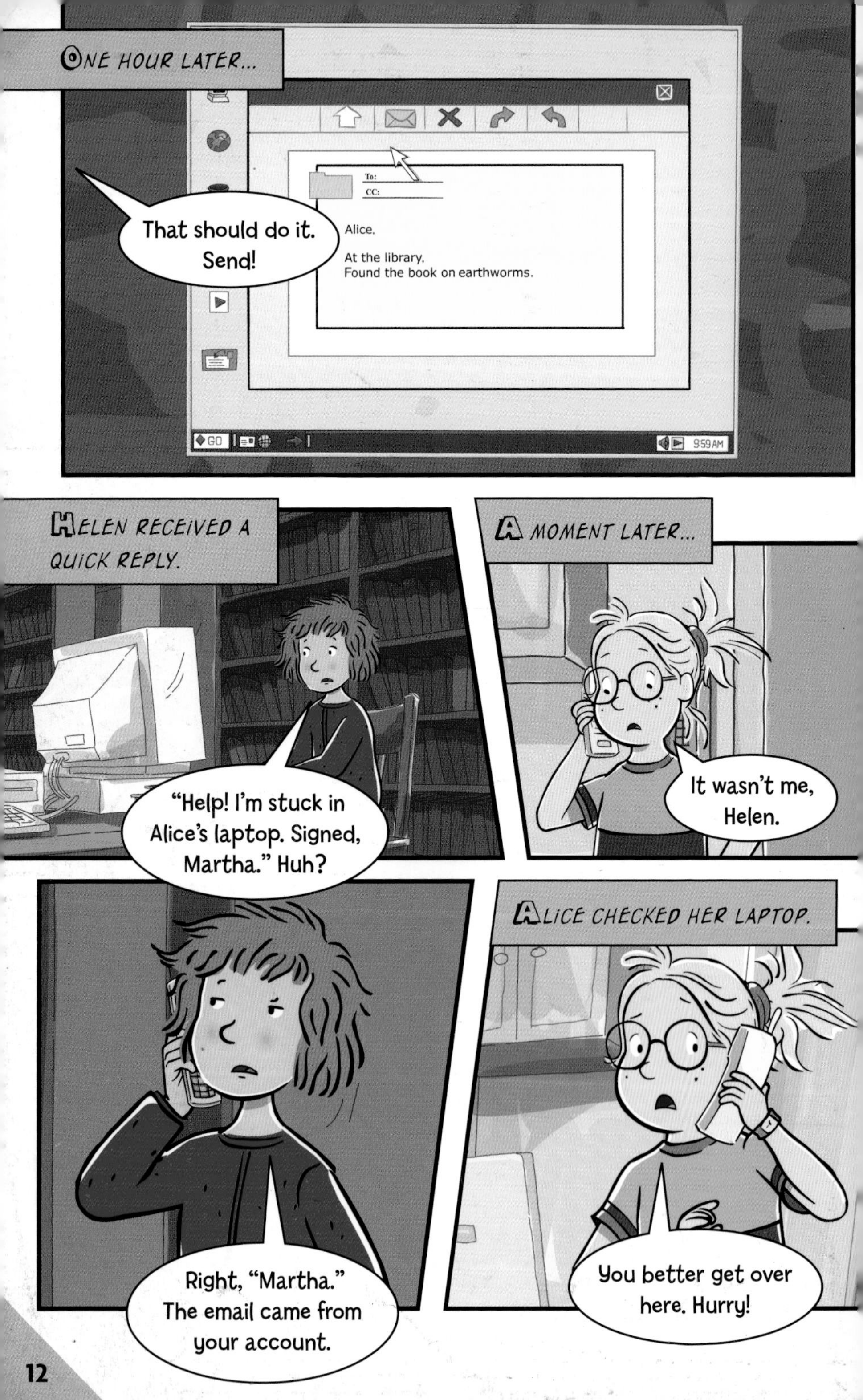
ONE HOUR LATER...
That should do it. Send!
To:
CC:
Alice,
At the library.
Found the book on earthworms.
GO
9:59 AM
HELEN RECEIVED A QUICK REPLY.
"Help! I'm stuck in Alice's laptop. Signed, Martha." Huh?
A MOMENT LATER...
It wasn't me, Helen.
Right, "Martha." The email came from your account.
ALICE CHECKED HER LAPTOP.
You better get over here. Hurry!

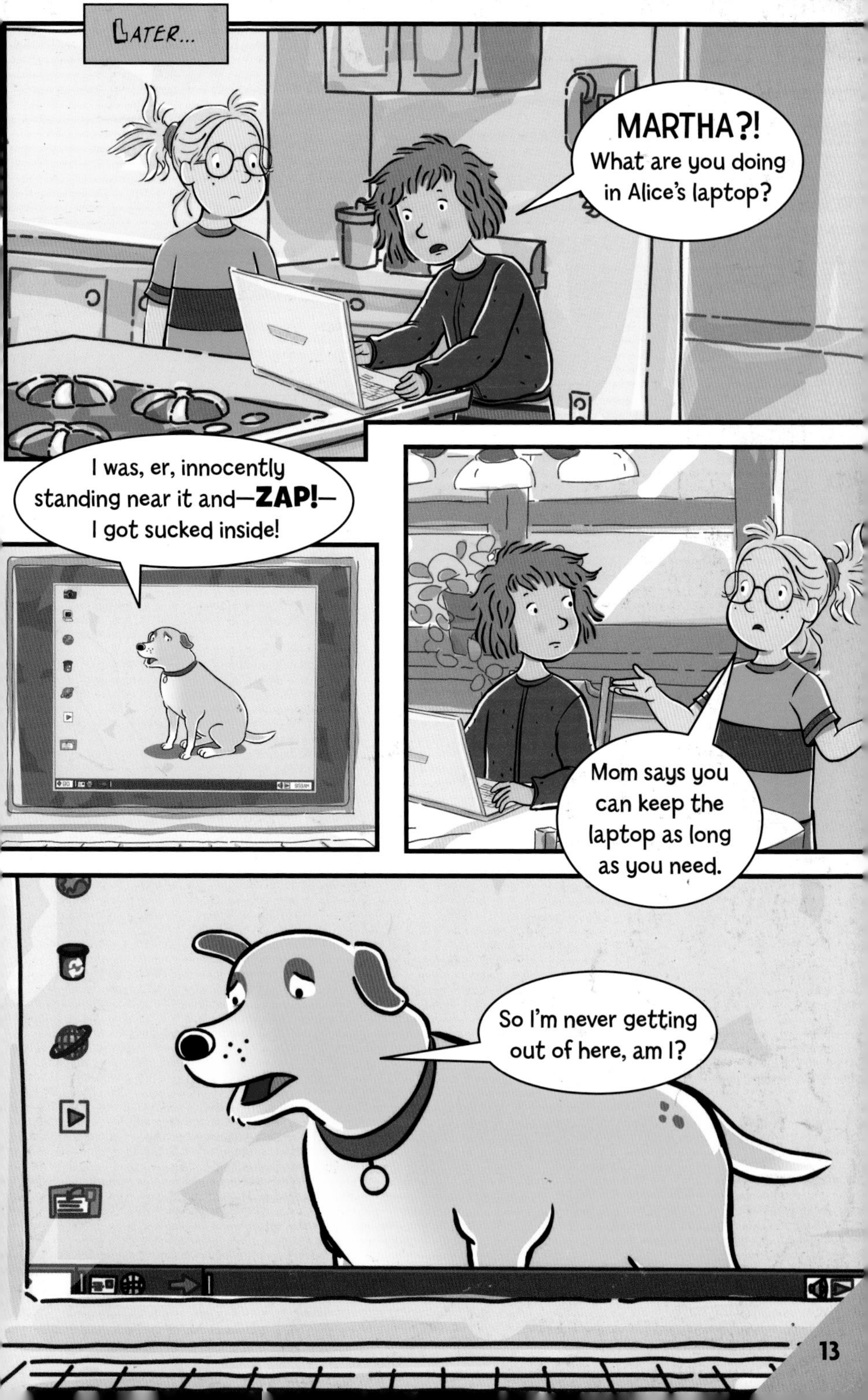
LATER...
MARTHA?! What are you doing in Alice's laptop?
I was, er, innocently standing near it and—ZAP!—I got sucked inside!
Mom says you can keep the laptop as long as you need.
So I'm never getting out of here, am I?

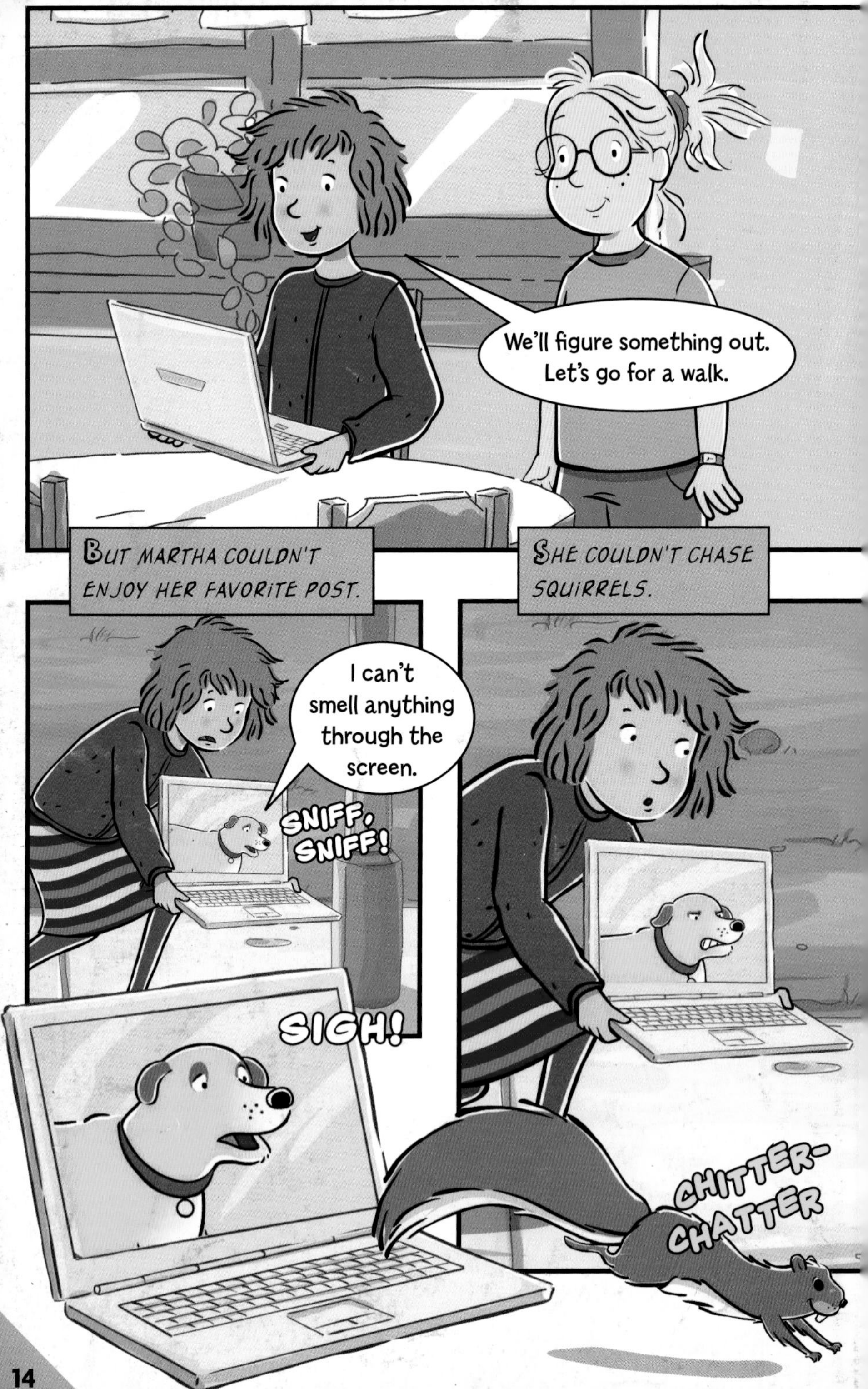
We'll figure something out. Let's go for a walk.
BUT MARTHA COULDN'T ENJOY HER FAVORITE POST.
I can't smell anything through the screen.
SNIFF, SNIFF!
SIGH!
SHE COULDN'T CHASE SQUIRRELS.
CHITTER-CHATTER

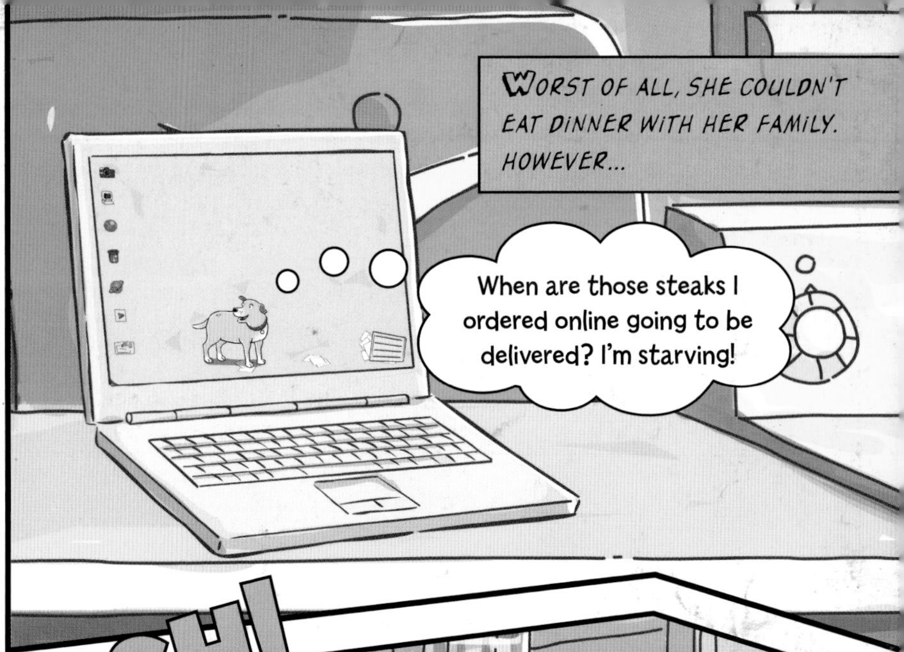
WORST OF ALL, SHE COULDN'T EAT DINNER WITH HER FAMILY. HOWEVER...
When are those steaks I ordered online going to be delivered? I'm starving!

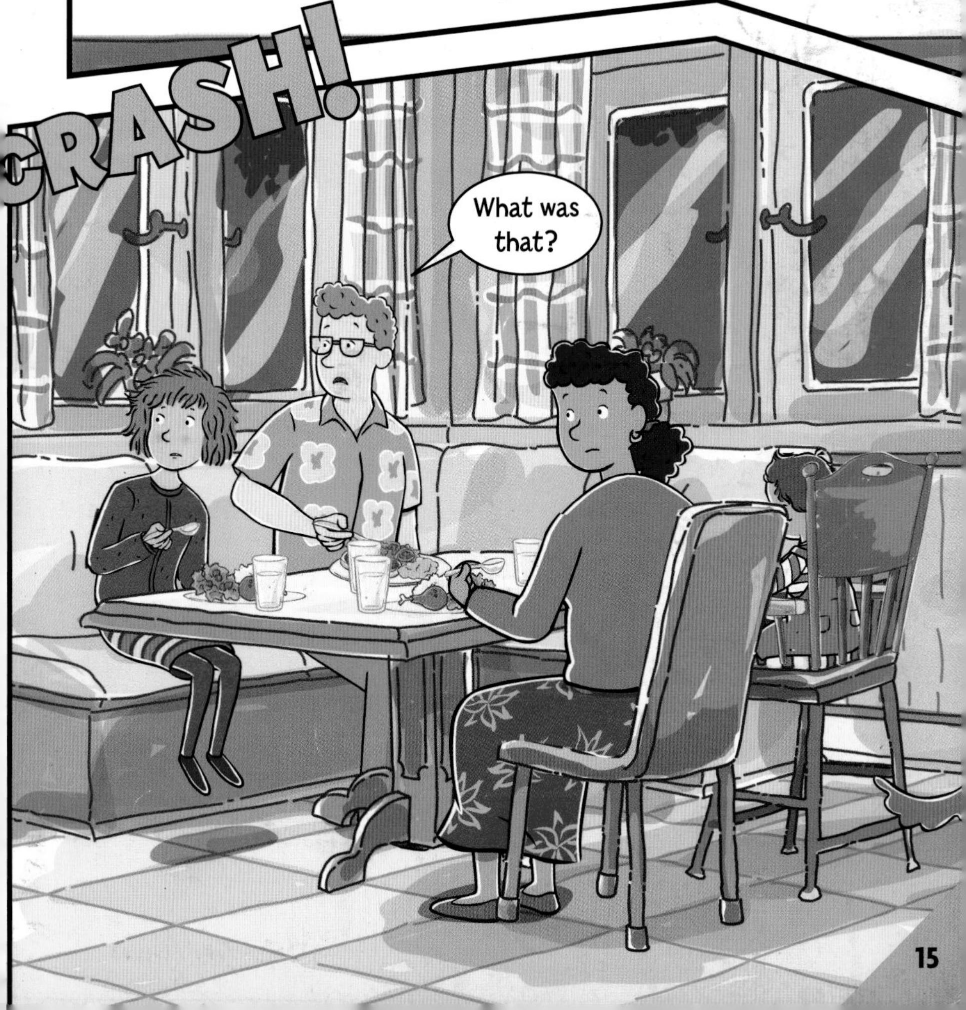
CRASH!
What was that?

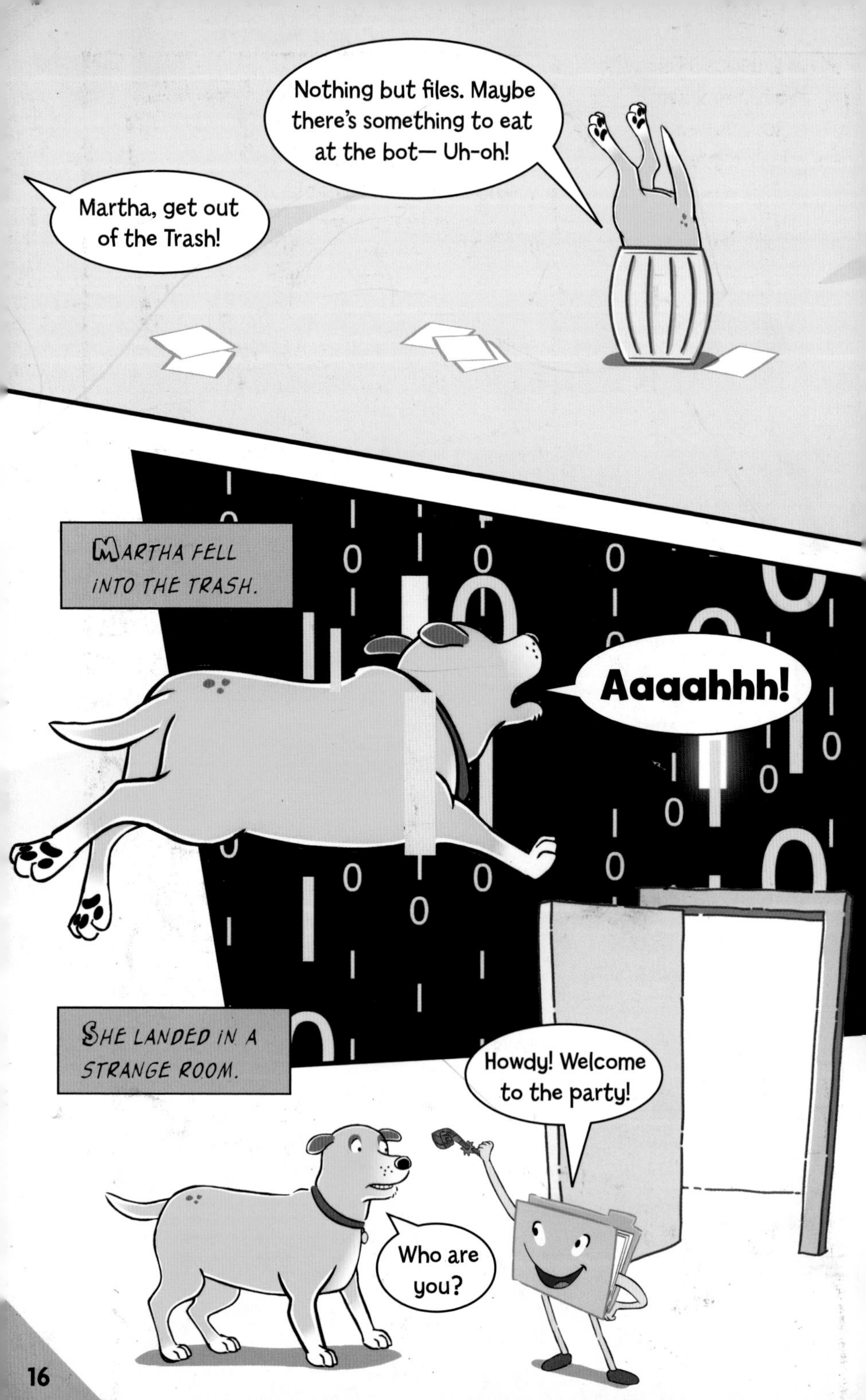
Martha, get out of the Trash!
Nothing but files. Maybe there's something to eat at the bot— Uh-oh!
MARTHA FELL INTO THE TRASH.
Aaaahhh!
SHE LANDED IN A STRANGE ROOM.
Howdy! Welcome to the party!
Who are you?

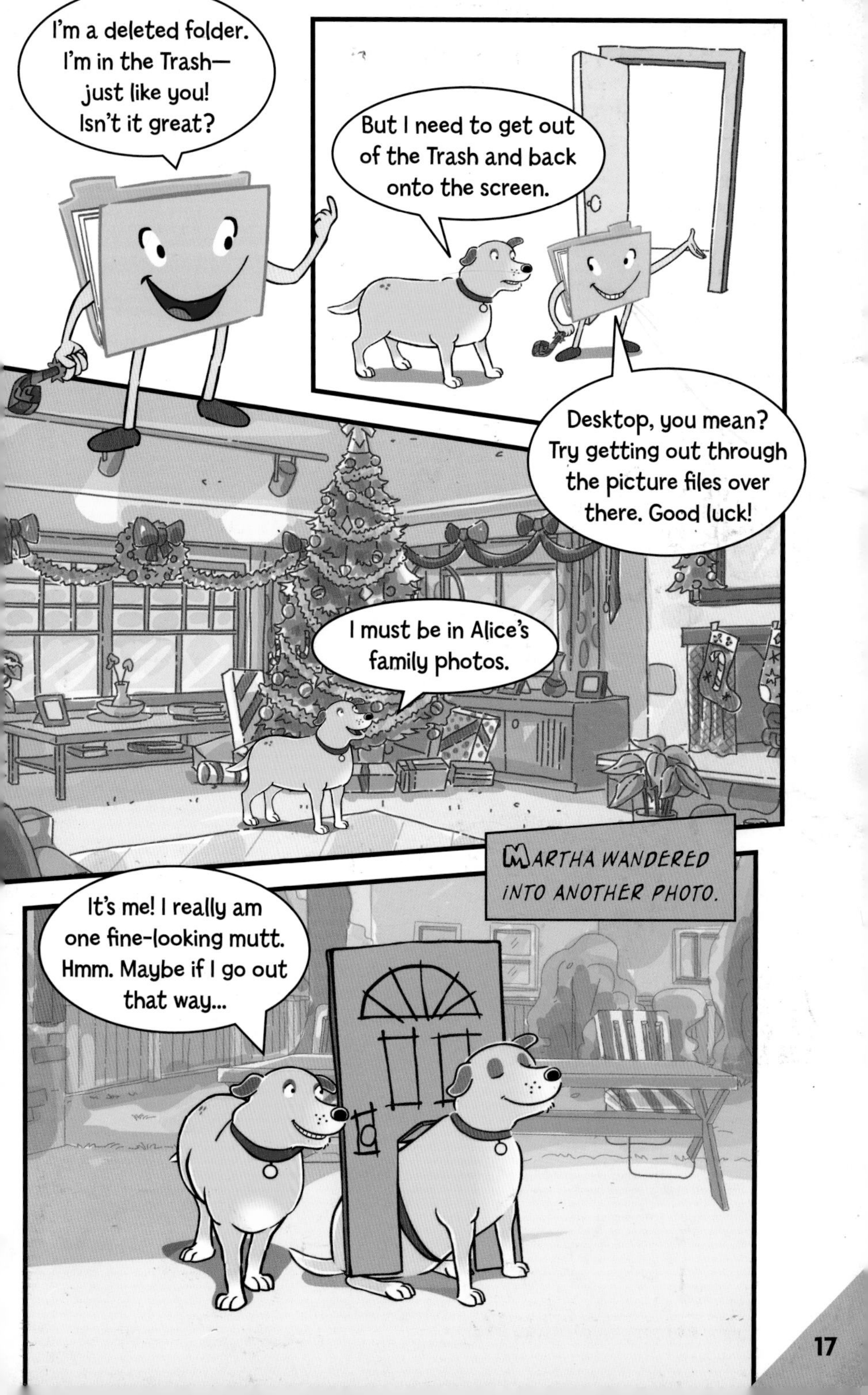
I'm a deleted folder. I'm in the Trash—just like you! Isn't it great?
But I need to get out of the Trash and back onto the screen.
Desktop, you mean? Try getting out through the picture files over there. Good luck!
I must be in Alice's family photos.
MARTHA WANDERED INTO ANOTHER PHOTO.
It's me! I really am one fine-looking mutt. Hmm. Maybe if I go out that way...

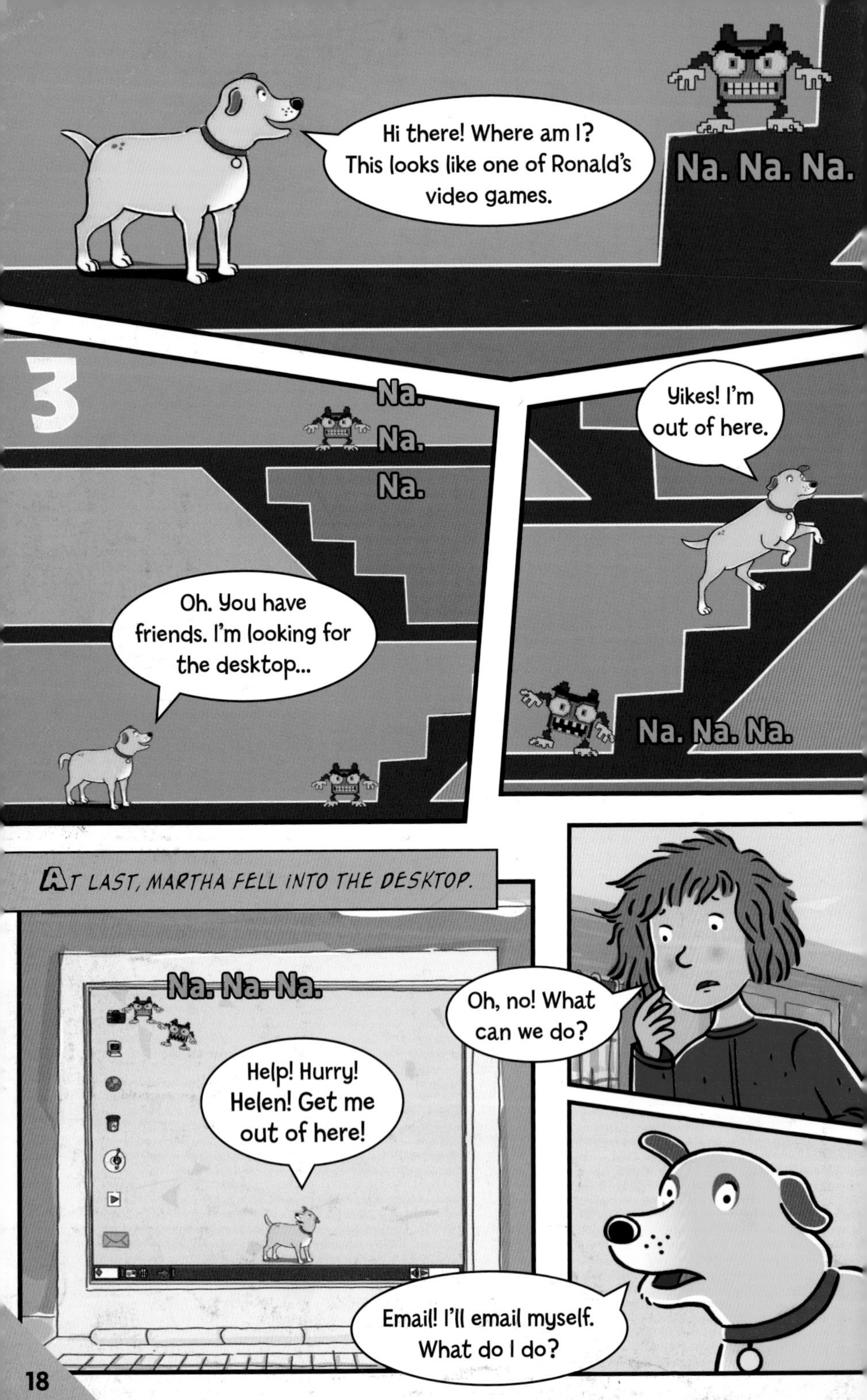
Hi there! Where am I? This looks like one of Ronald's video games.
Na. Na. Na.
3
Na.
Na.
Na.
Oh. You have friends. I'm looking for the desktop...
Yikes! I'm out of here.
Na. Na. Na.
AT LAST, MARTHA FELL INTO THE DESKTOP.
Na. Na. Na.
Help! Hurry! Helen! Get me out of here!
Oh, no! What can we do?
Email! I'll email myself. What do I do?

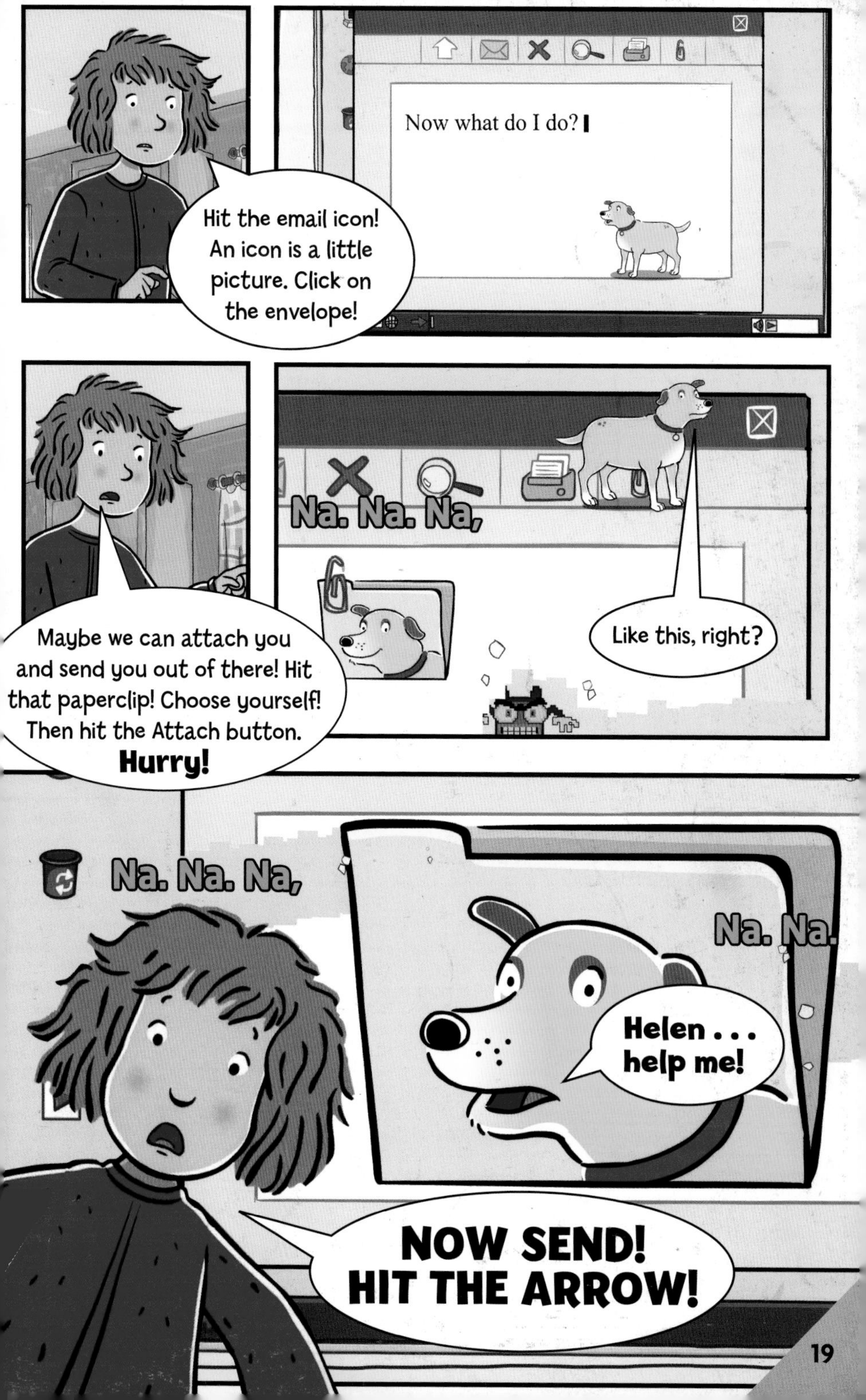

Now what do I do?
Hit the email icon! An icon is a little picture. Click on the envelope!
Na. Na. Na,
Maybe we can attach you and send you out of there! Hit that paperclip! Choose yourself! Then hit the Attach button. **Hurry!**
Like this, right?
Na. Na. Na,
Na. Na.
Helen . . . help me!
NOW SEND! HIT THE ARROW!

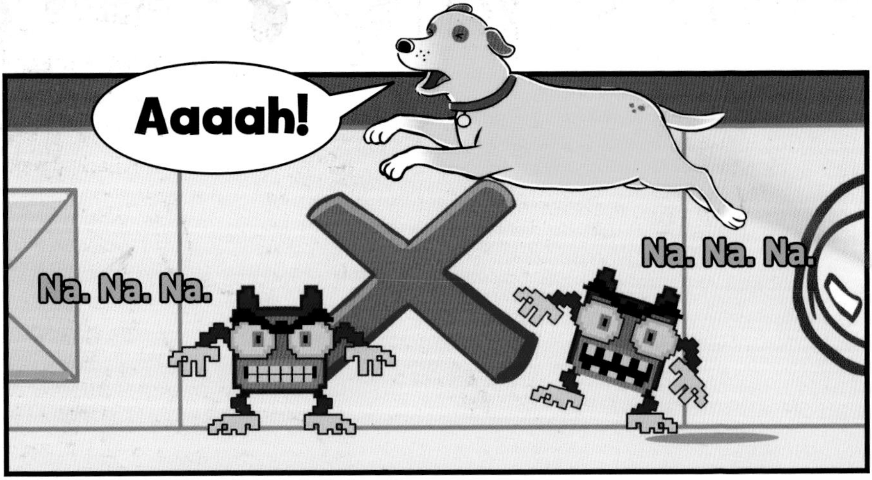
Aaaah!
Na. Na. Na.
Na. Na. Na.

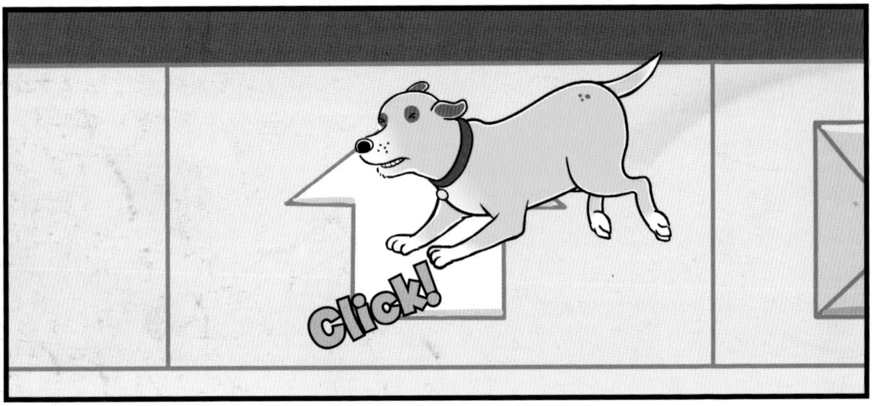
Click!

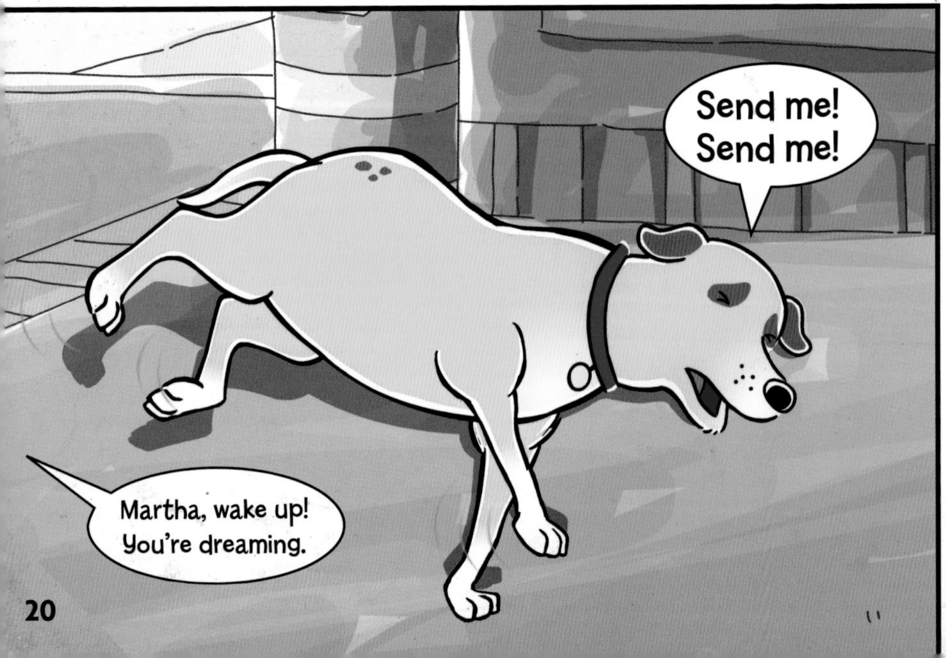
Send me!
Send me!
Martha, wake up!
You're dreaming.

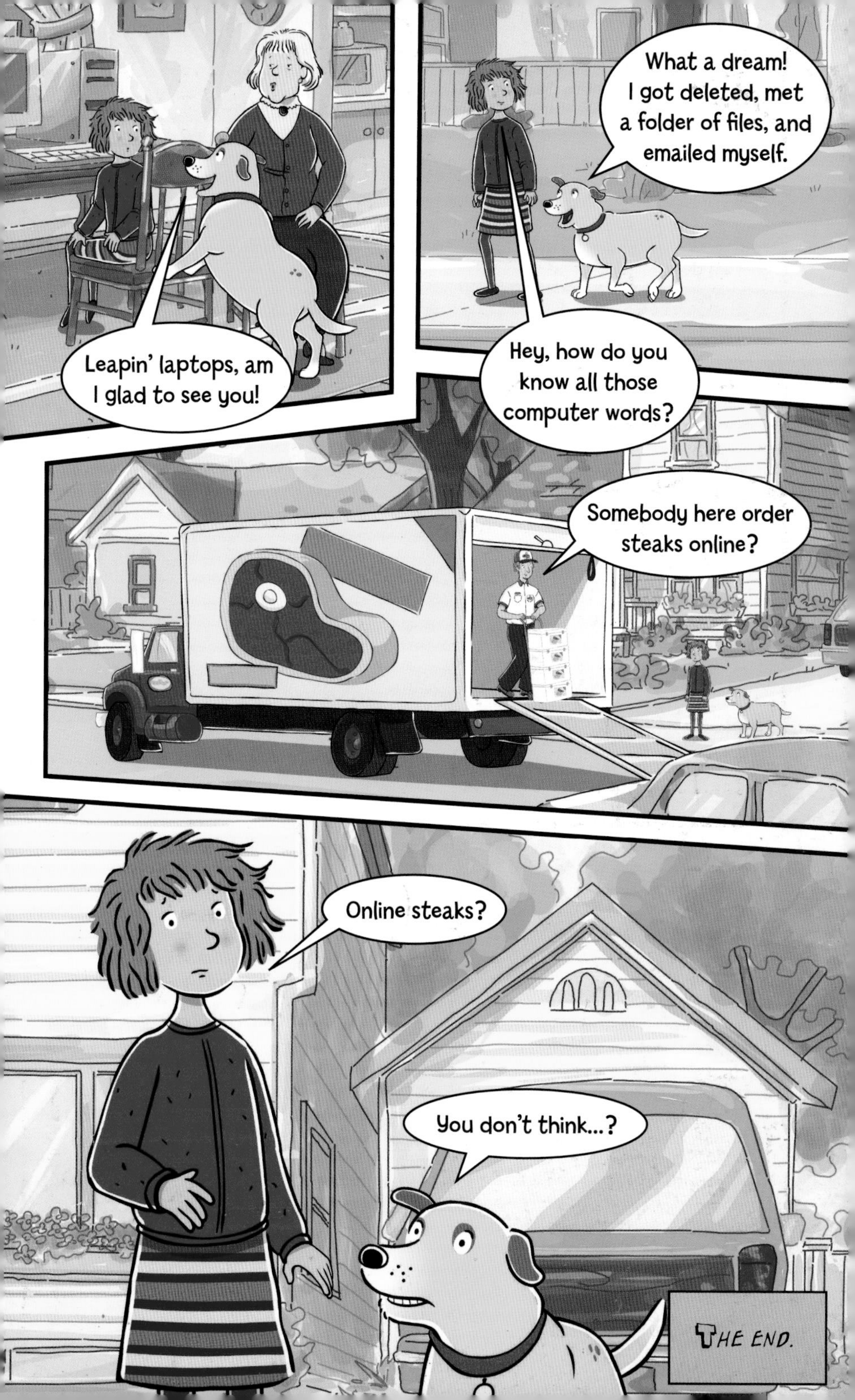
Leapin' laptops, am I glad to see you!
What a dream! I got deleted, met a folder of files, and emailed myself.
Hey, how do you know all those computer words?
Somebody here order steaks online?
Online steaks?
You don't think...?
THE END.

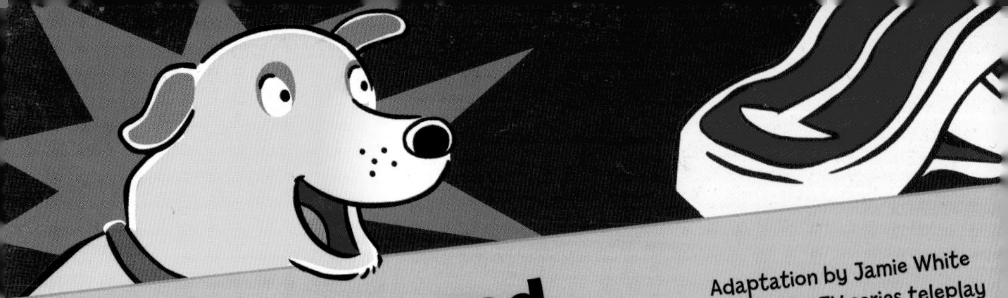

2 Martha and the Meat Heist

Adaptation by Jamie White
Based on a TV series teleplay
written by Peter K. Hirsch

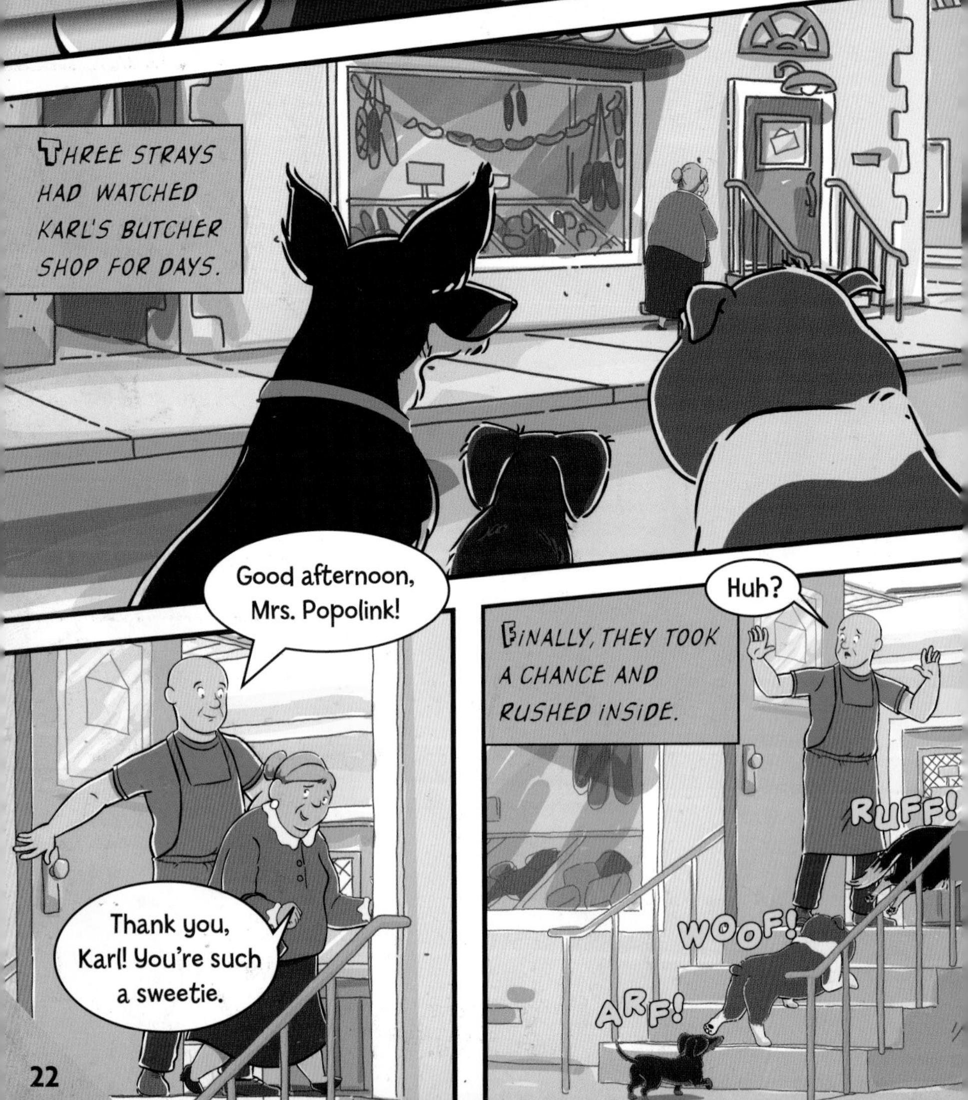

THREE STRAYS HAD WATCHED KARL'S BUTCHER SHOP FOR DAYS.
Good afternoon, Mrs. Popolink!
Thank you, Karl! You're such a sweetie.
FINALLY, THEY TOOK A CHANCE AND RUSHED INSIDE.
Huh?
RUFF!
WOOF!
ARF!

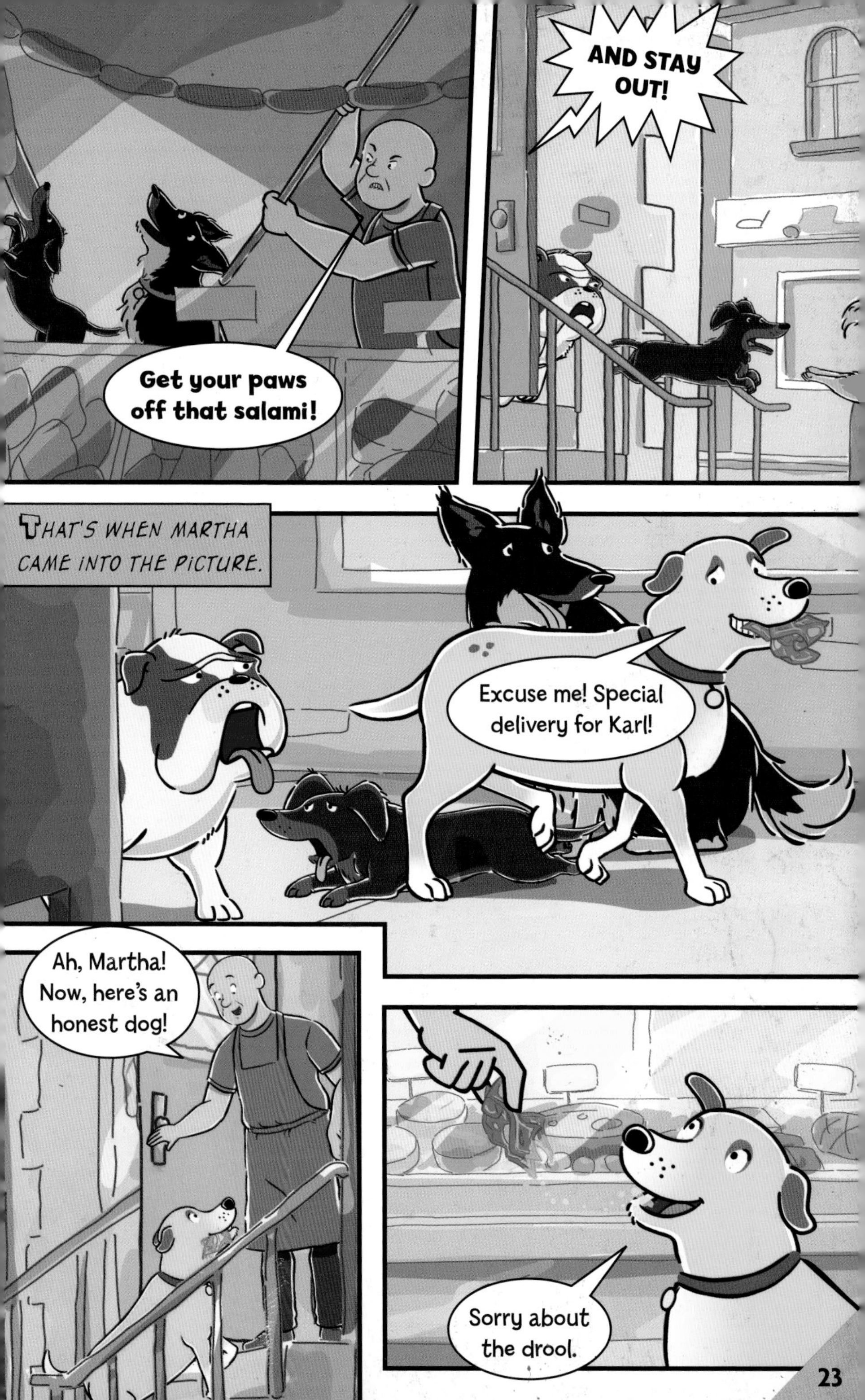

Get your paws off that salami!
AND STAY OUT!
THAT'S WHEN MARTHA CAME INTO THE PICTURE.
Excuse me! Special delivery for Karl!
Ah, Martha! Now, here's an honest dog!
Sorry about the drool.

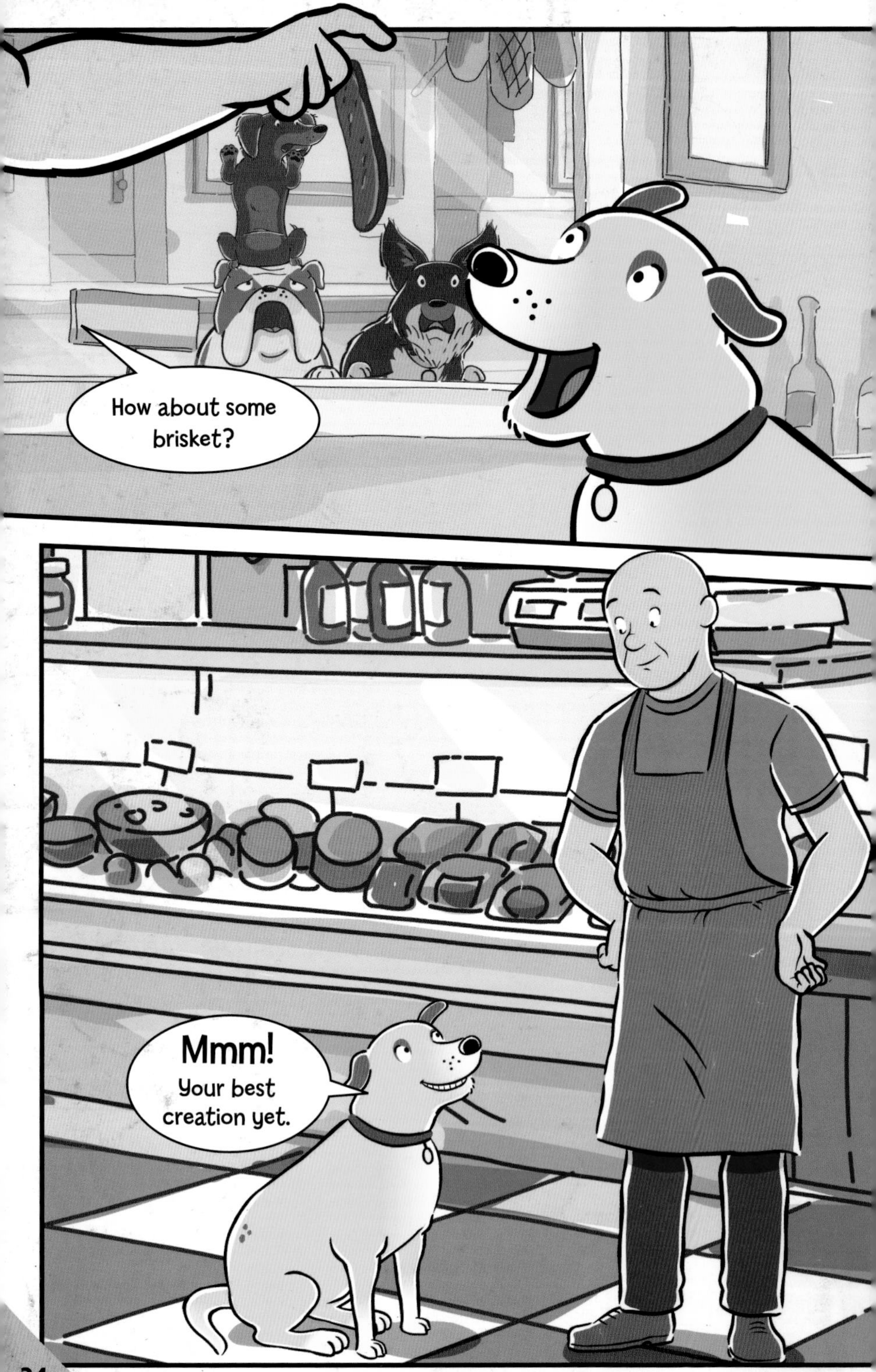
How about some brisket?
Mmm! Your best creation yet.

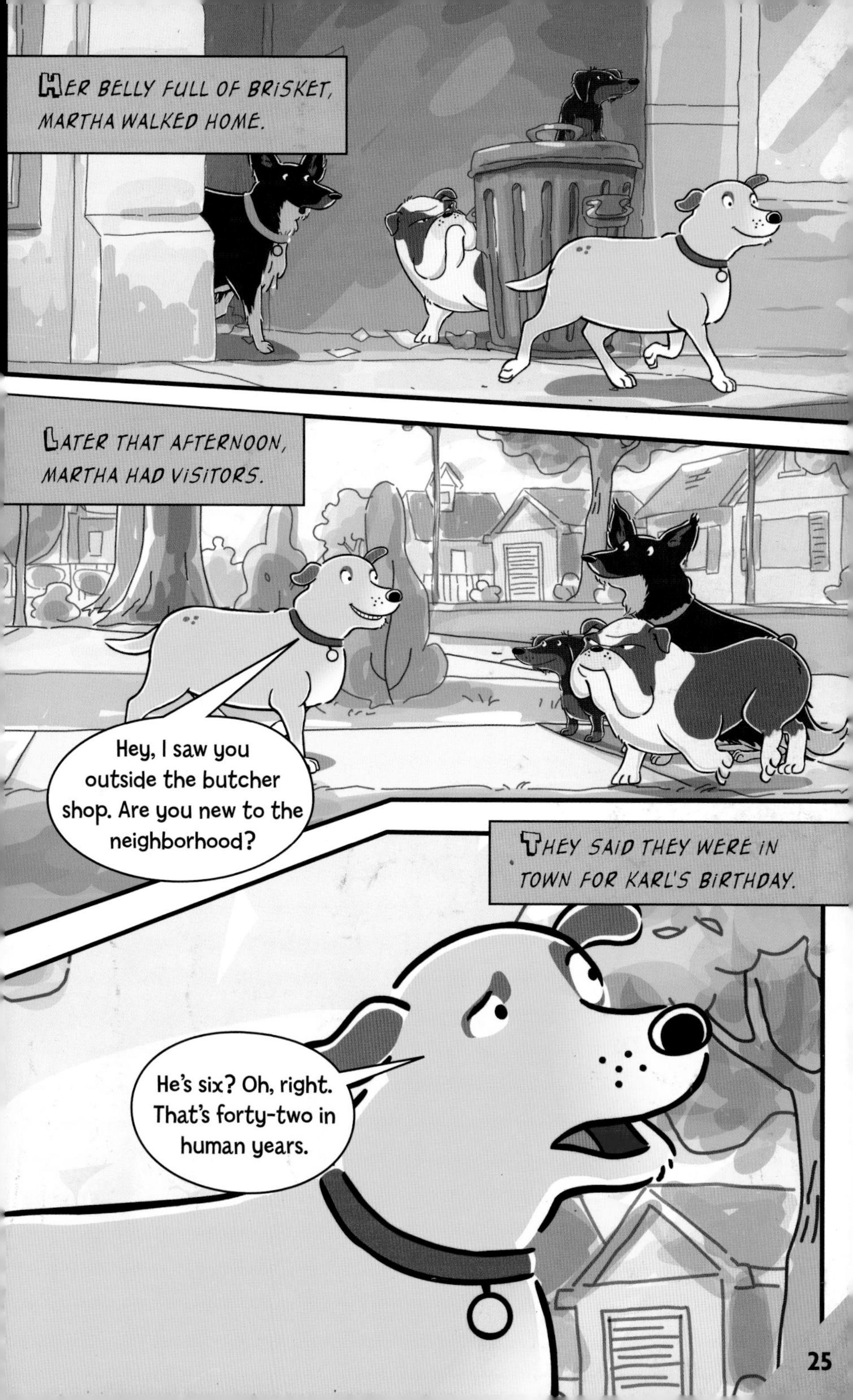
HER BELLY FULL OF BRISKET, MARTHA WALKED HOME.
LATER THAT AFTERNOON, MARTHA HAD VISITORS.
Hey, I saw you outside the butcher shop. Are you new to the neighborhood?
THEY SAID THEY WERE IN TOWN FOR KARL'S BIRTHDAY.
He's six? Oh, right. That's forty-two in human years.

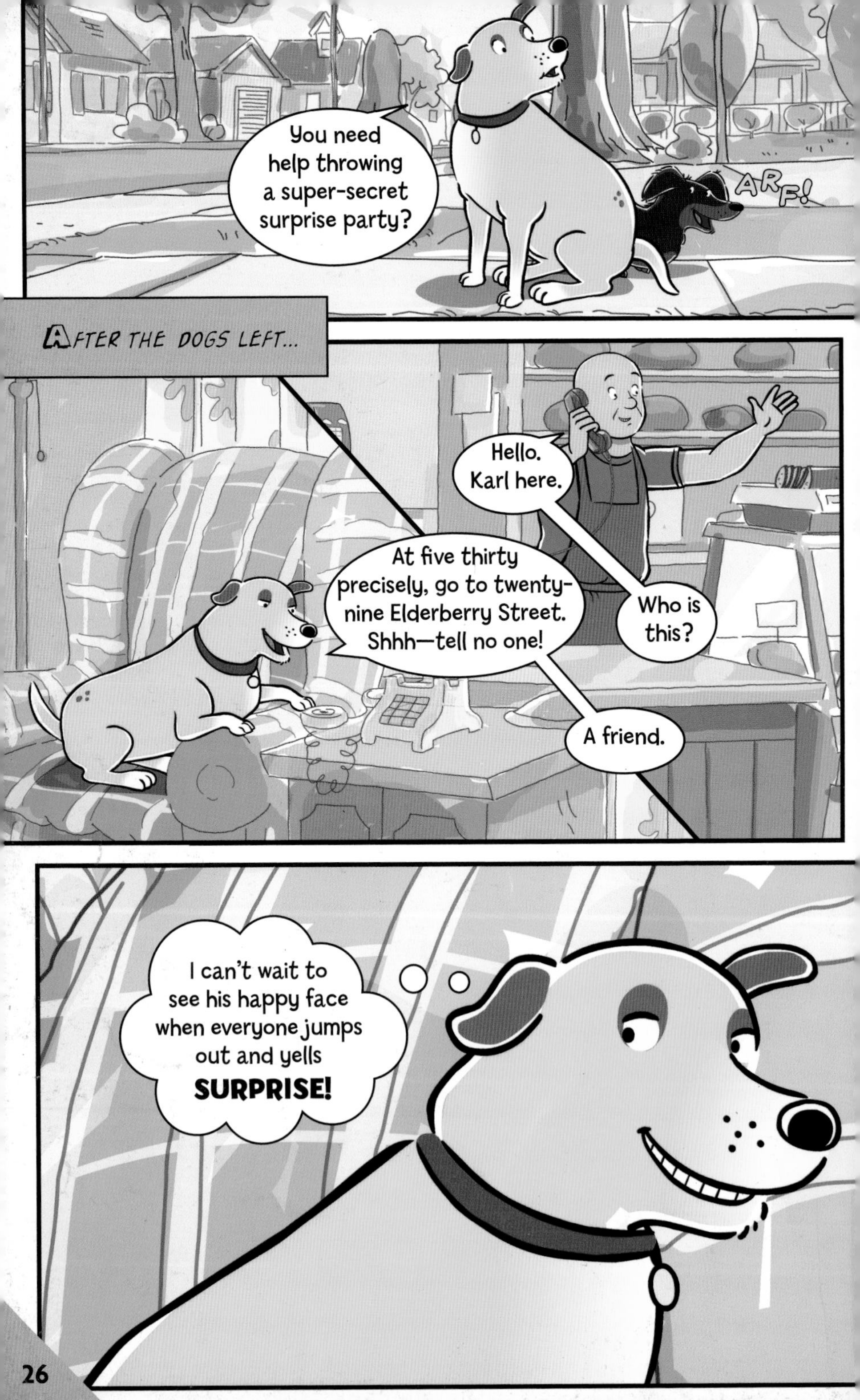
You need help throwing a super-secret surprise party?
ARF!
AFTER THE DOGS LEFT...
Hello. Karl here.
At five thirty precisely, go to twenty-nine Elderberry Street. Shhh—tell no one!
Who is this?
A friend.
I can't wait to see his happy face when everyone jumps out and yells
SURPRISE!

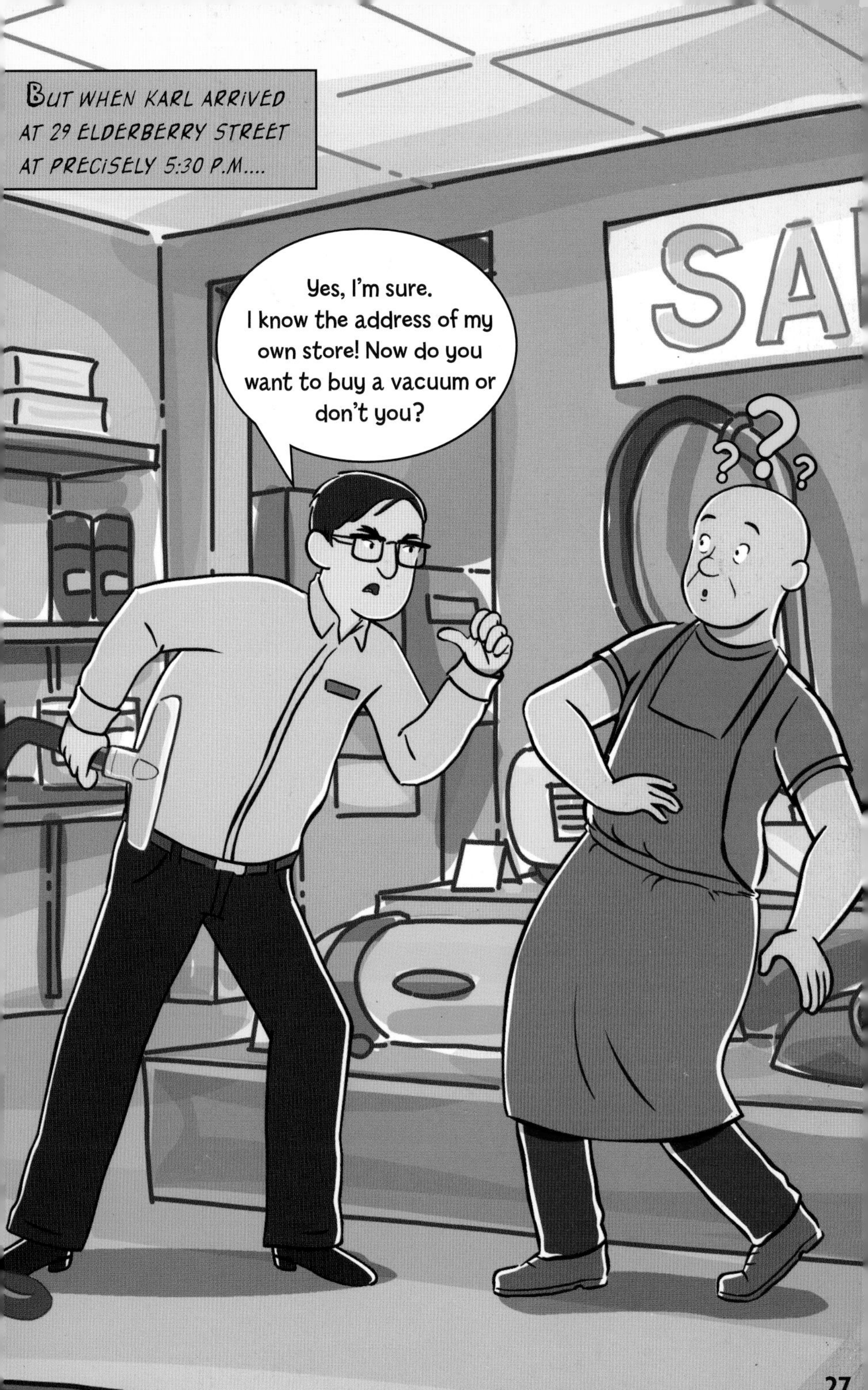
BUT WHEN KARL ARRIVED AT 29 ELDERBERRY STREET AT PRECISELY 5:30 P.M....
Yes, I'm sure. I know the address of my own store! Now do you want to buy a vacuum or don't you?
SA

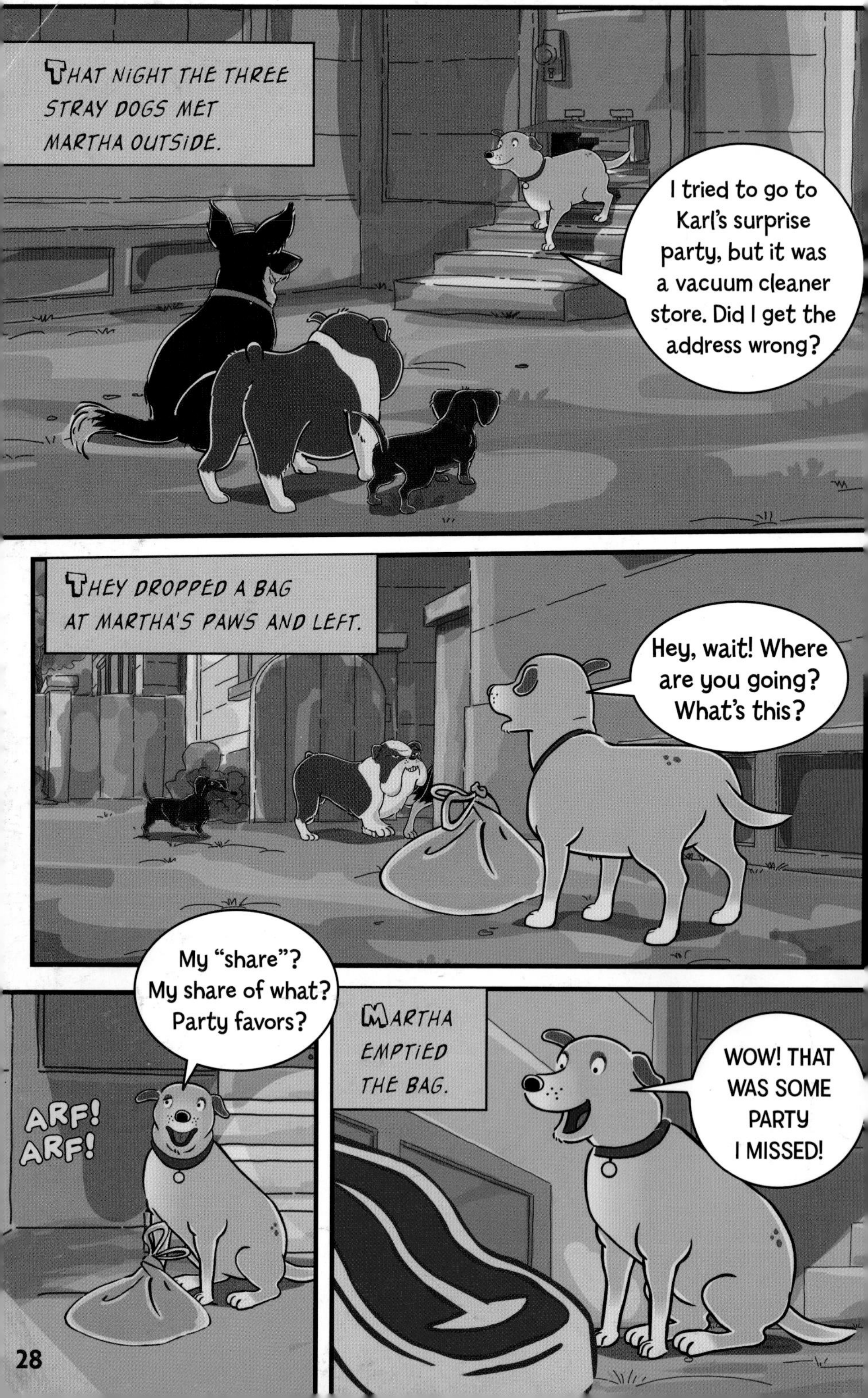
THAT NIGHT THE THREE STRAY DOGS MET MARTHA OUTSIDE.
I tried to go to Karl's surprise party, but it was a vacuum cleaner store. Did I get the address wrong?
THEY DROPPED A BAG AT MARTHA'S PAWS AND LEFT.
Hey, wait! Where are you going? What's this?
My "share"? My share of what? Party favors?
ARF! ARF!
MARTHA EMPTIED THE BAG.
WOW! THAT WAS SOME PARTY I MISSED!

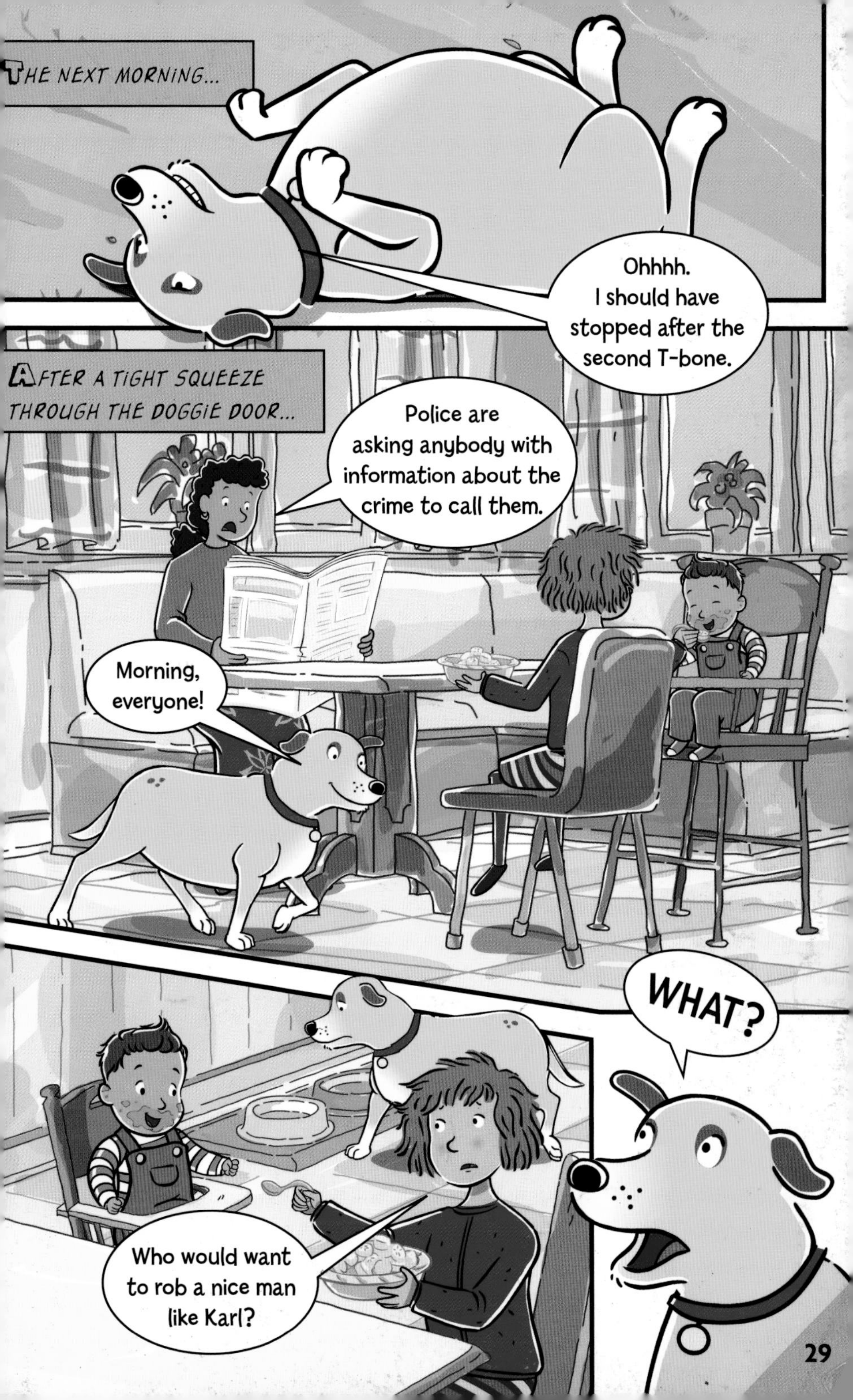
THE NEXT MORNING...
Ohhhh. I should have stopped after the second T-bone.
AFTER A TIGHT SQUEEZE THROUGH THE DOGGIE DOOR...
Police are asking anybody with information about the crime to call them.
Morning, everyone!
WHAT?
Who would want to rob a nice man like Karl?

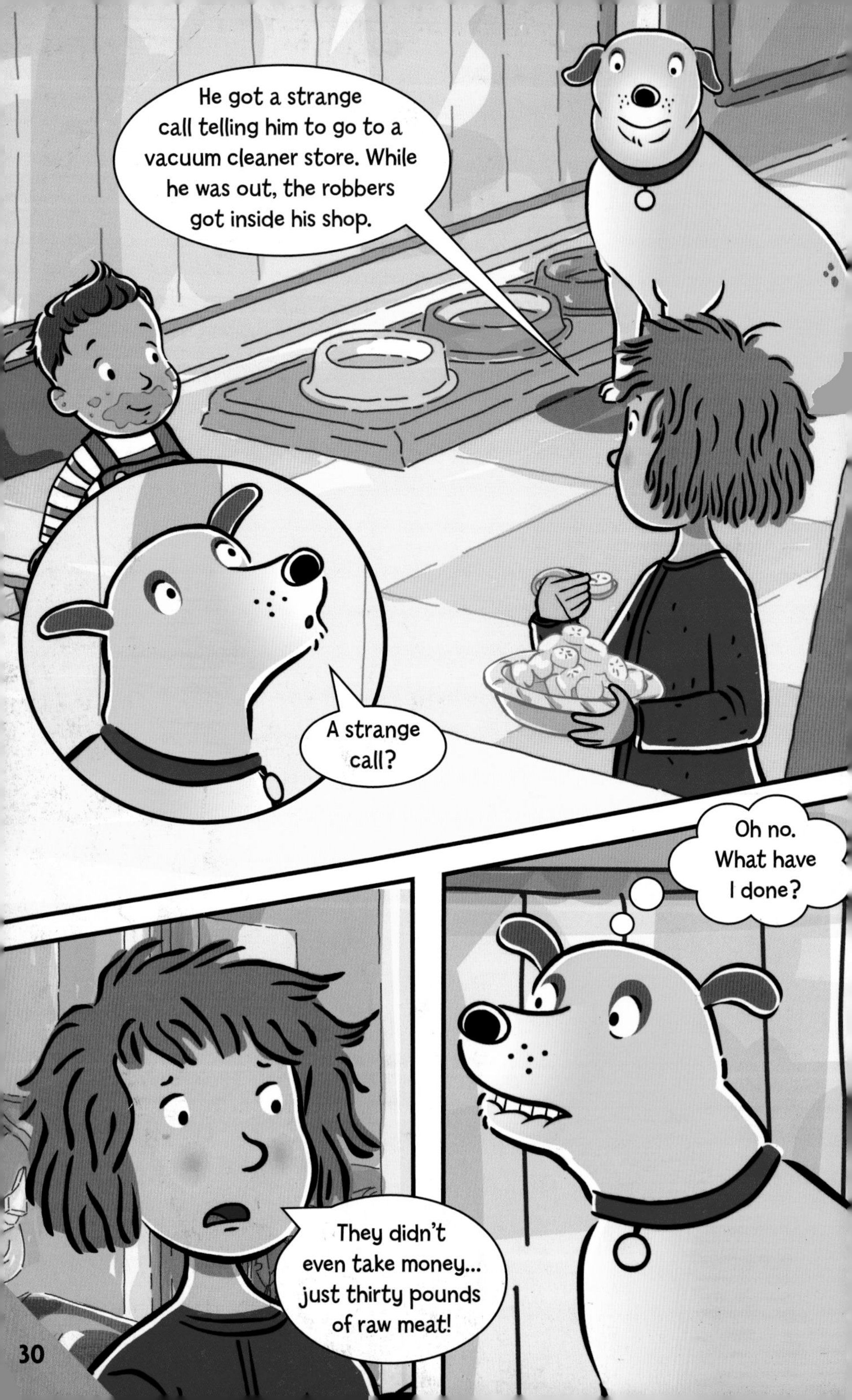
He got a strange call telling him to go to a vacuum cleaner store. While he was out, the robbers got inside his shop.
A strange call?
Oh no. What have I done?
They didn't even take money... just thirty pounds of raw meat!

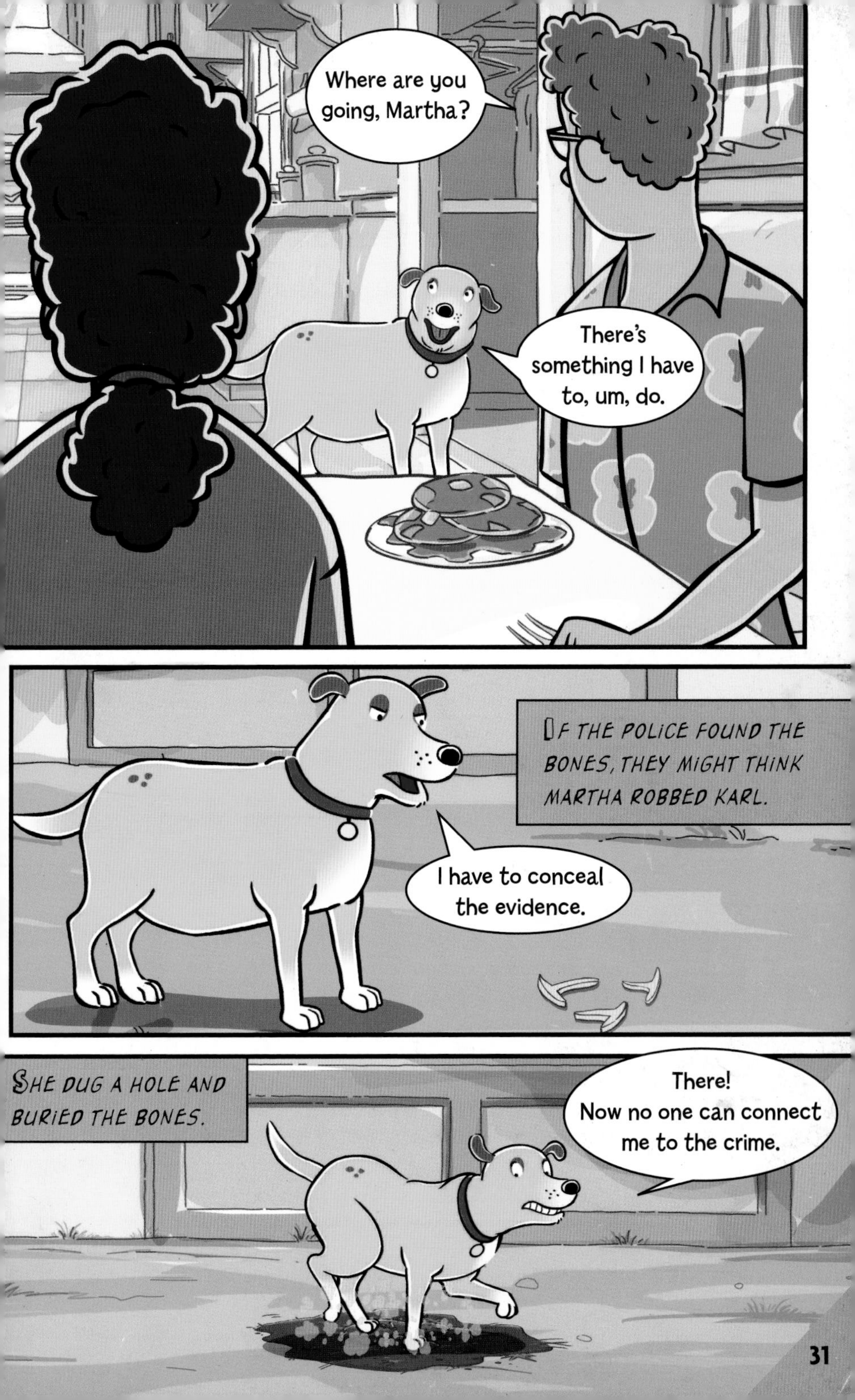
Where are you going, Martha?
There's something I have to, um, do.
IF THE POLICE FOUND THE BONES, THEY MIGHT THINK MARTHA ROBBED KARL.
I have to conceal the evidence.
SHE DUG A HOLE AND BURIED THE BONES.
There! Now no one can connect me to the crime.

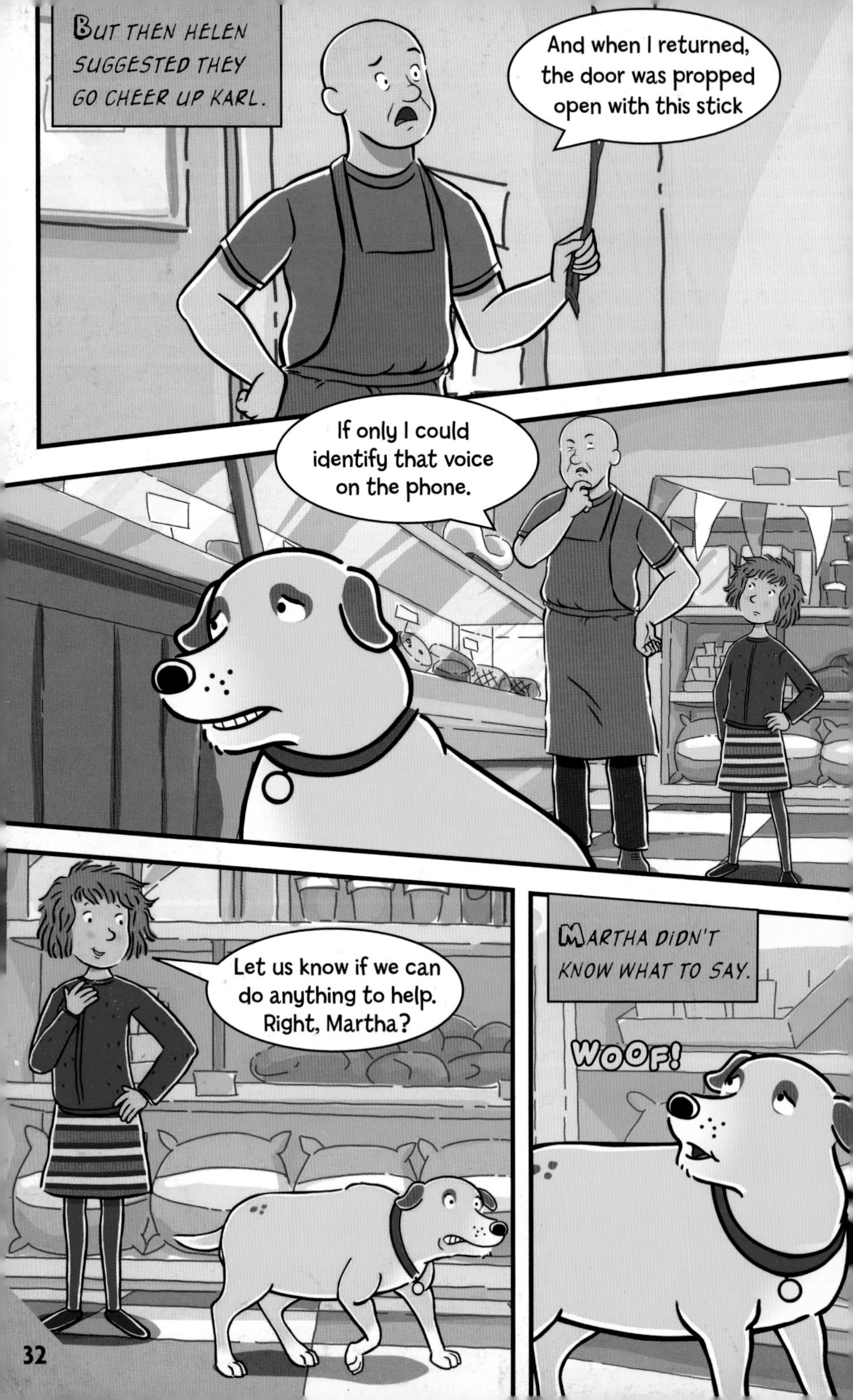
BUT THEN HELEN SUGGESTED THEY GO CHEER UP KARL.
And when I returned, the door was propped open with this stick
If only I could identify that voice on the phone.
Let us know if we can do anything to help. Right, Martha?
MARTHA DIDN'T KNOW WHAT TO SAY.
WOOF!

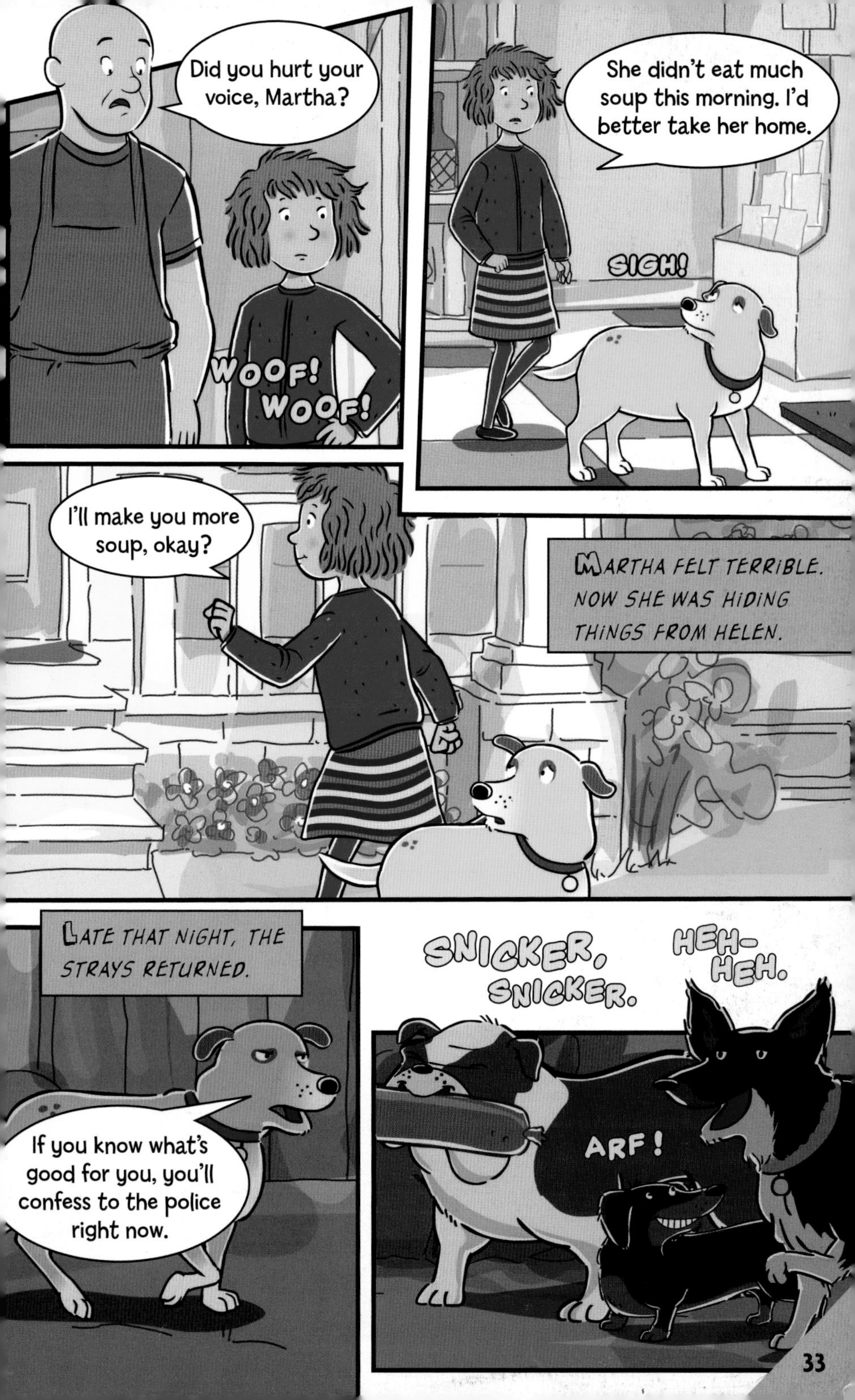
Did you hurt your voice, Martha?
WOOF! WOOF!
She didn't eat much soup this morning. I'd better take her home.
SIGH!
I'll make you more soup, okay?
MARTHA FELT TERRIBLE. NOW SHE WAS HIDING THINGS FROM HELEN.
LATE THAT NIGHT, THE STRAYS RETURNED.
If you know what's good for you, you'll confess to the police right now.
SNICKER, SNICKER.
HEH-HEH.
ARF!

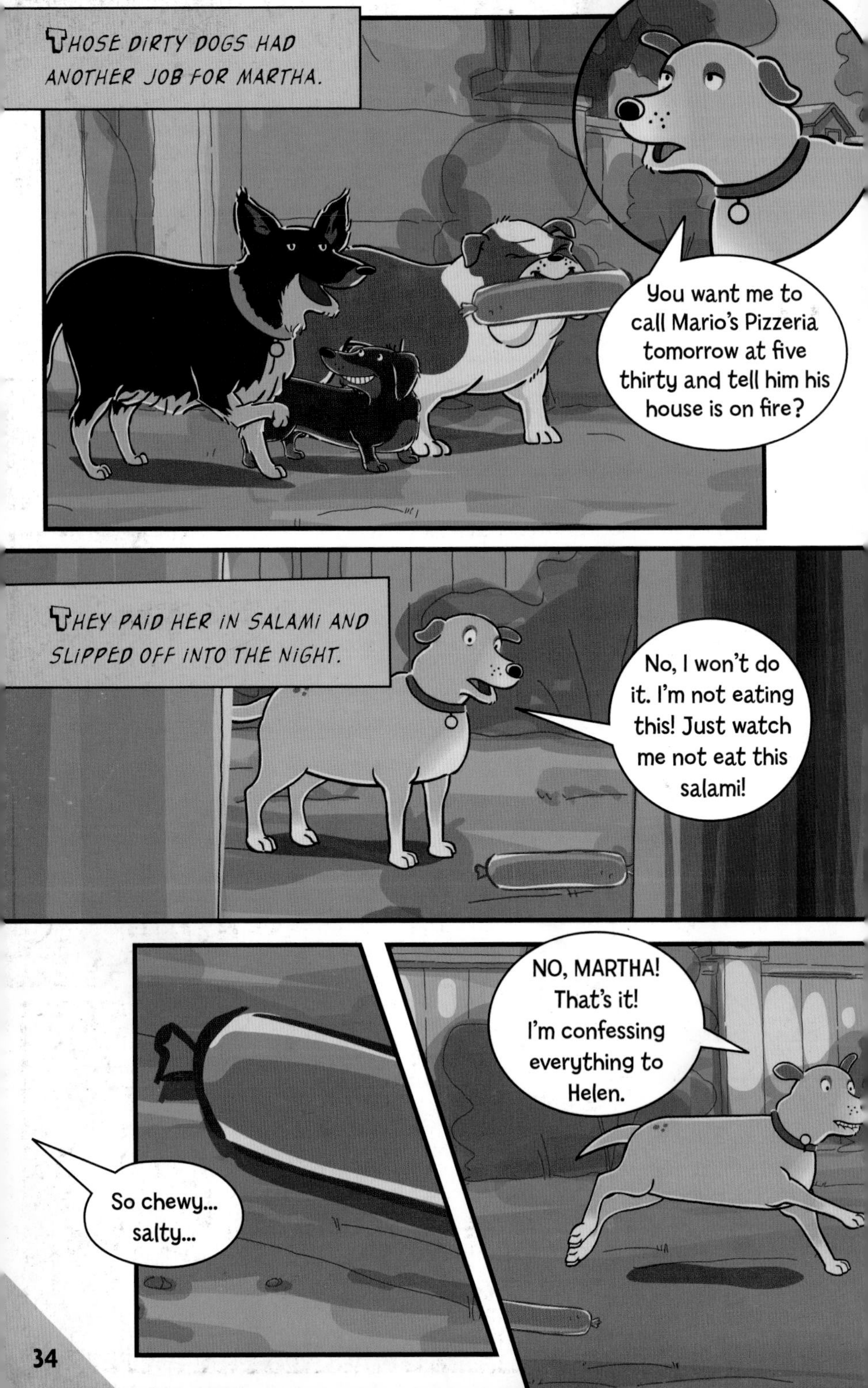
THOSE DIRTY DOGS HAD ANOTHER JOB FOR MARTHA.
You want me to call Mario's Pizzeria tomorrow at five thirty and tell him his house is on fire?
THEY PAID HER IN SALAMI AND SLIPPED OFF INTO THE NIGHT.
No, I won't do it. I'm not eating this! Just watch me not eat this salami!
So chewy... salty...
NO, MARTHA! That's it! I'm confessing everything to Helen.

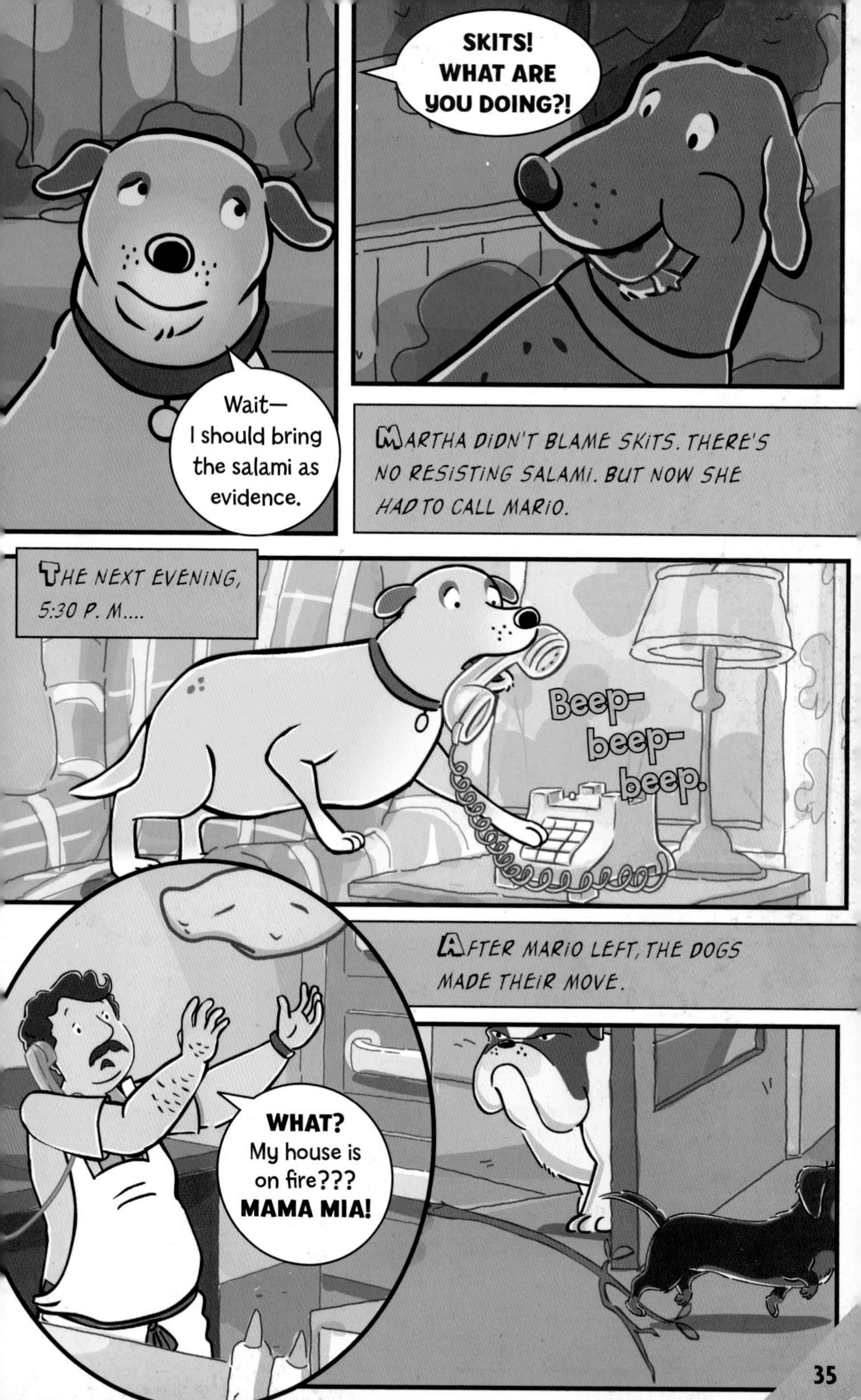
SKITS! WHAT ARE YOU DOING?!
Wait— I should bring the salami as evidence.
MARTHA DIDN'T BLAME SKITS. THERE'S NO RESISTING SALAMI. BUT NOW SHE HAD TO CALL MARIO.
THE NEXT EVENING, 5:30 P. M....
Beep-beep-beep.
AFTER MARIO LEFT, THE DOGS MADE THEIR MOVE.
WHAT? My house is on fire??? MAMA MIA!

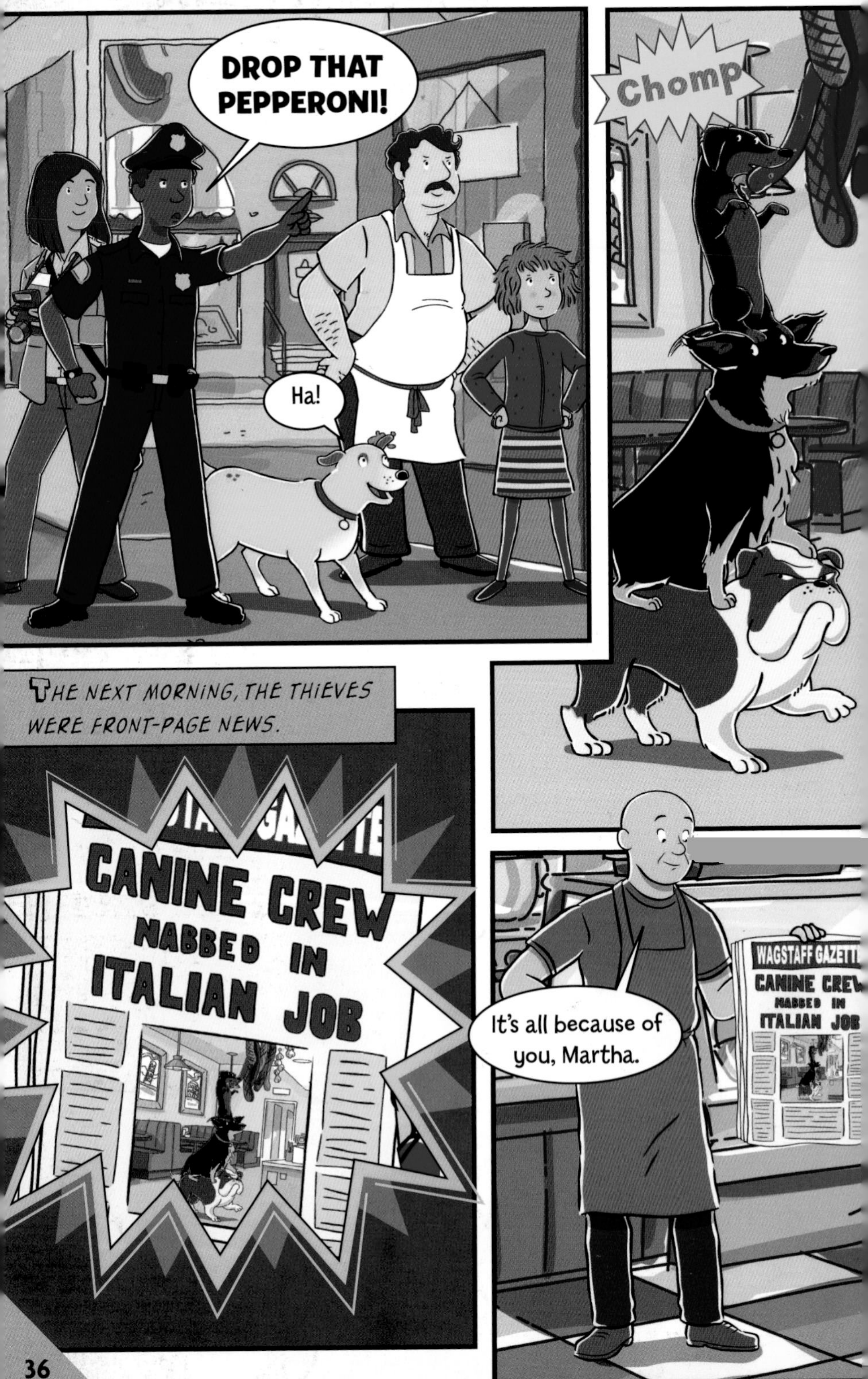
DROP THAT PEPPERONI!
Ha!
Chomp
THE NEXT MORNING, THE THIEVES WERE FRONT-PAGE NEWS.
CANINE CREW NABBED IN ITALIAN JOB
It's all because of you, Martha.
CANINE CREW NABBED IN ITALIAN JOB

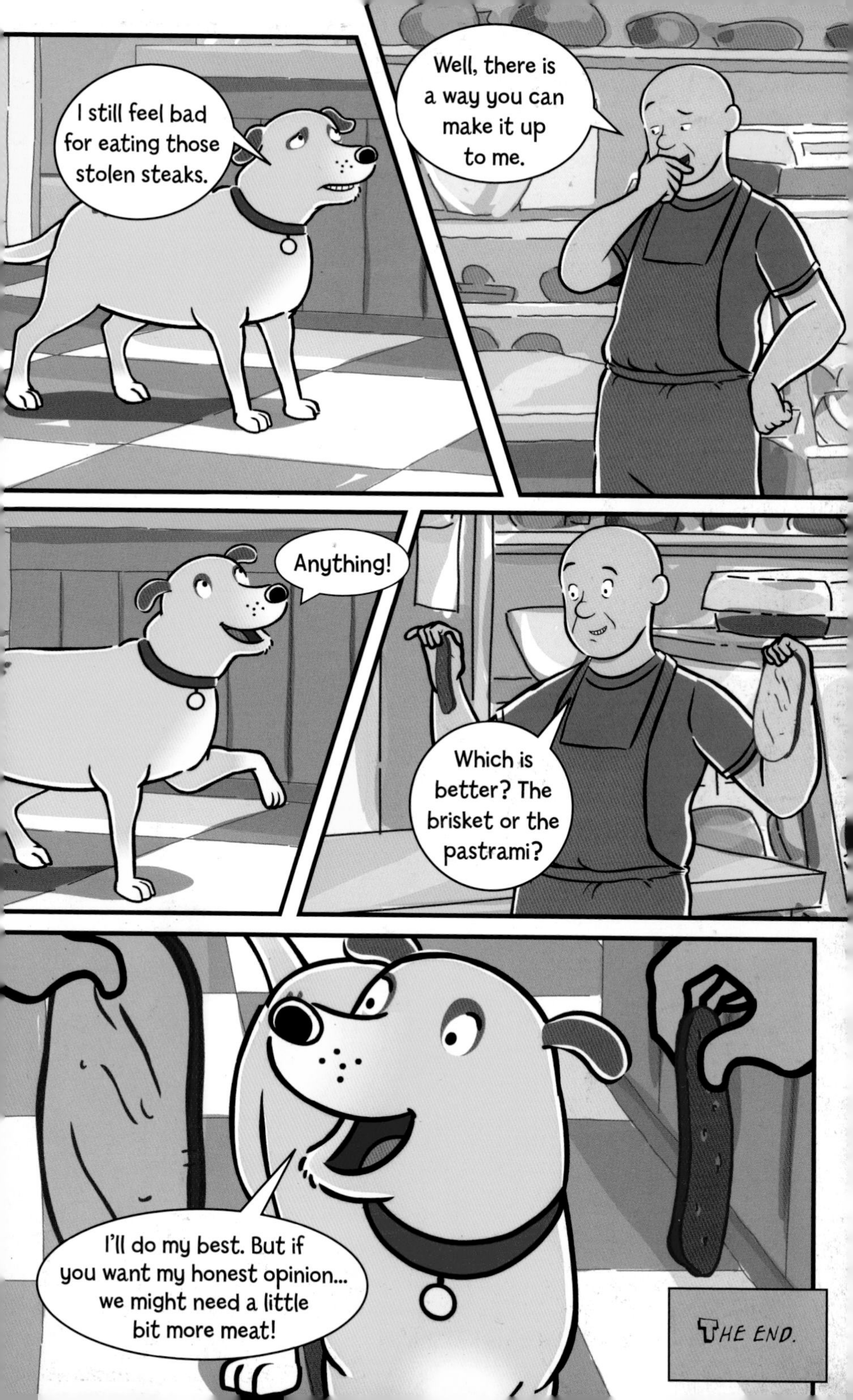
I still feel bad for eating those stolen steaks.
Well, there is a way you can make it up to me.
Anything!
Which is better? The brisket or the pastrami?
I'll do my best. But if you want my honest opinion... we might need a little bit more meat!
THE END.

3 Martha Fails the Course

Adaptation by Jamie White
Based on a TV series teleplay
written by Raye Lankford

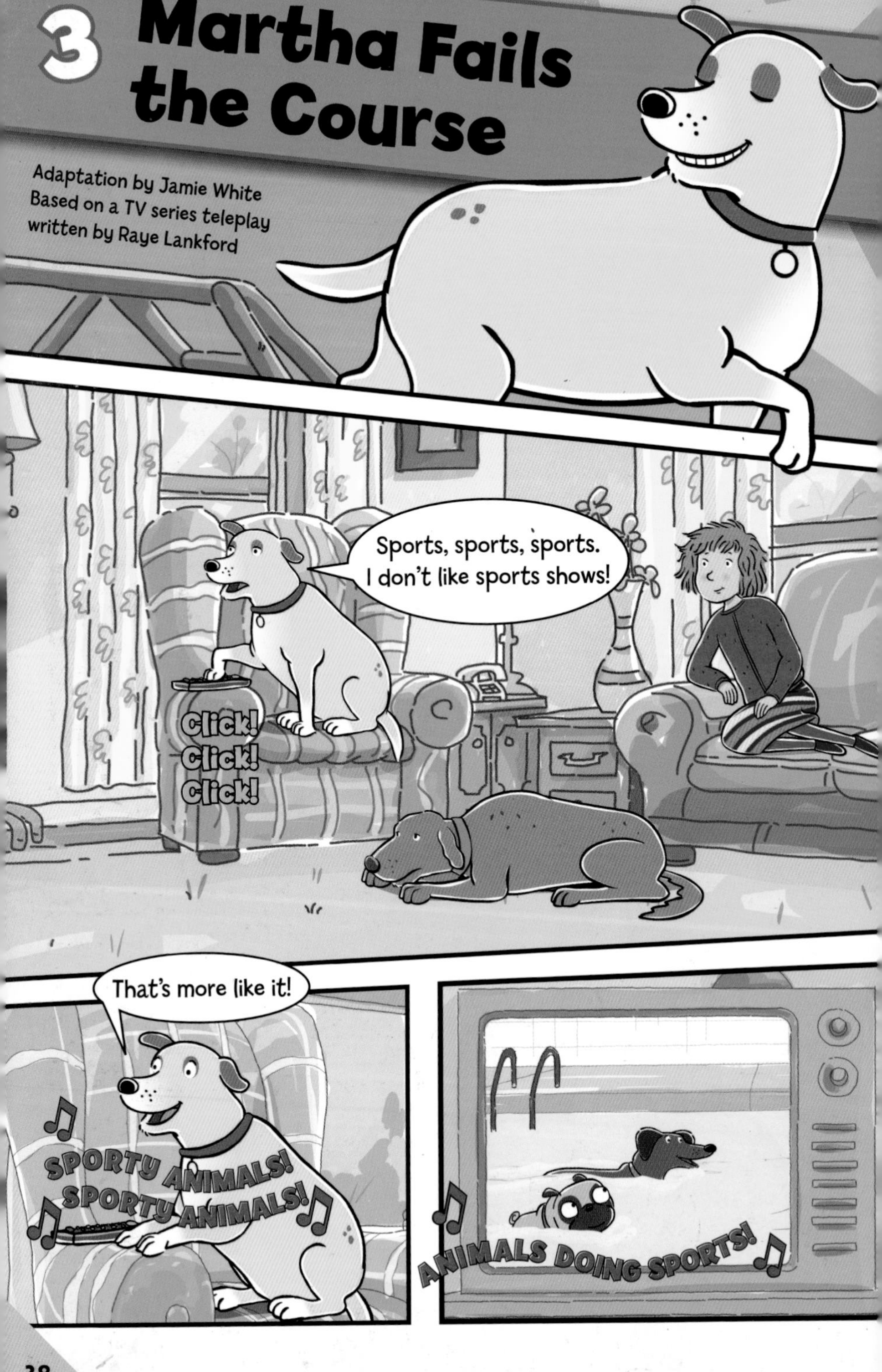
Sports, sports, sports.
I don't like sports shows!
Click!
Click!
Click!
That's more like it!
SPORTY ANIMALS!
SPORTY ANIMALS!
ANIMALS DOING SPORTS!

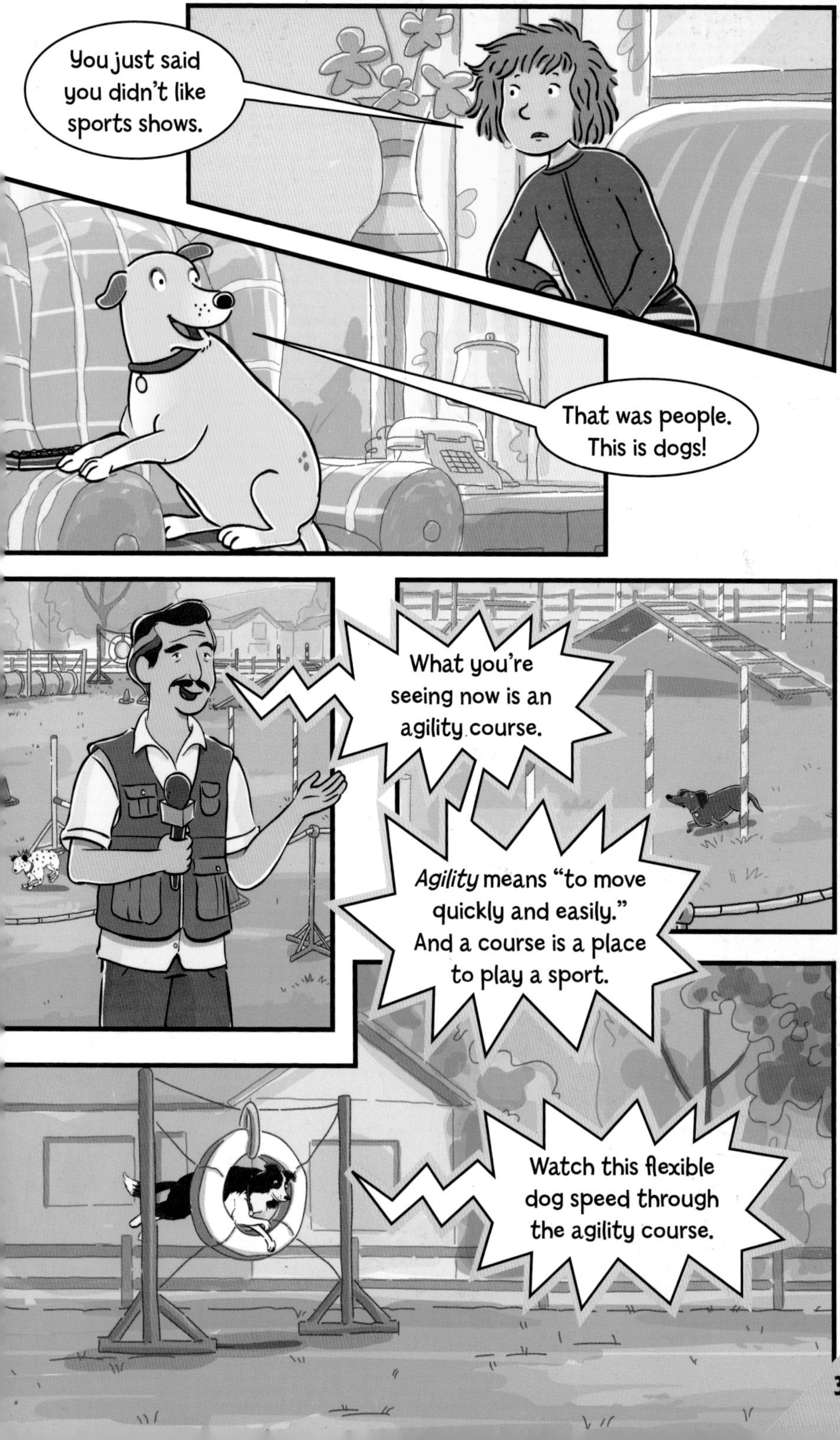
You just said you didn't like sports shows.
That was people. This is dogs!
What you're seeing now is an agility course.
Agility means "to move quickly and easily." And a course is a place to play a sport.
Watch this flexible dog speed through the agility course.

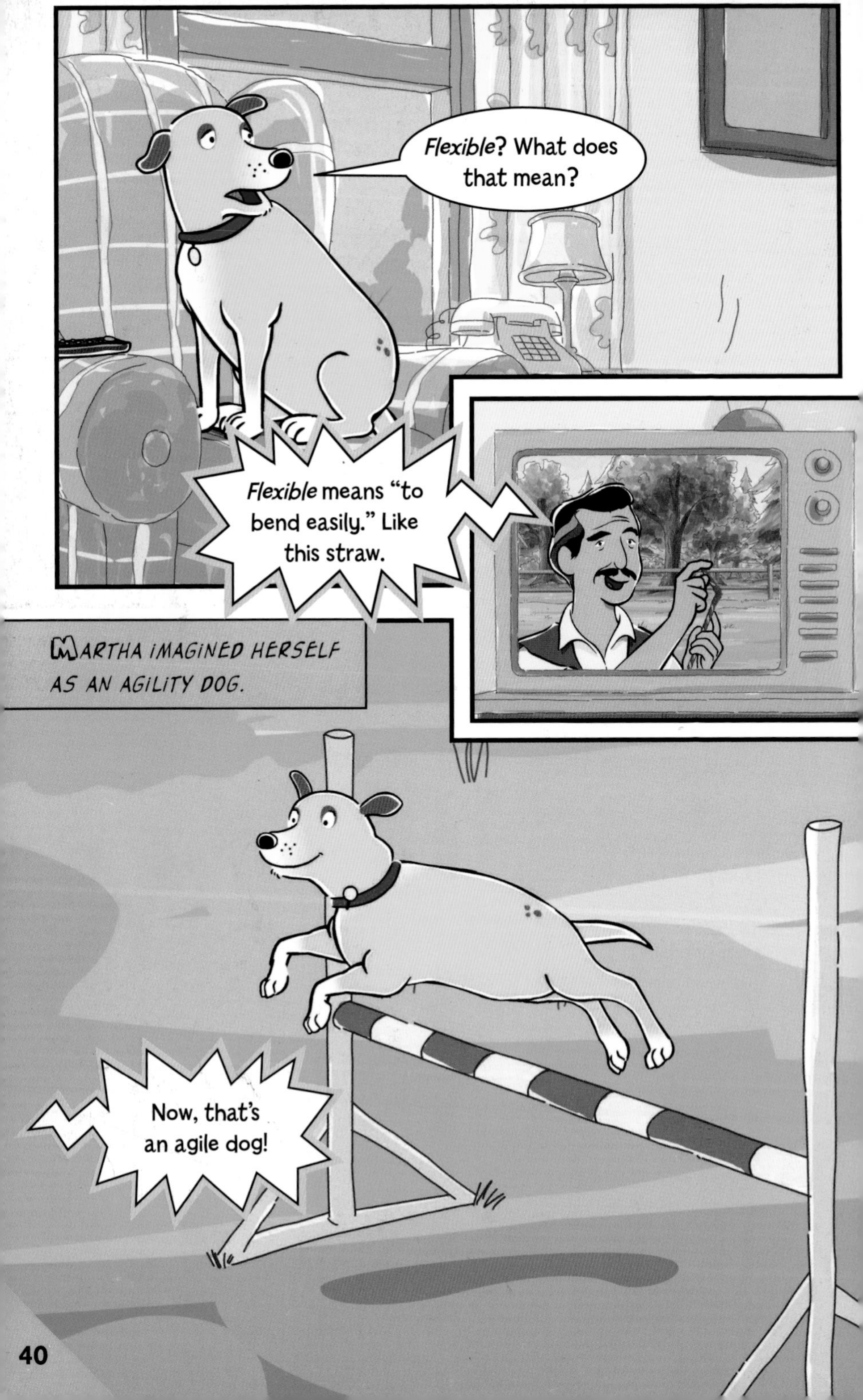
Flexible? What does that mean?
Flexible means "to bend easily." Like this straw.
MARTHA IMAGINED HERSELF AS AN AGILITY DOG.
Now, that's an agile dog!

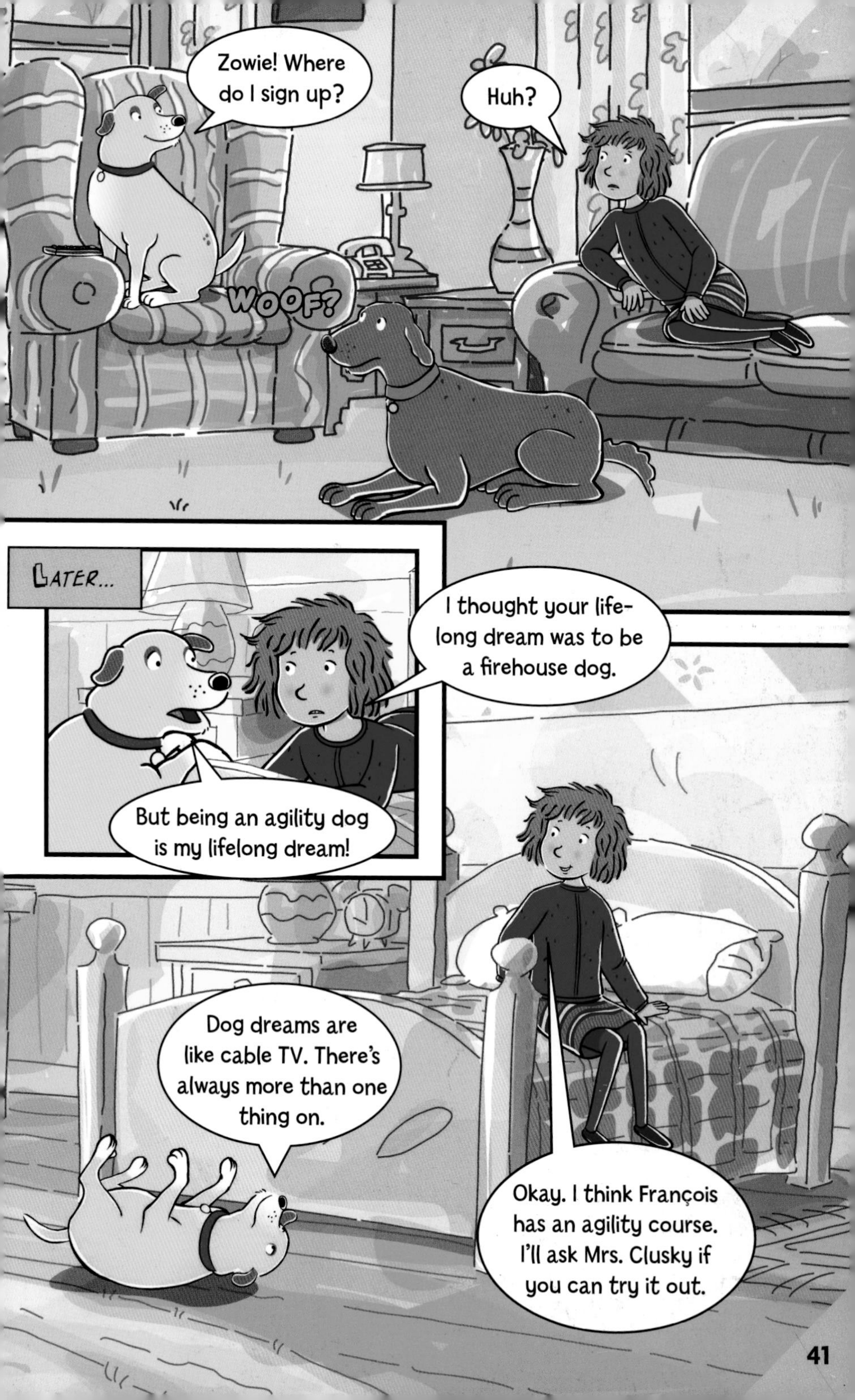
Zowie! Where do I sign up?
Huh?
WOOF?
LATER...
I thought your life-long dream was to be a firehouse dog.
But being an agility dog is my lifelong dream!
Dog dreams are like cable TV. There's always more than one thing on.
Okay. I think François has an agility course. I'll ask Mrs. Clusky if you can try it out.

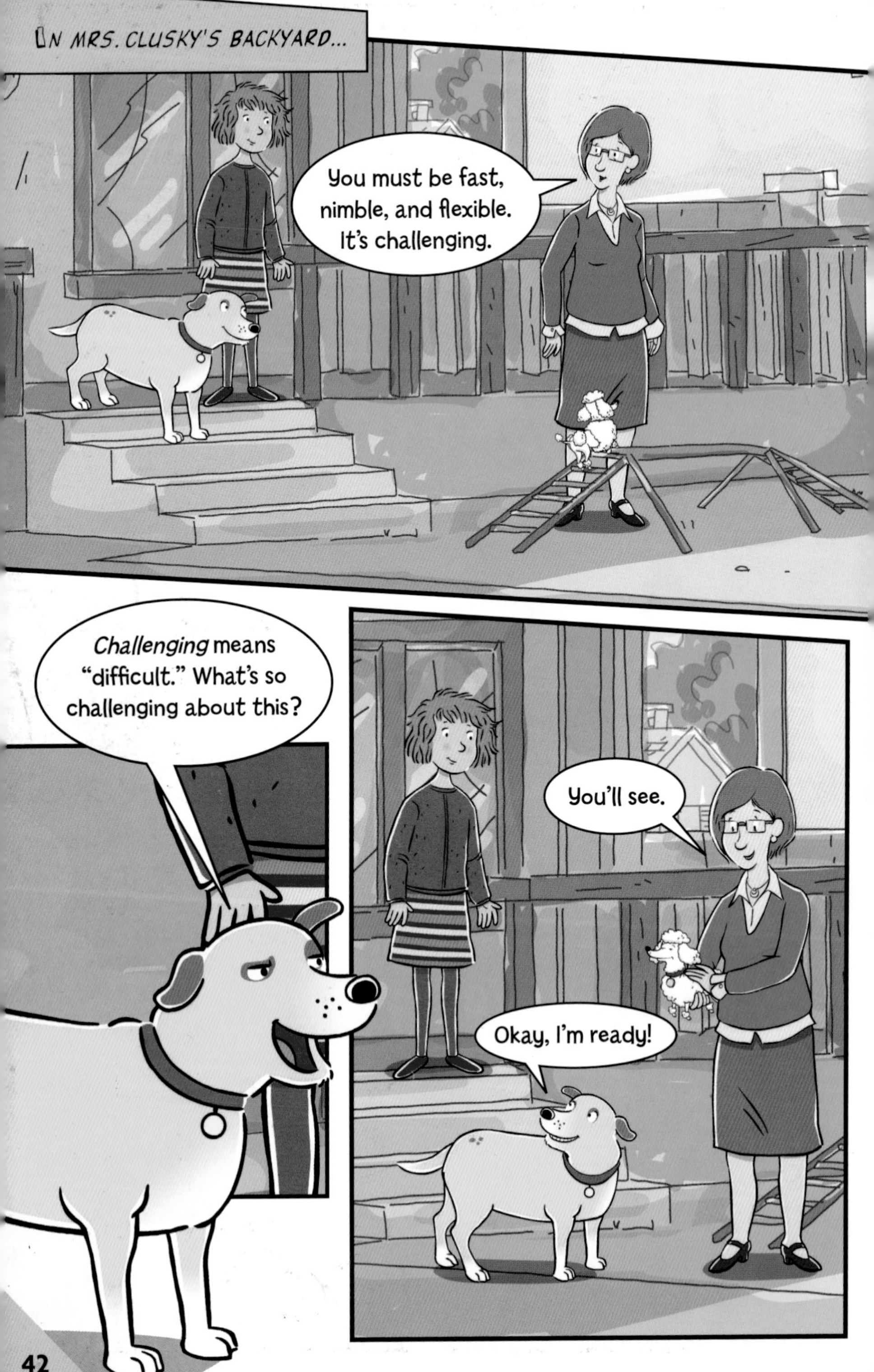
IN MRS. CLUSKY'S BACKYARD...
You must be fast, nimble, and flexible. It's challenging.
Challenging means "difficult." What's so challenging about this?
You'll see.
Okay, I'm ready!

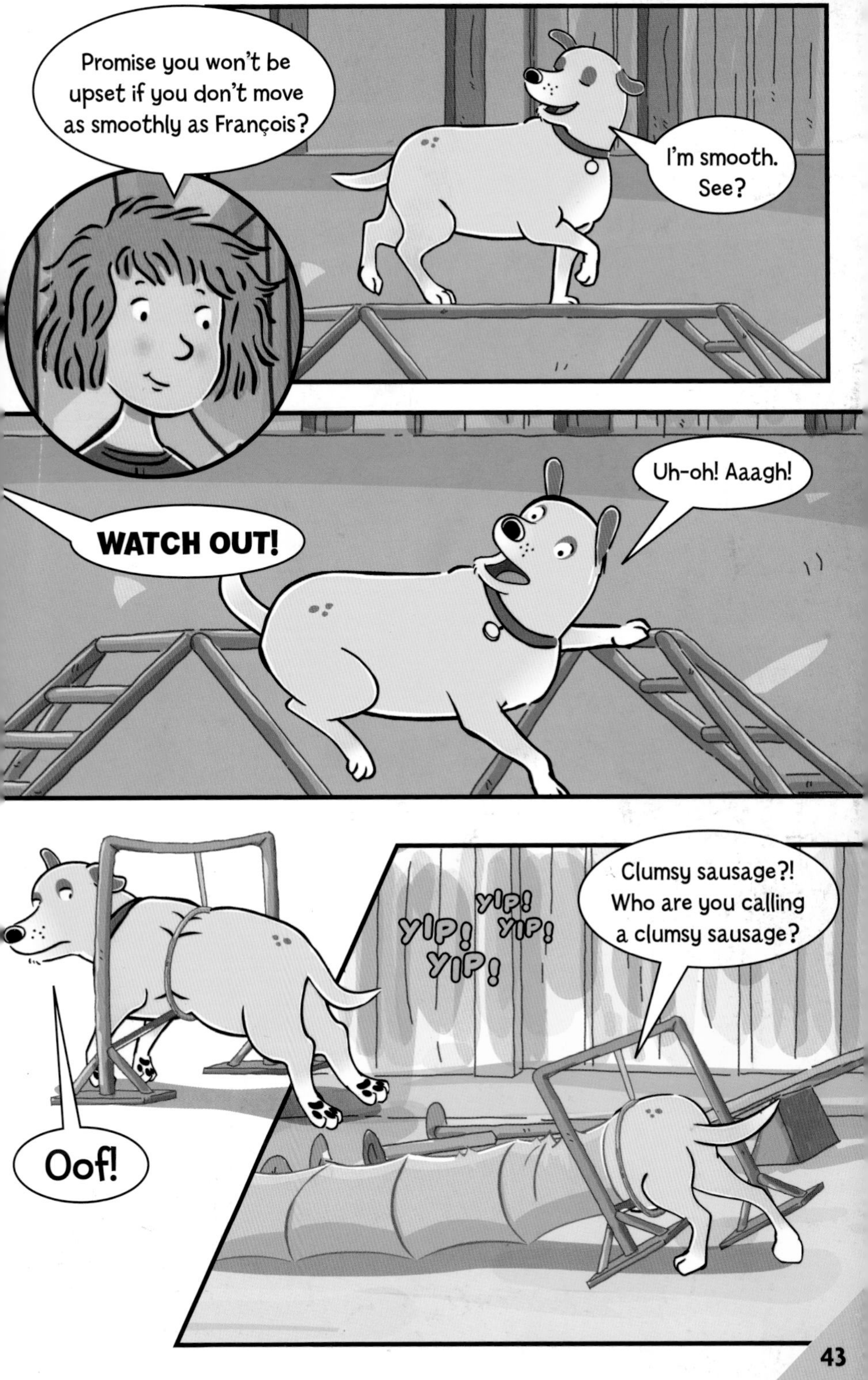
Promise you won't be upset if you don't move as smoothly as François?
I'm smooth. See?
WATCH OUT!
Uh-oh! Aaagh!
Oof!
YIP! YIP! YIP! YIP!
Clumsy sausage?! Who are you calling a clumsy sausage?

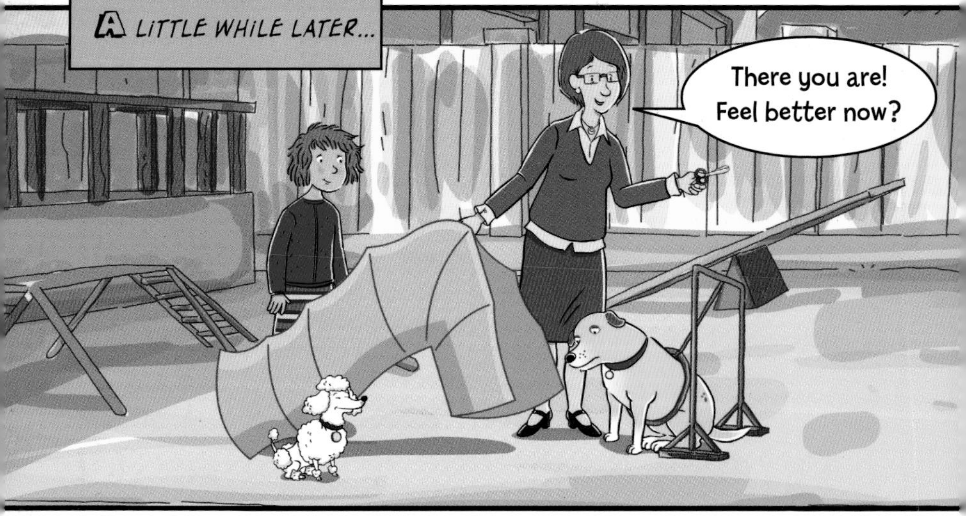
A LITTLE WHILE LATER...
There you are!
Feel better now?

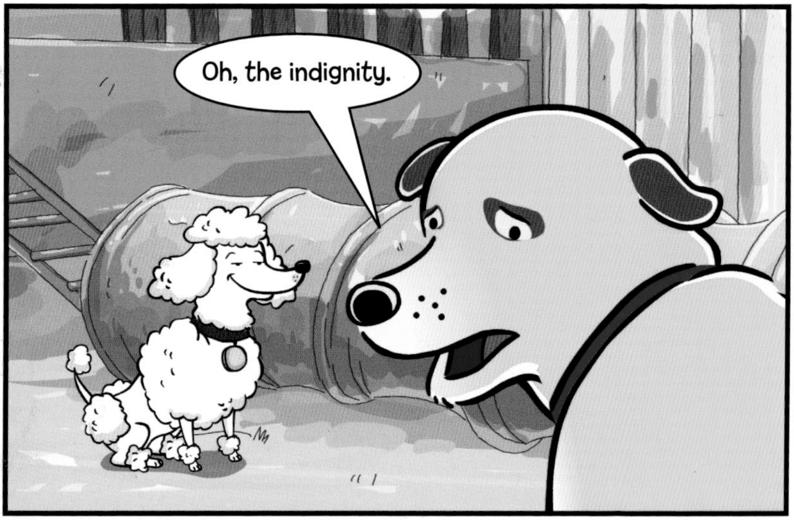
Oh, the indignity.

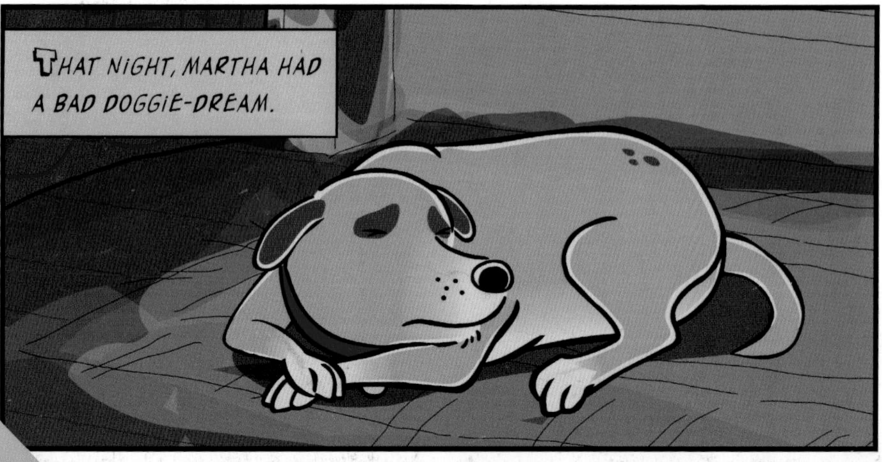
THAT NIGHT, MARTHA HAD
A BAD DOGGIE-DREAM.

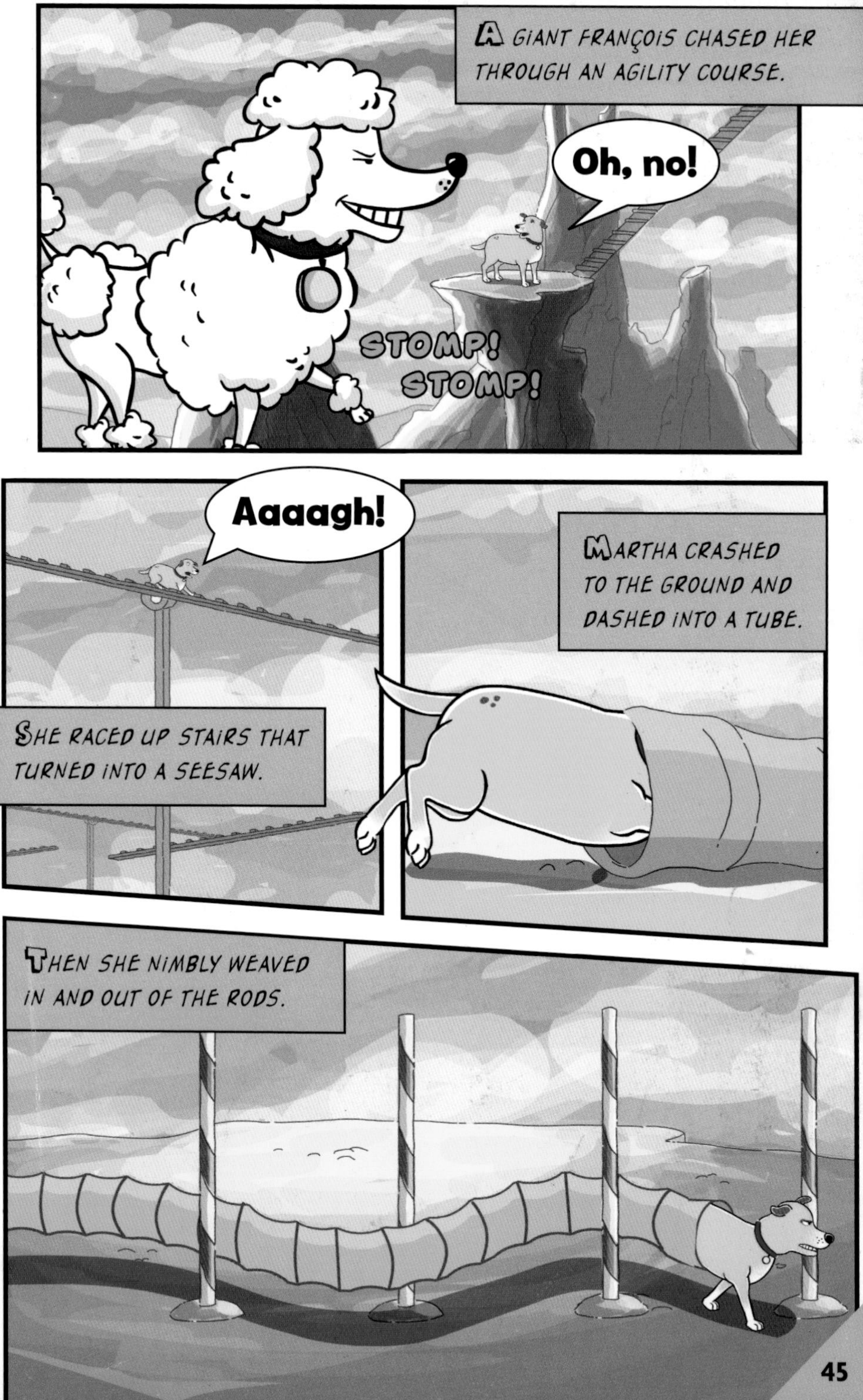
A GIANT FRANÇOIS CHASED HER THROUGH AN AGILITY COURSE.
Oh, no!
STOMP! STOMP!
SHE RACED UP STAIRS THAT TURNED INTO A SEESAW.
Aaaagh!
MARTHA CRASHED TO THE GROUND AND DASHED INTO A TUBE.
THEN SHE NIMBLY WEAVED IN AND OUT OF THE RODS.

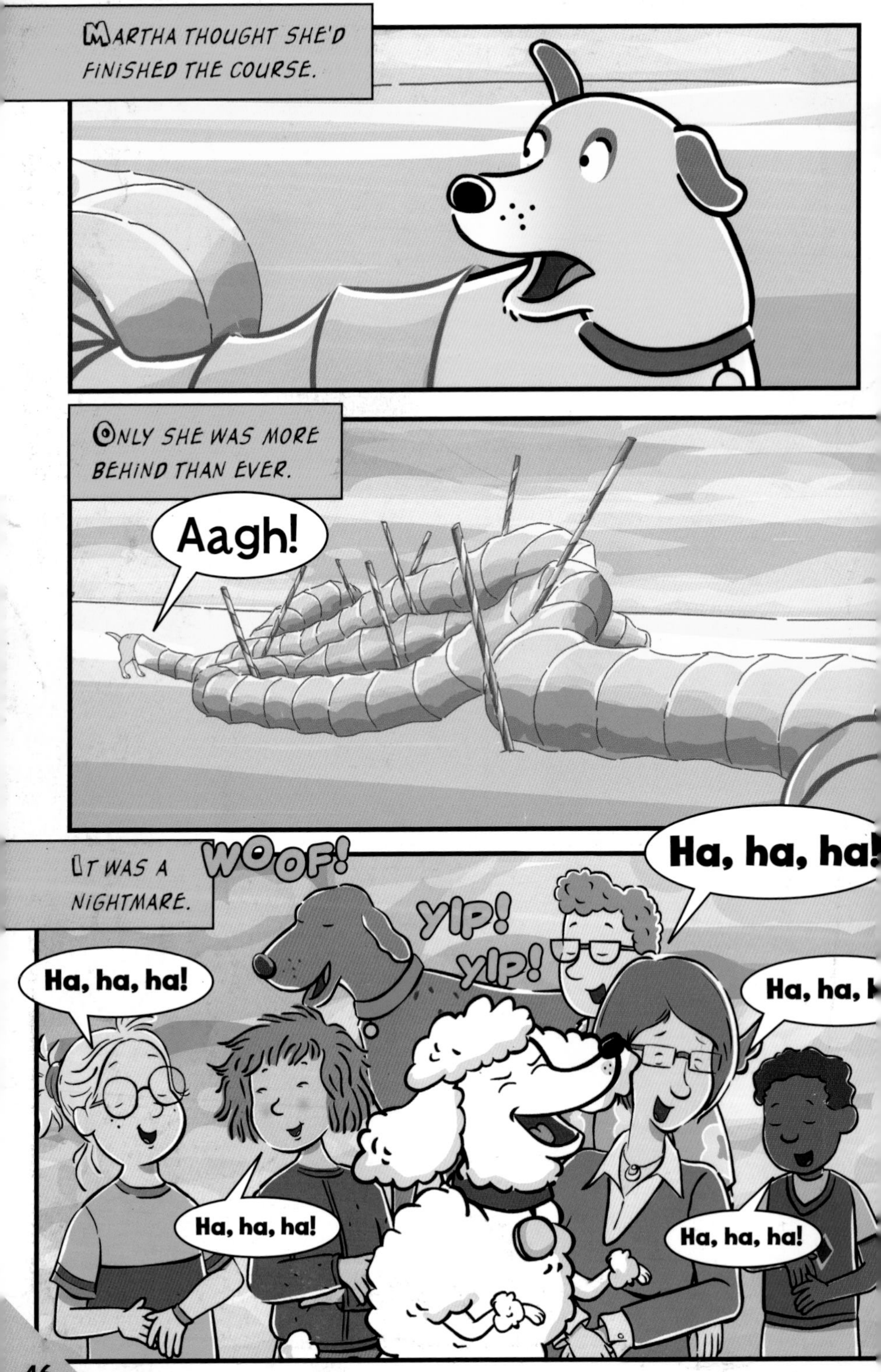
MARTHA THOUGHT SHE'D FINISHED THE COURSE.
ONLY SHE WAS MORE BEHIND THAN EVER.
Aagh!
IT WAS A NIGHTMARE.
WOOF!
Ha, ha, ha!
YIP!
YIP!
Ha, ha, ha!
Ha, ha,
Ha, ha, ha!
Ha, ha, ha!

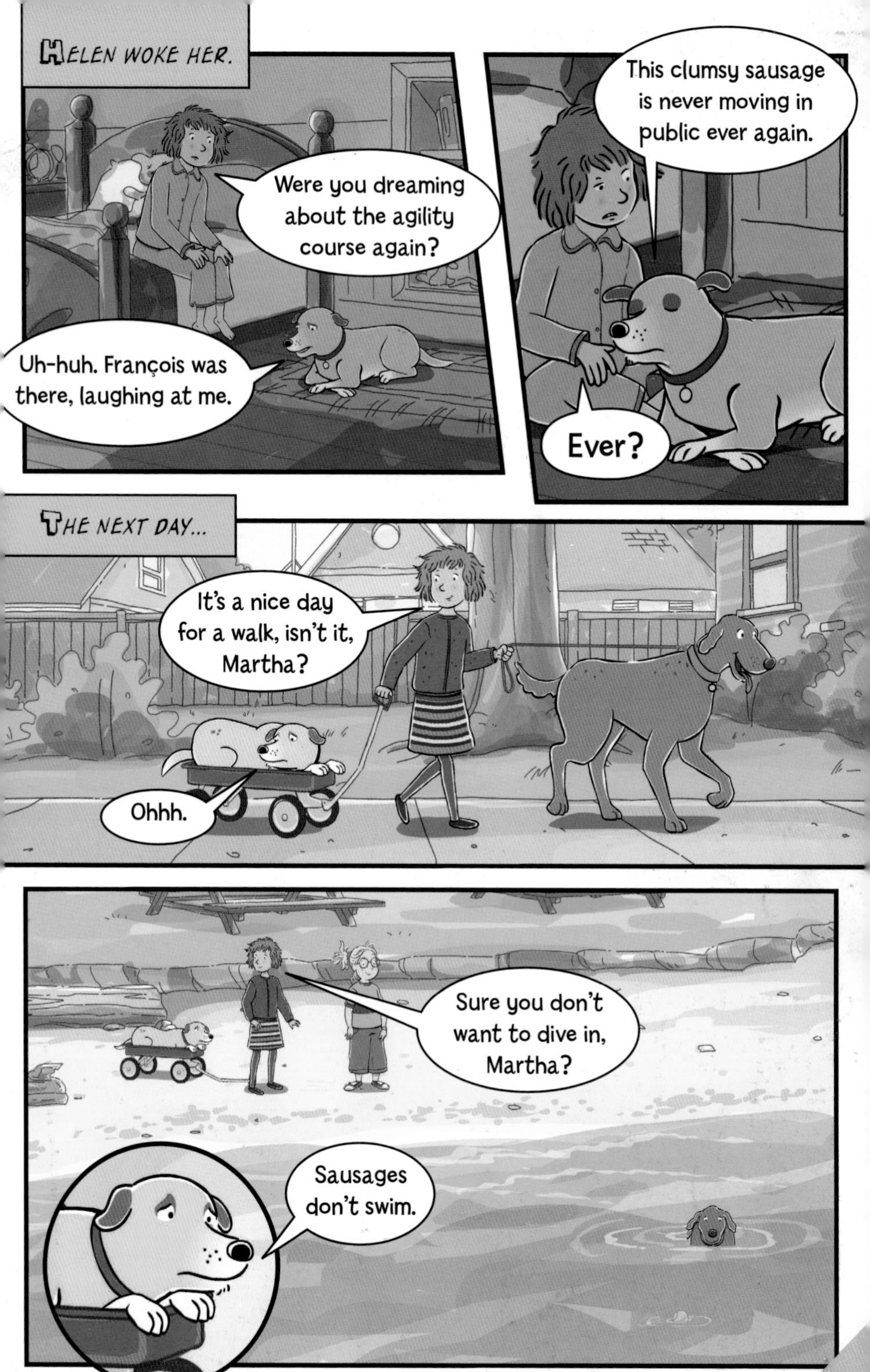
HELEN WOKE HER.
Were you dreaming about the agility course again?
Uh-huh. François was there, laughing at me.
This clumsy sausage is never moving in public ever again.
Ever?
THE NEXT DAY...
It's a nice day for a walk, isn't it, Martha?
Ohhh.
Sure you don't want to dive in, Martha?
Sausages don't swim.

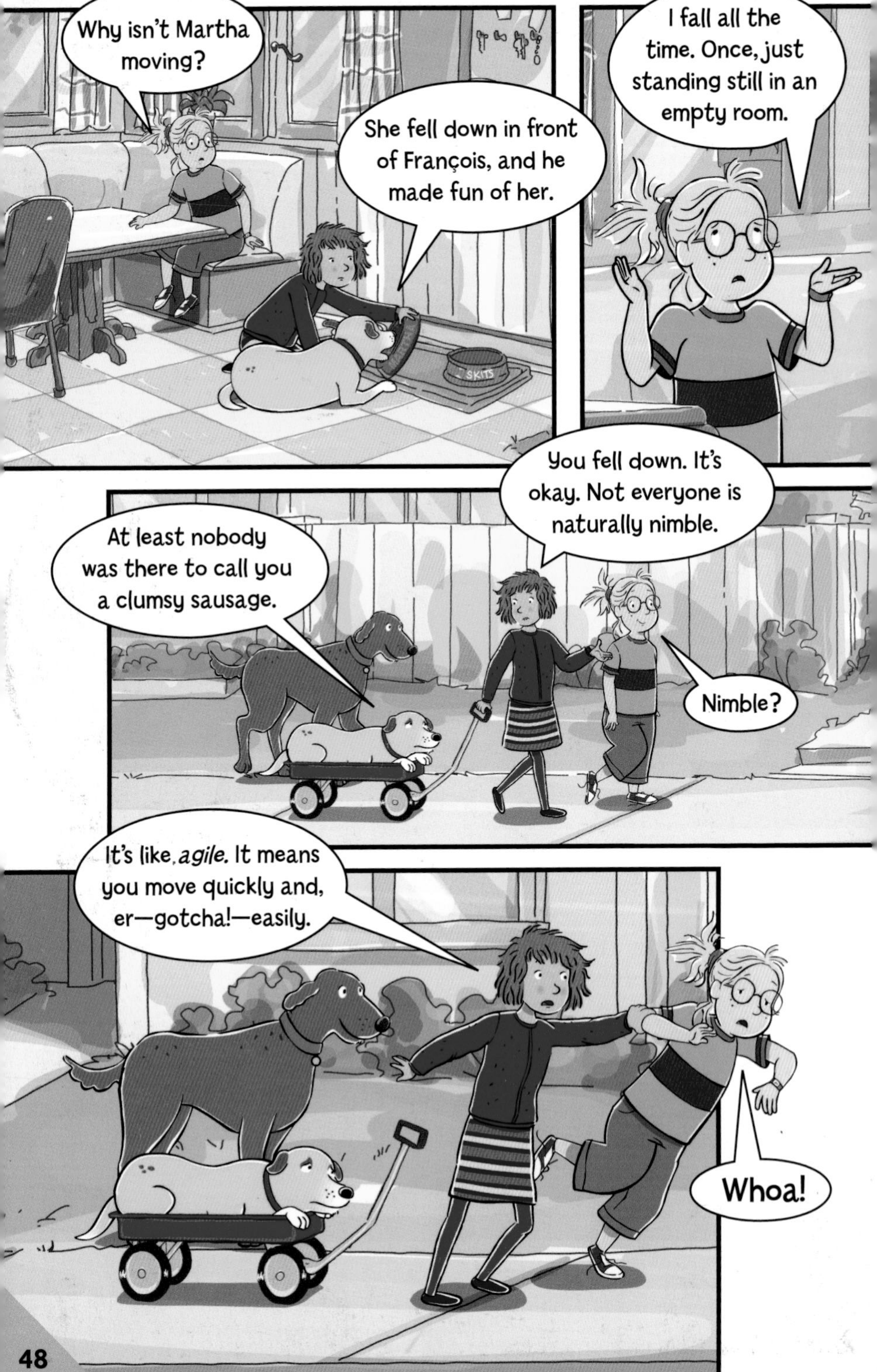
Why isn't Martha moving?
She fell down in front of François, and he made fun of her.
SKITS
I fall all the time. Once, just standing still in an empty room.
You fell down. It's okay. Not everyone is naturally nimble.
At least nobody was there to call you a clumsy sausage.
Nimble?
It's like, *agile.* It means you move quickly and, er—gotcha!—easily.
Whoa!

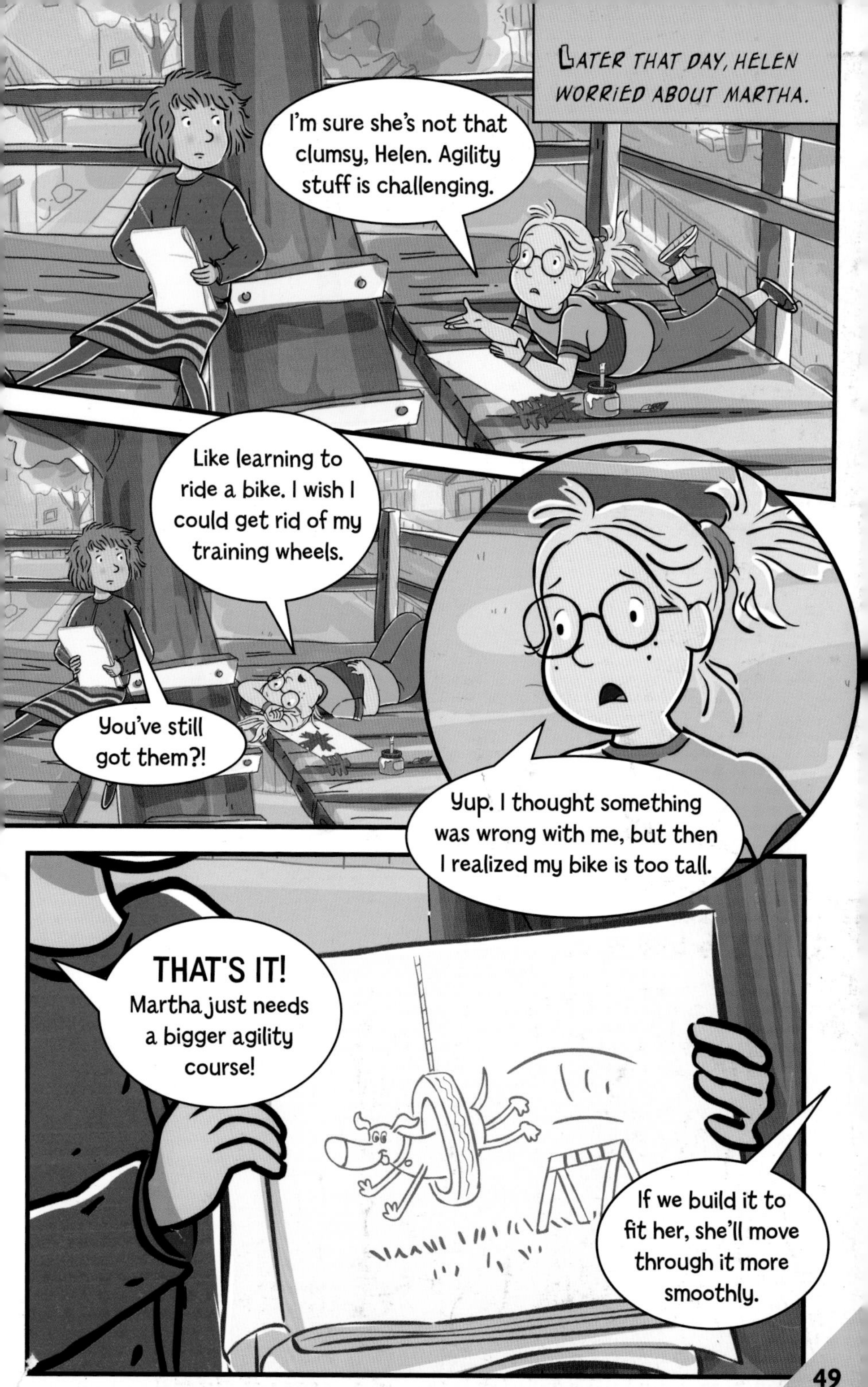
LATER THAT DAY, HELEN WORRIED ABOUT MARTHA.
I'm sure she's not that clumsy, Helen. Agility stuff is challenging.
Like learning to ride a bike. I wish I could get rid of my training wheels.
You've still got them?!
Yup. I thought something was wrong with me, but then I realized my bike is too tall.
THAT'S IT! Martha just needs a bigger agility course!
If we build it to fit her, she'll move through it more smoothly.

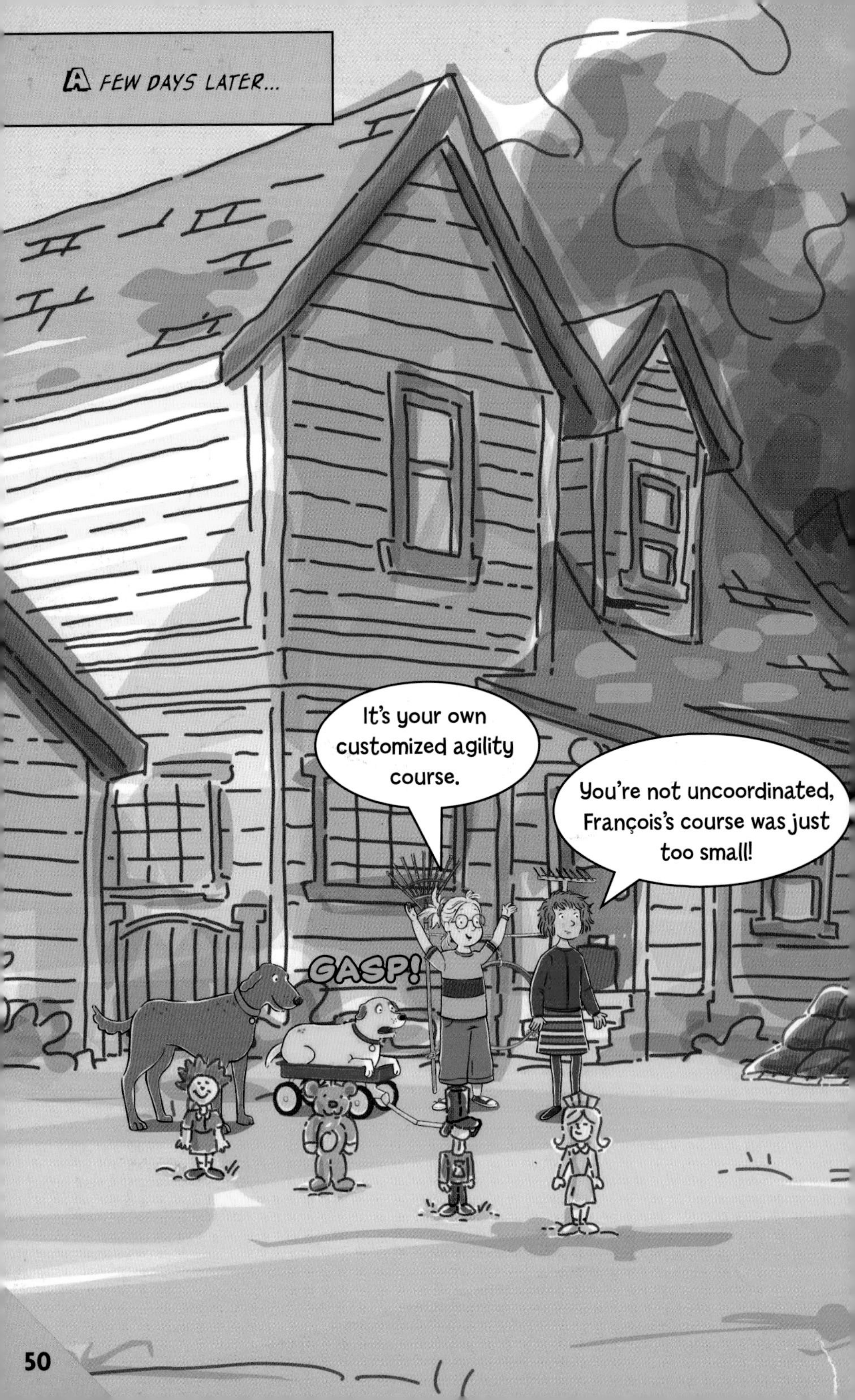
A FEW DAYS LATER...
It's your own customized agility course.
You're not uncoordinated, François's course was just too small!
GASP!

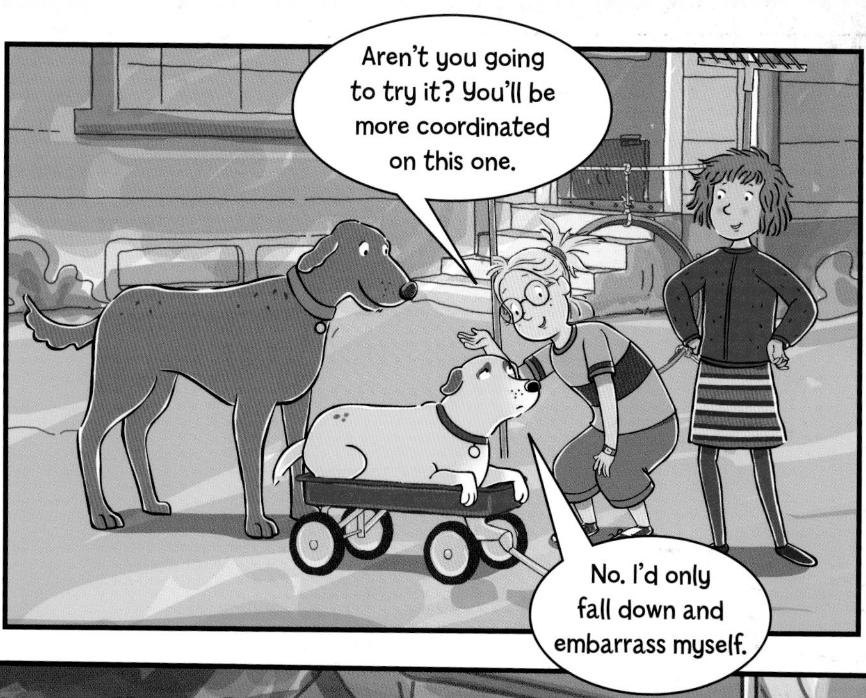
Aren't you going to try it? You'll be more coordinated on this one.
No. I'd only fall down and embarrass myself.

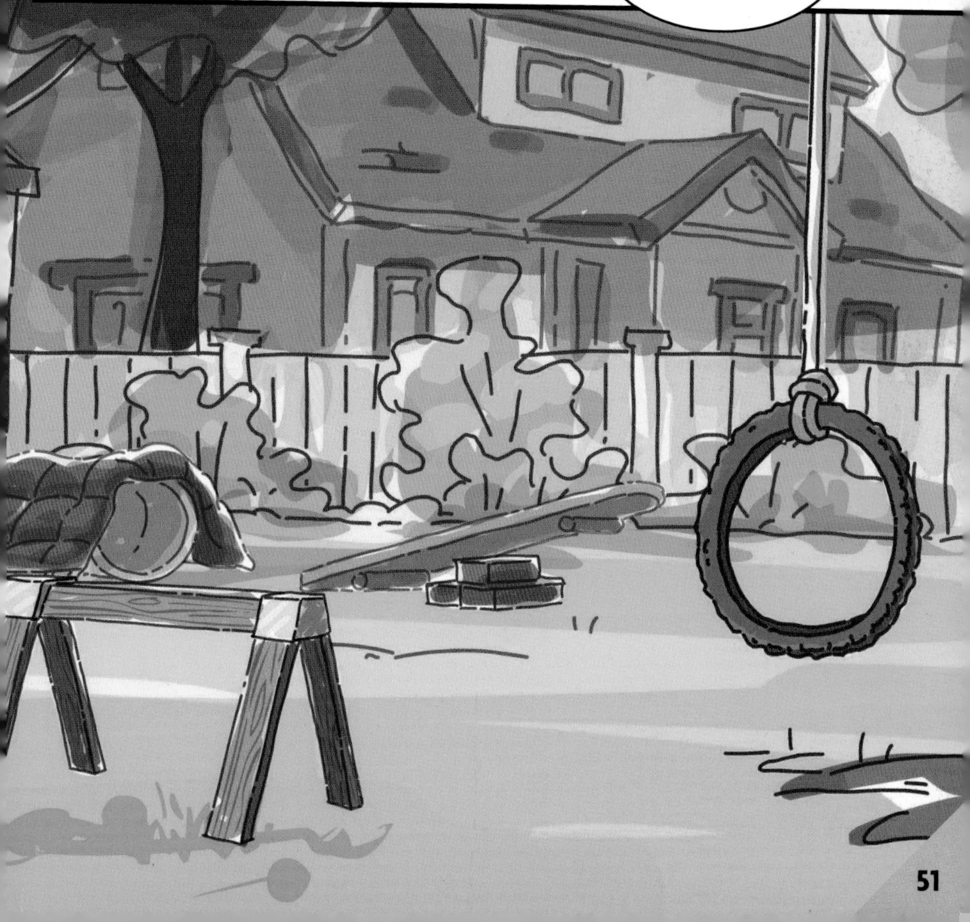

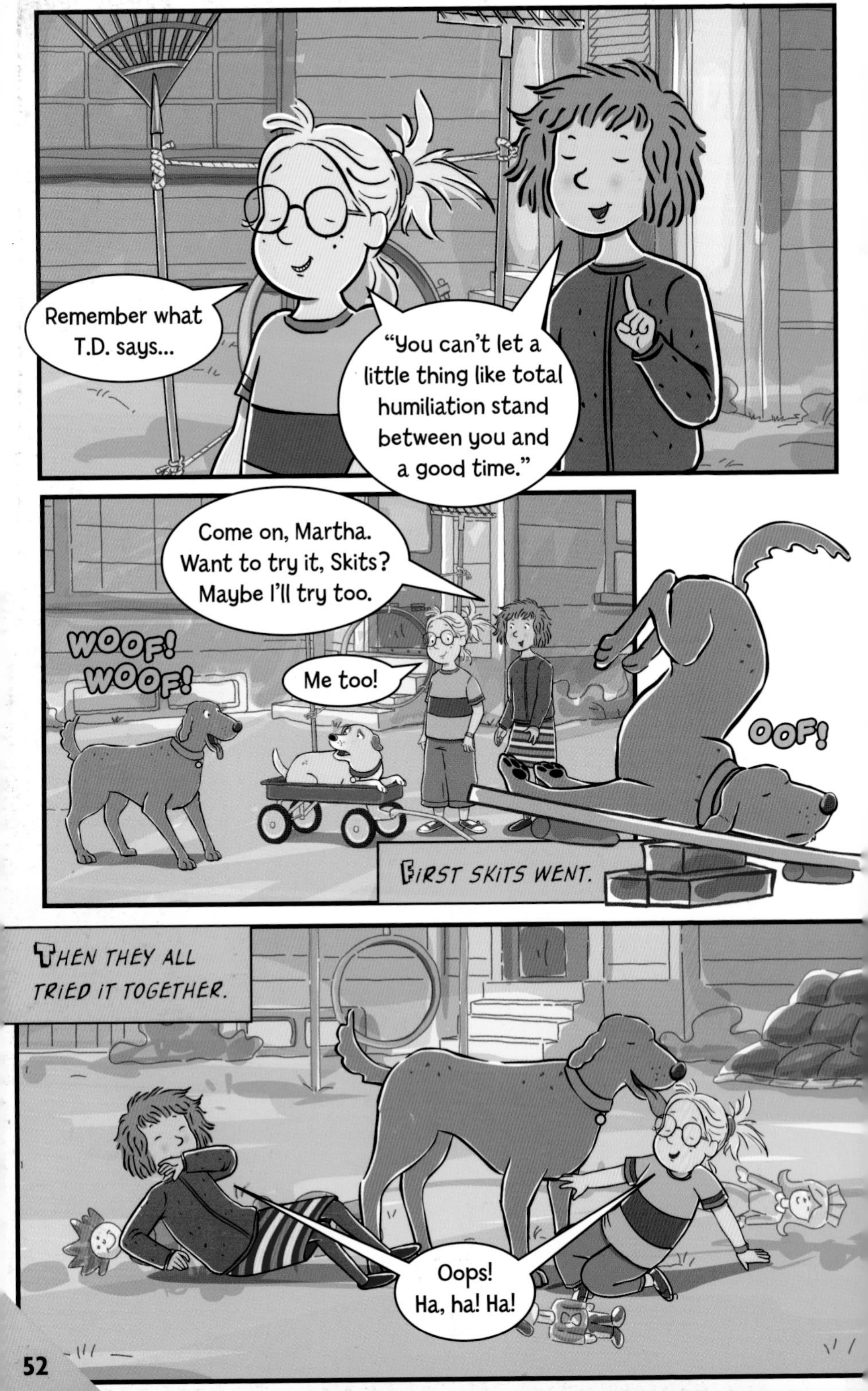
Remember what T.D. says...
"You can't let a little thing like total humiliation stand between you and a good time."
Come on, Martha. Want to try it, Skits? Maybe I'll try too.
WOOF! WOOF!
Me too!
OOF!
FIRST SKITS WENT.
THEN THEY ALL TRIED IT TOGETHER.
Oops! Ha, ha! Ha!

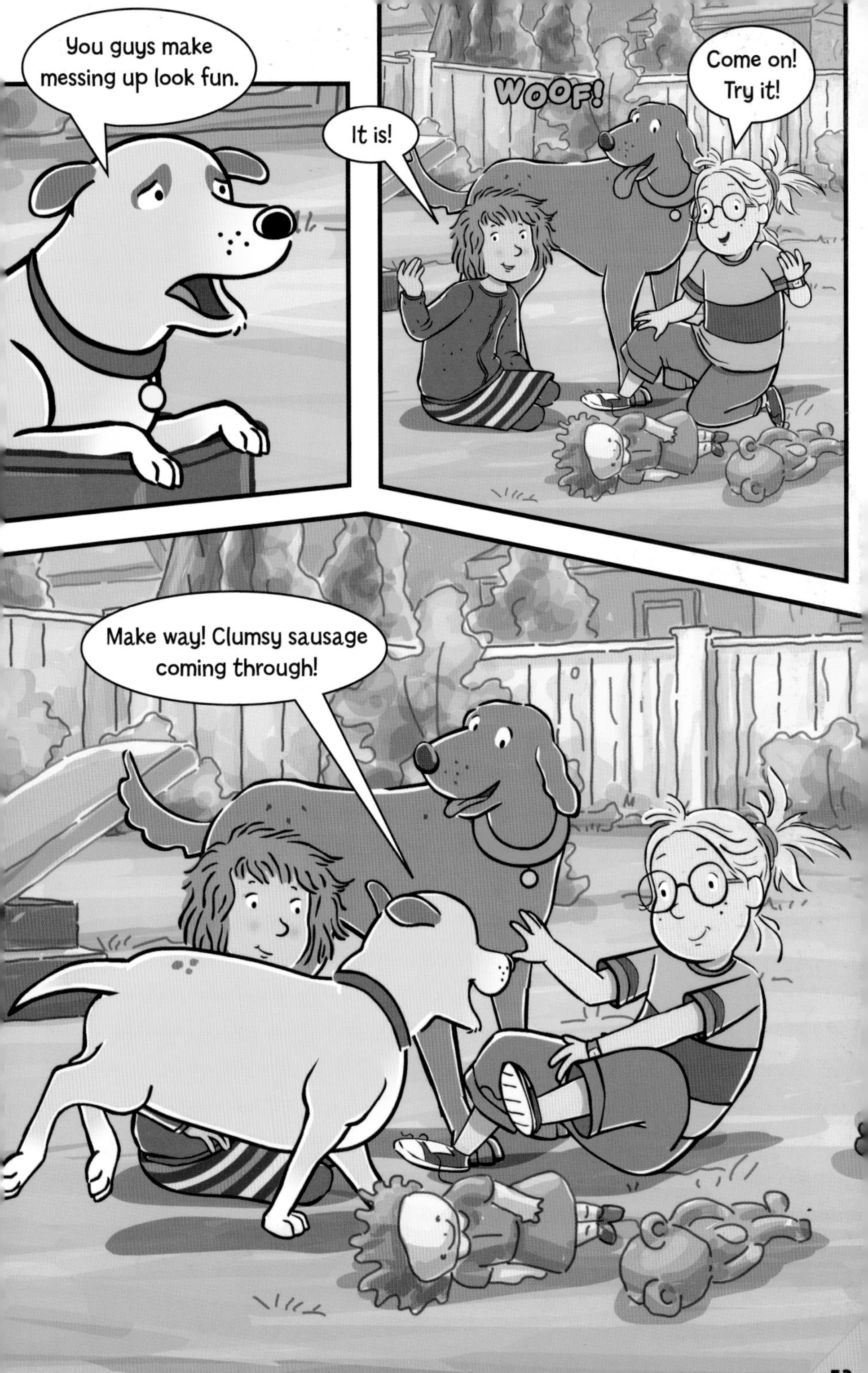
You guys make messing up look fun.
It is!
WOOF!
Come on! Try it!
Make way! Clumsy sausage coming through!

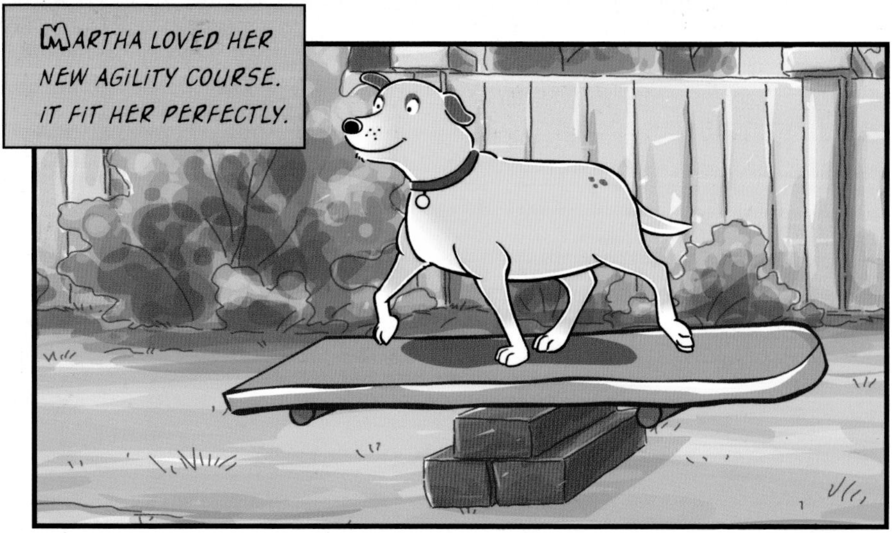
MARTHA LOVED HER NEW AGILITY COURSE. IT FIT HER PERFECTLY.

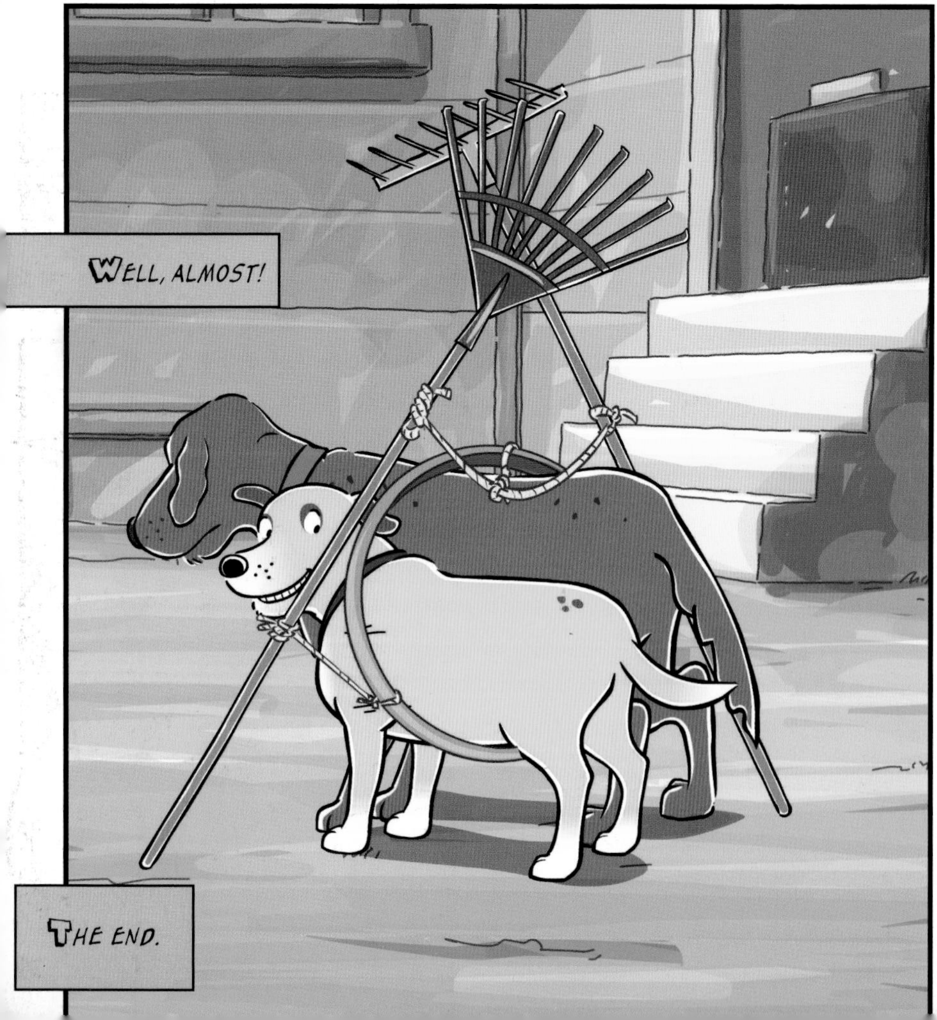
WELL, ALMOST!
THE END.

4 Best in Show

Adaptation by Jamie White
Based on a TV series teleplay
written by Maria Finn & Raye Lankford

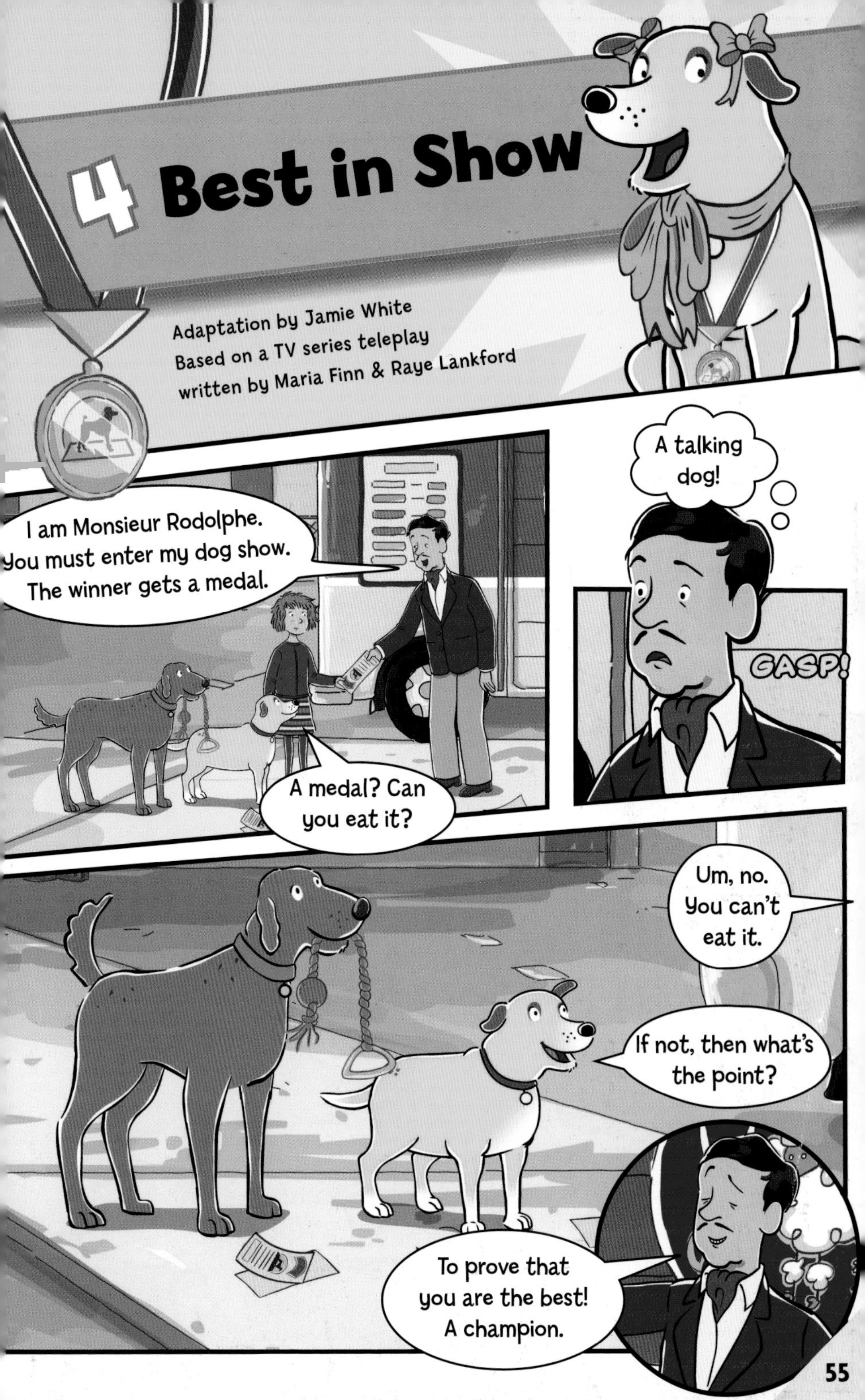

I am Monsieur Rodolphe. You must enter my dog show. The winner gets a medal.
A medal? Can you eat it?
A talking dog!
GASP!
Um, no. You can't eat it.
If not, then what's the point?
To prove that you are the best! A champion.

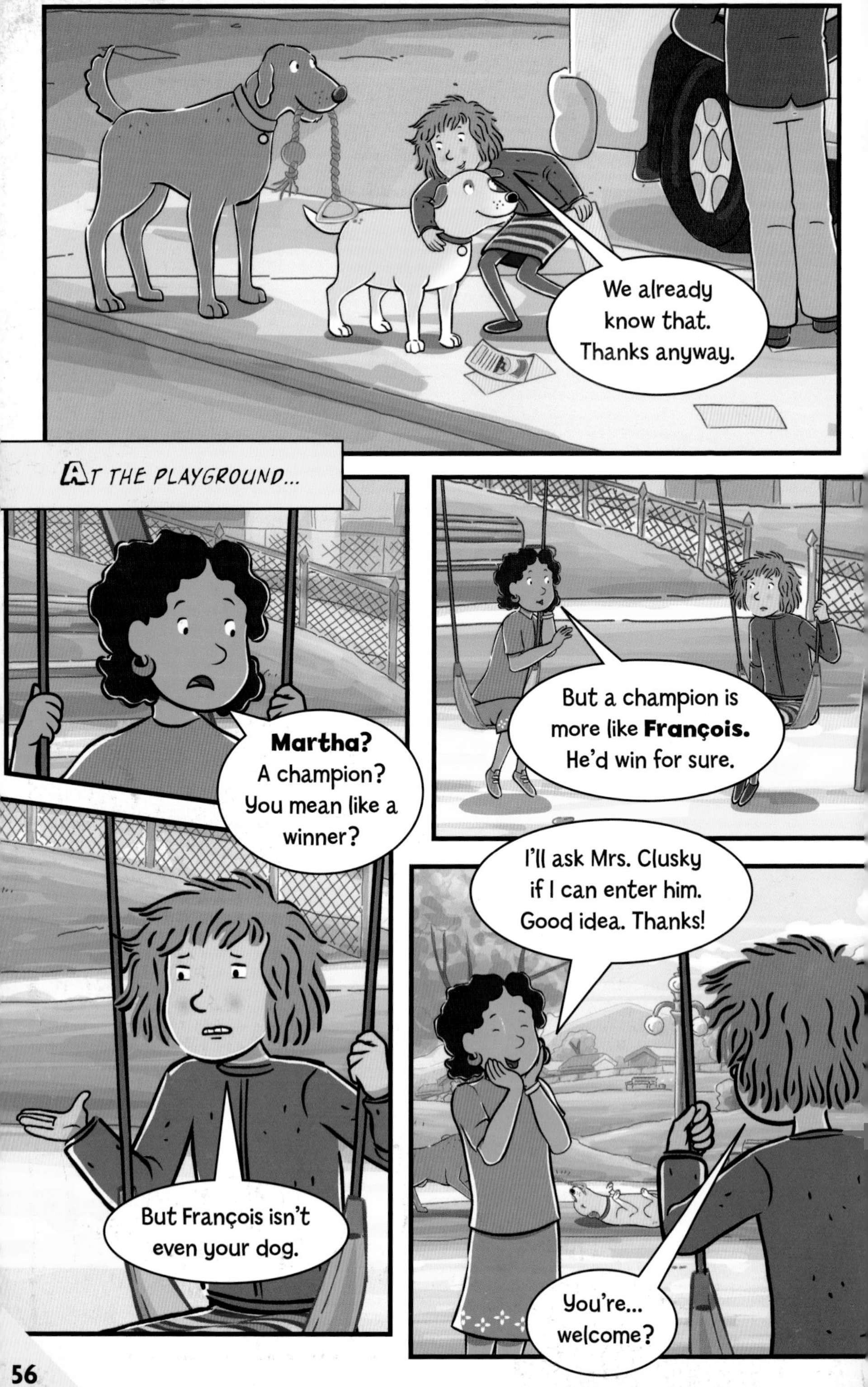

We already know that. Thanks anyway.
AT THE PLAYGROUND...
Martha? A champion? You mean like a winner?
But a champion is more like **François.** He'd win for sure.
But François isn't even your dog.
I'll ask Mrs. Clusky if I can enter him. Good idea. Thanks!
You're... welcome?

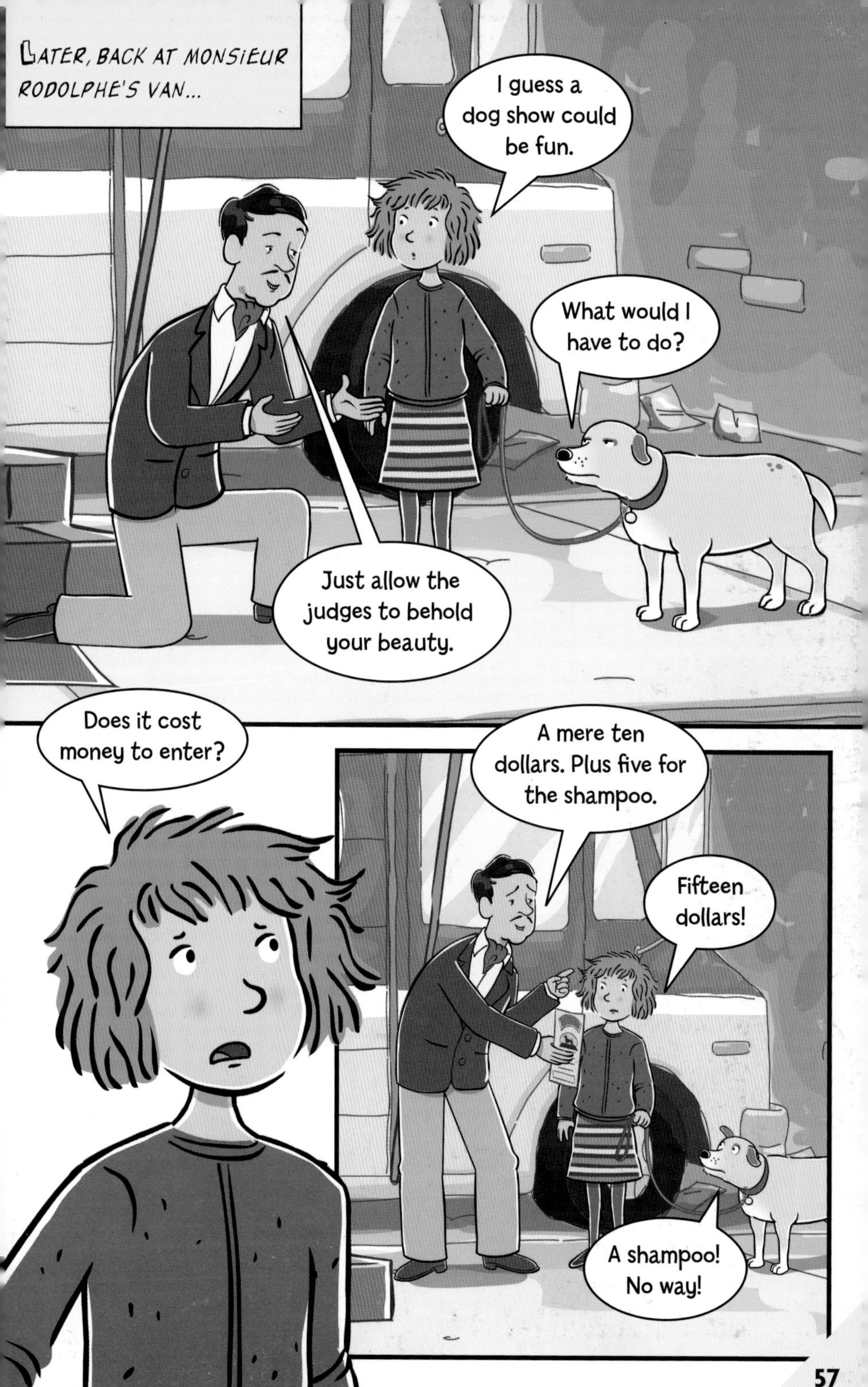
LATER, BACK AT MONSIEUR RODOLPHE'S VAN...
I guess a dog show could be fun.
What would I have to do?
Just allow the judges to behold your beauty.
Does it cost money to enter?
A mere ten dollars. Plus five for the shampoo.
Fifteen dollars!
A shampoo! No way!

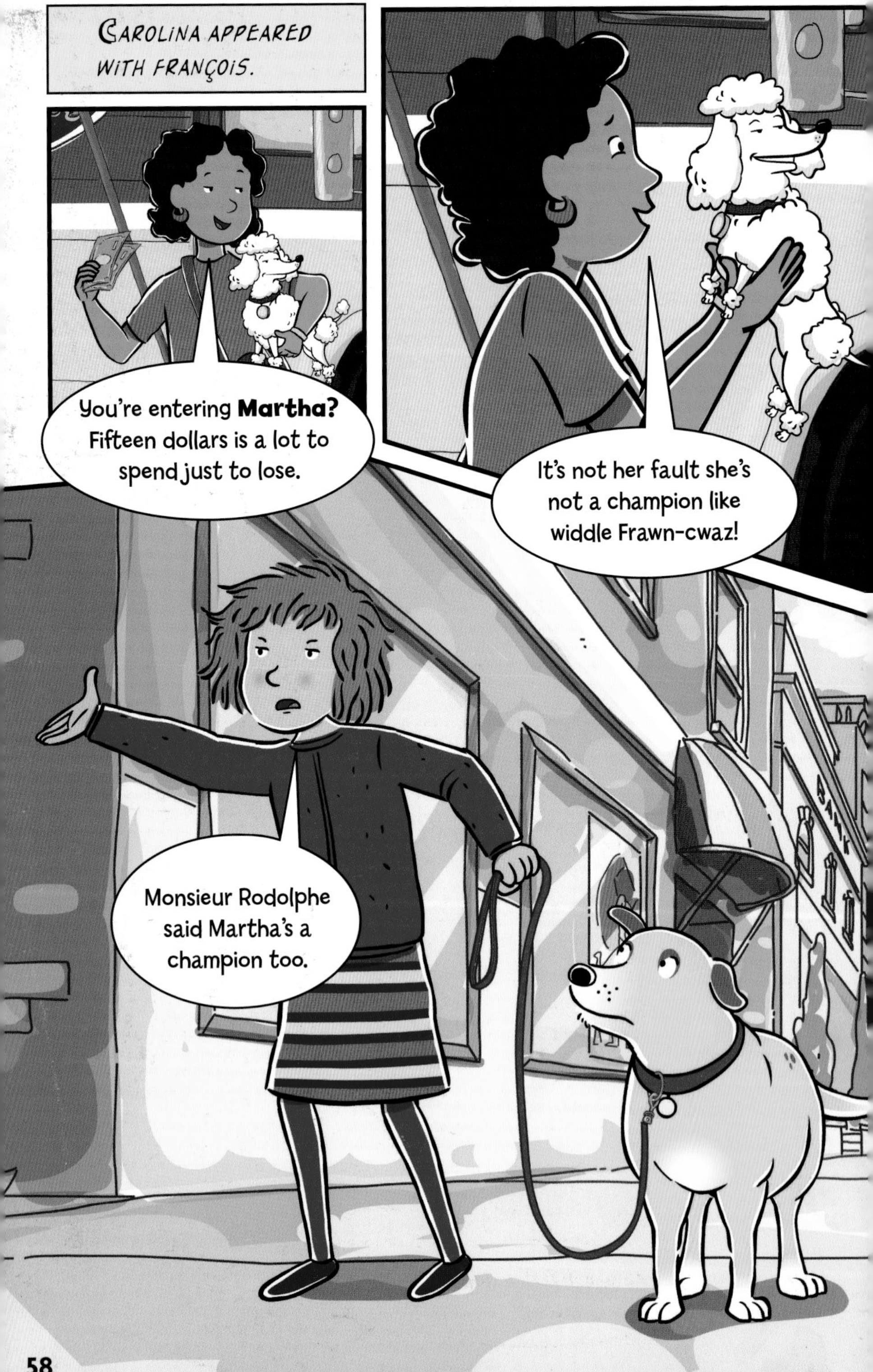
CAROLINA APPEARED WITH FRANÇOIS.
You're entering **Martha?** Fifteen dollars is a lot to spend just to lose.
It's not her fault she's not a champion like widdle Frawn-cwaz!
Monsieur Rodolphe said Martha's a champion too.
BANK

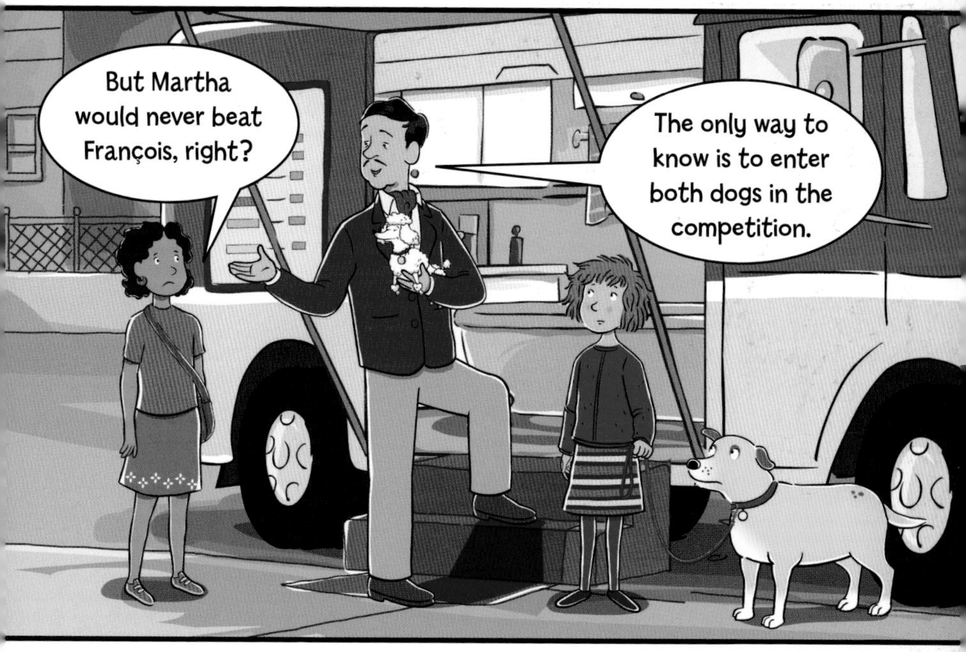
But Martha would never beat François, right?
The only way to know is to enter both dogs in the competition.

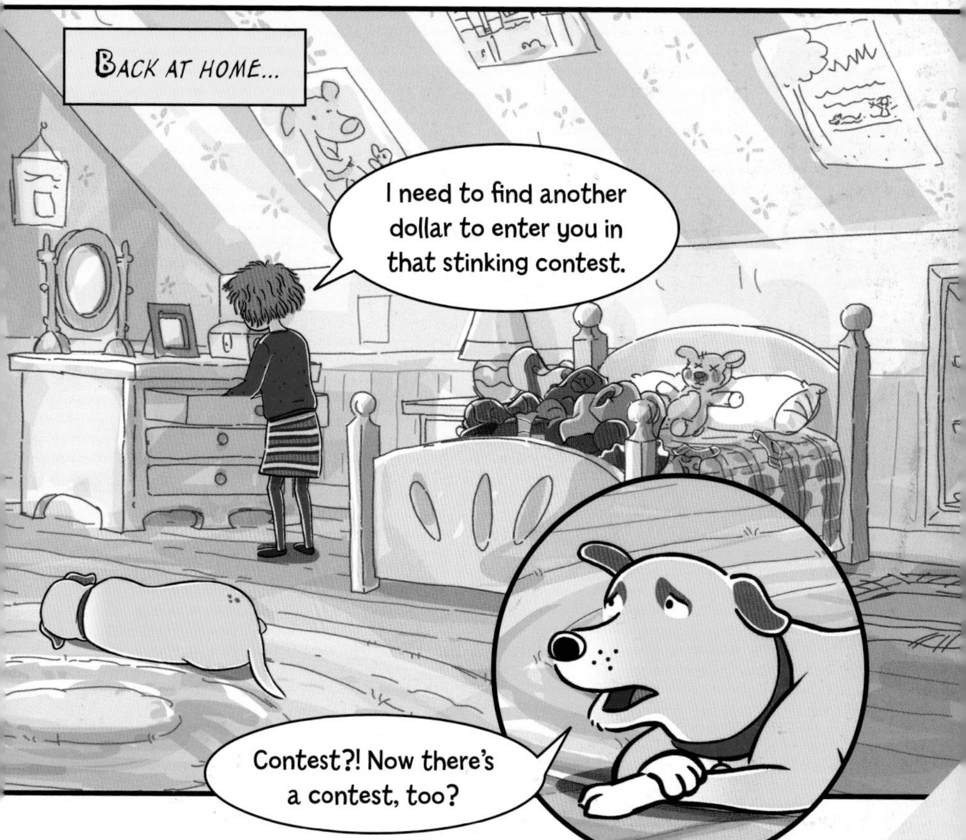
BACK AT HOME...
I need to find another dollar to enter you in that stinking contest.
Contest?! Now there's a contest, too?

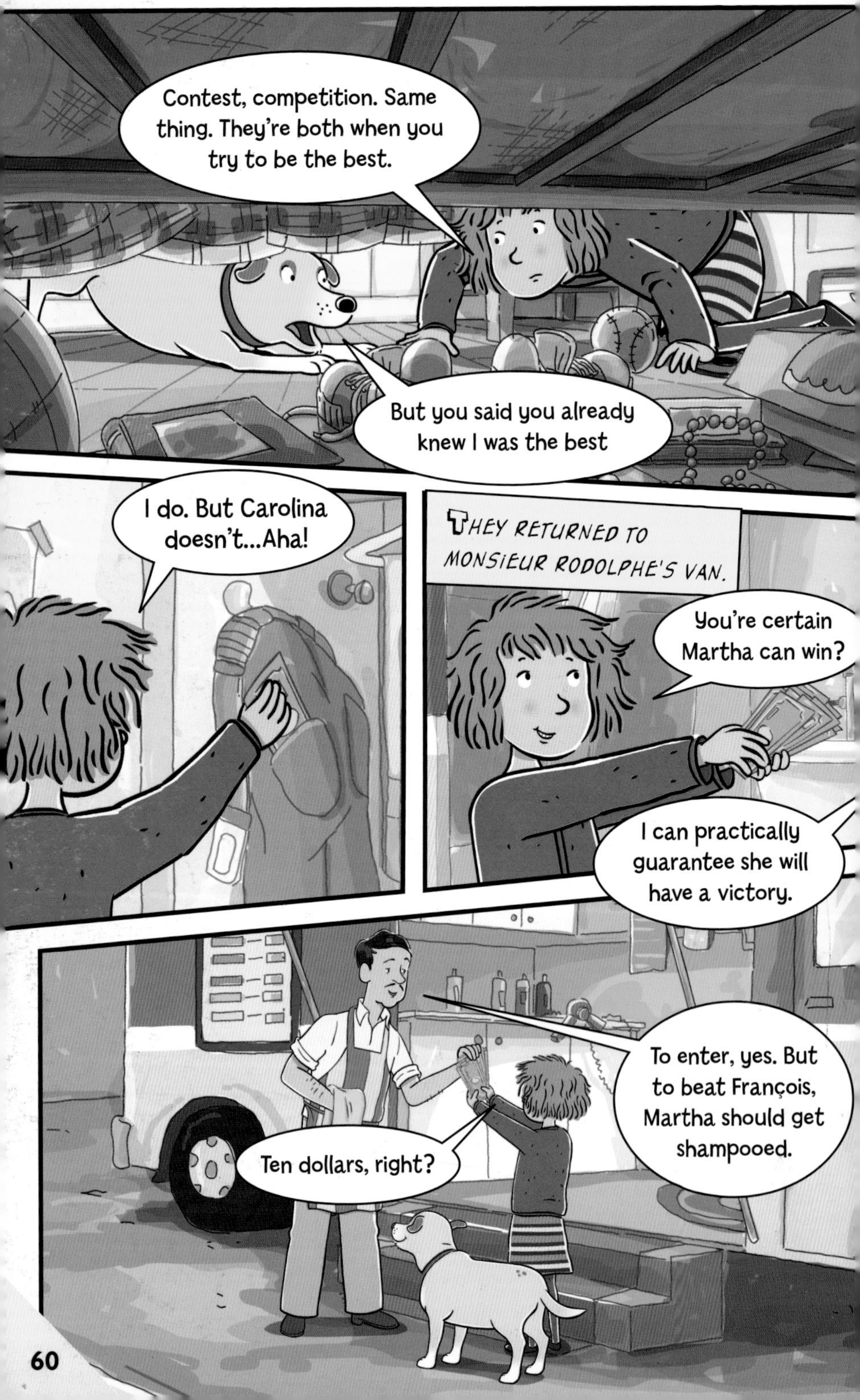
Contest, competition. Same thing. They're both when you try to be the best.
But you said you already knew I was the best
I do. But Carolina doesn't...Aha!
THEY RETURNED TO MONSIEUR RODOLPHE'S VAN.
You're certain Martha can win?
I can practically guarantee she will have a victory.
To enter, yes. But to beat François, Martha should get shampooed.
Ten dollars, right?

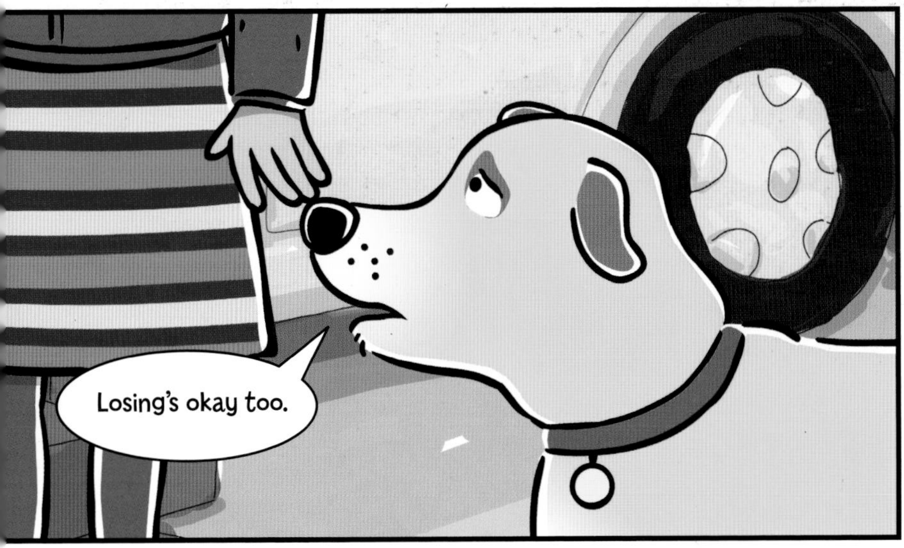
Losing's okay too.

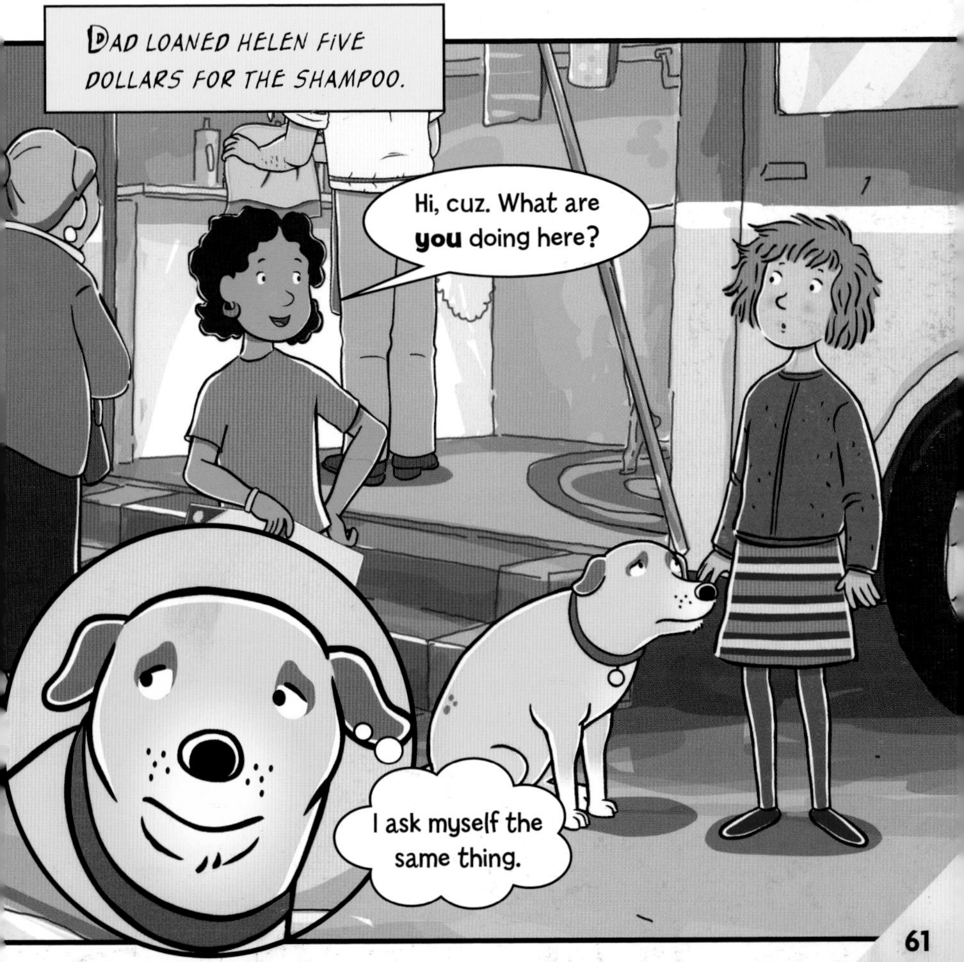
DAD LOANED HELEN FIVE DOLLARS FOR THE SHAMPOO.
Hi, cuz. What are **you** doing here?
I ask myself the same thing.

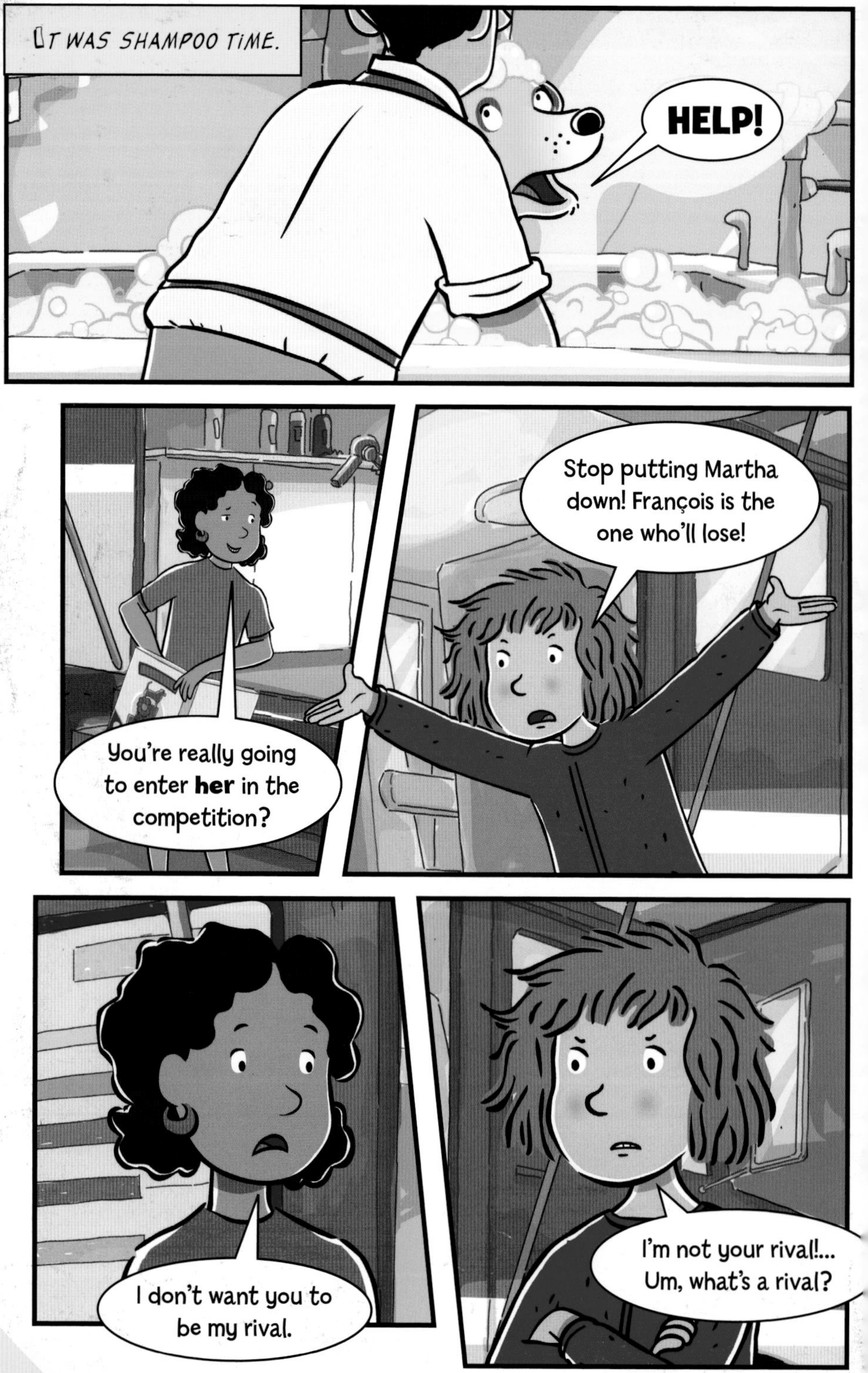
IT WAS SHAMPOO TIME.
HELP!
You're really going to enter **her** in the competition?
Stop putting Martha down! François is the one who'll lose!
I don't want you to be my rival.
I'm not your rival!... Um, what's a rival?

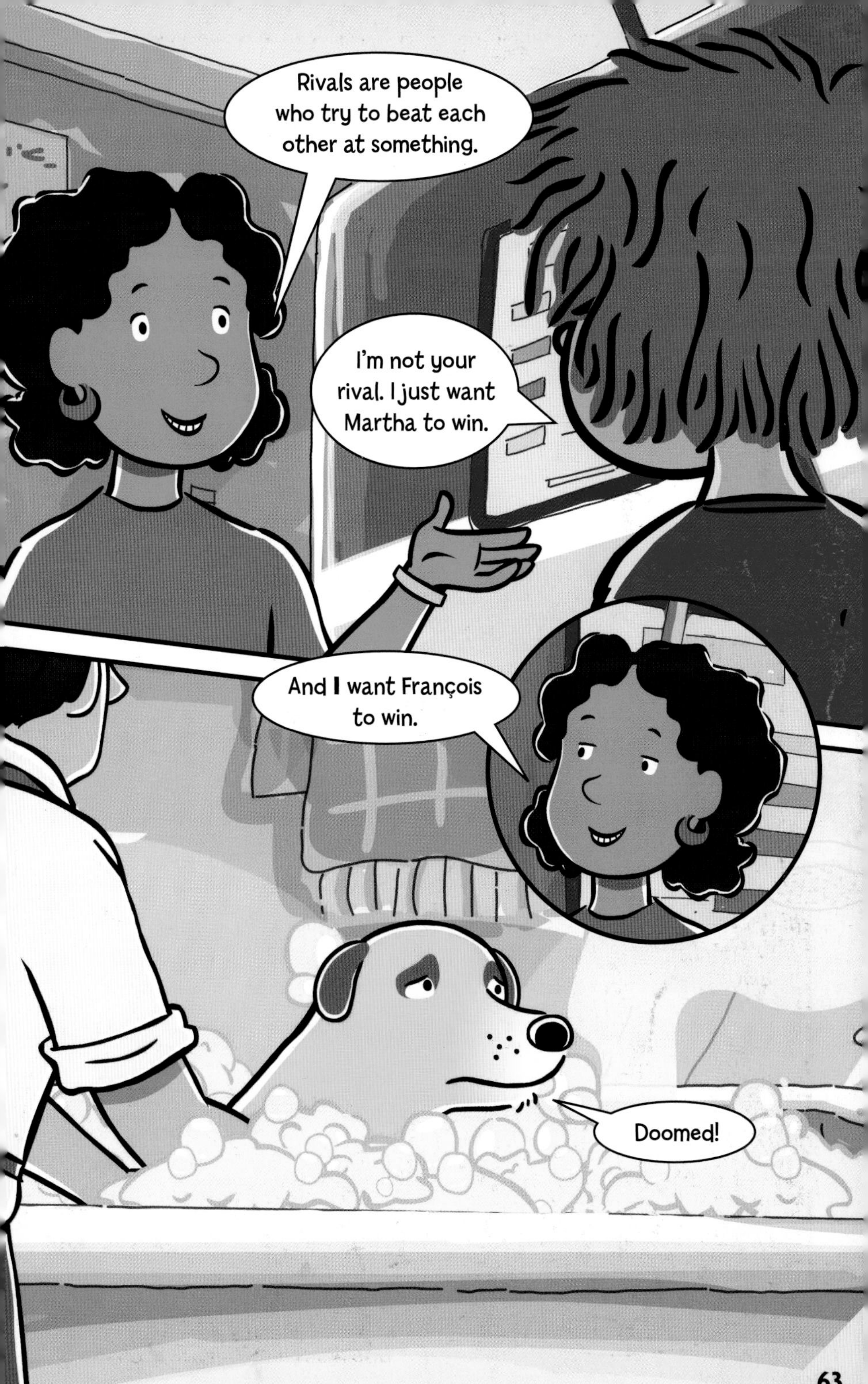
Rivals are people who try to beat each other at something.
I'm not your rival. I just want Martha to win.
And I want François to win.
Doomed!

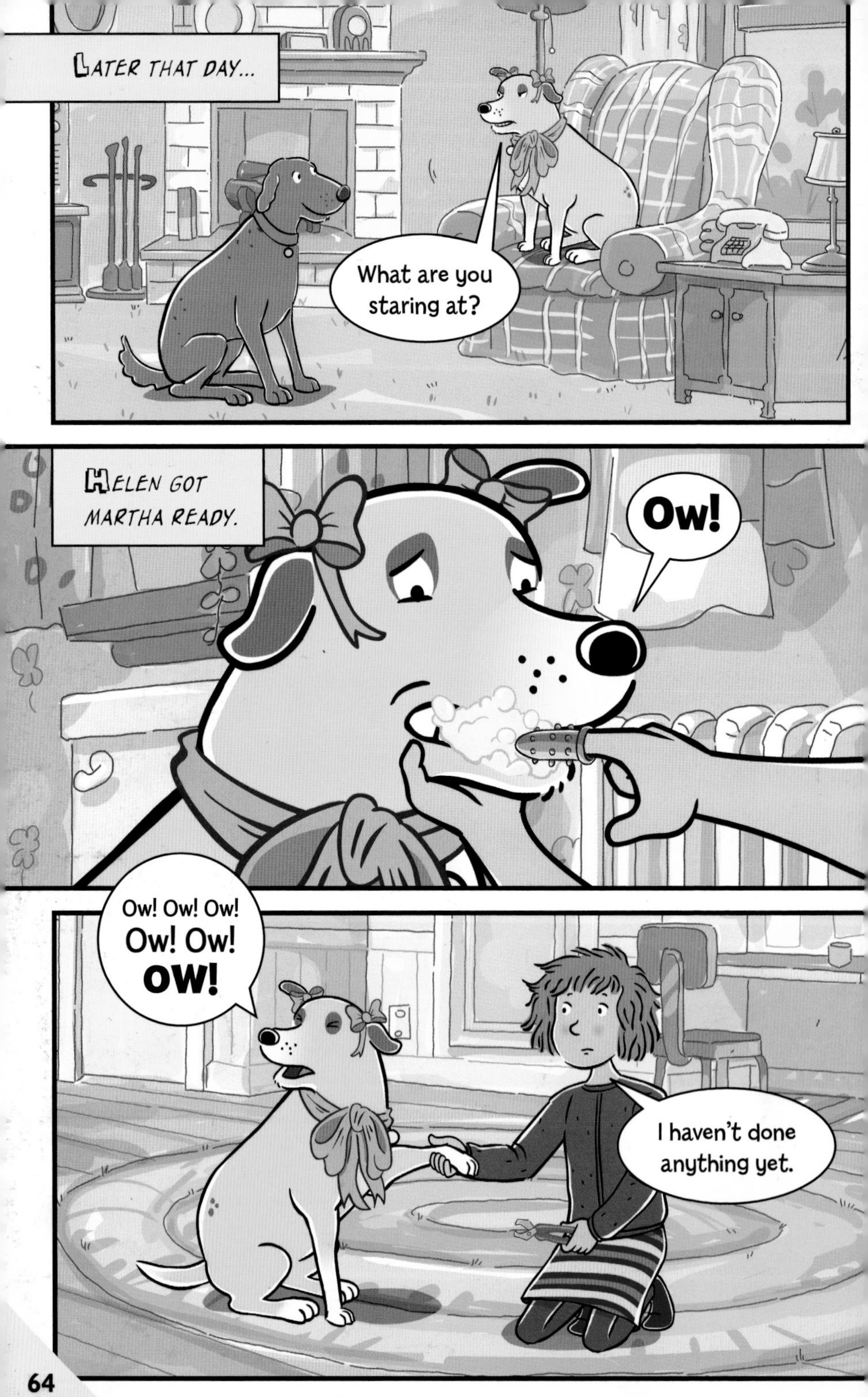
LATER THAT DAY...
What are you staring at?
HELEN GOT MARTHA READY.
Ow!
Ow! Ow! Ow! Ow! Ow! OW!
I haven't done anything yet.

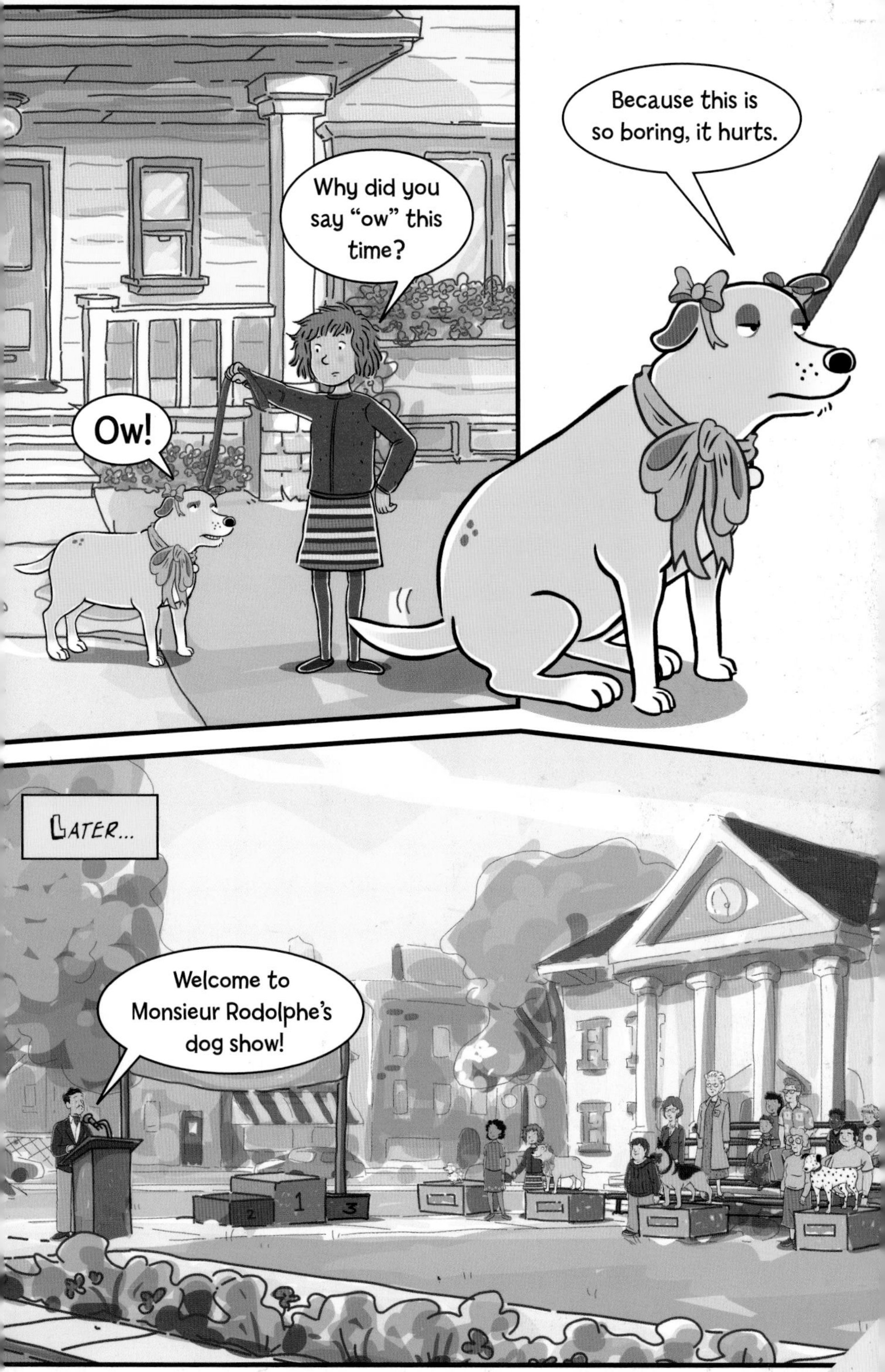

Ow!
Why did you say "ow" this time?
Because this is so boring, it hurts.
LATER...
Welcome to Monsieur Rodolphe's dog show!

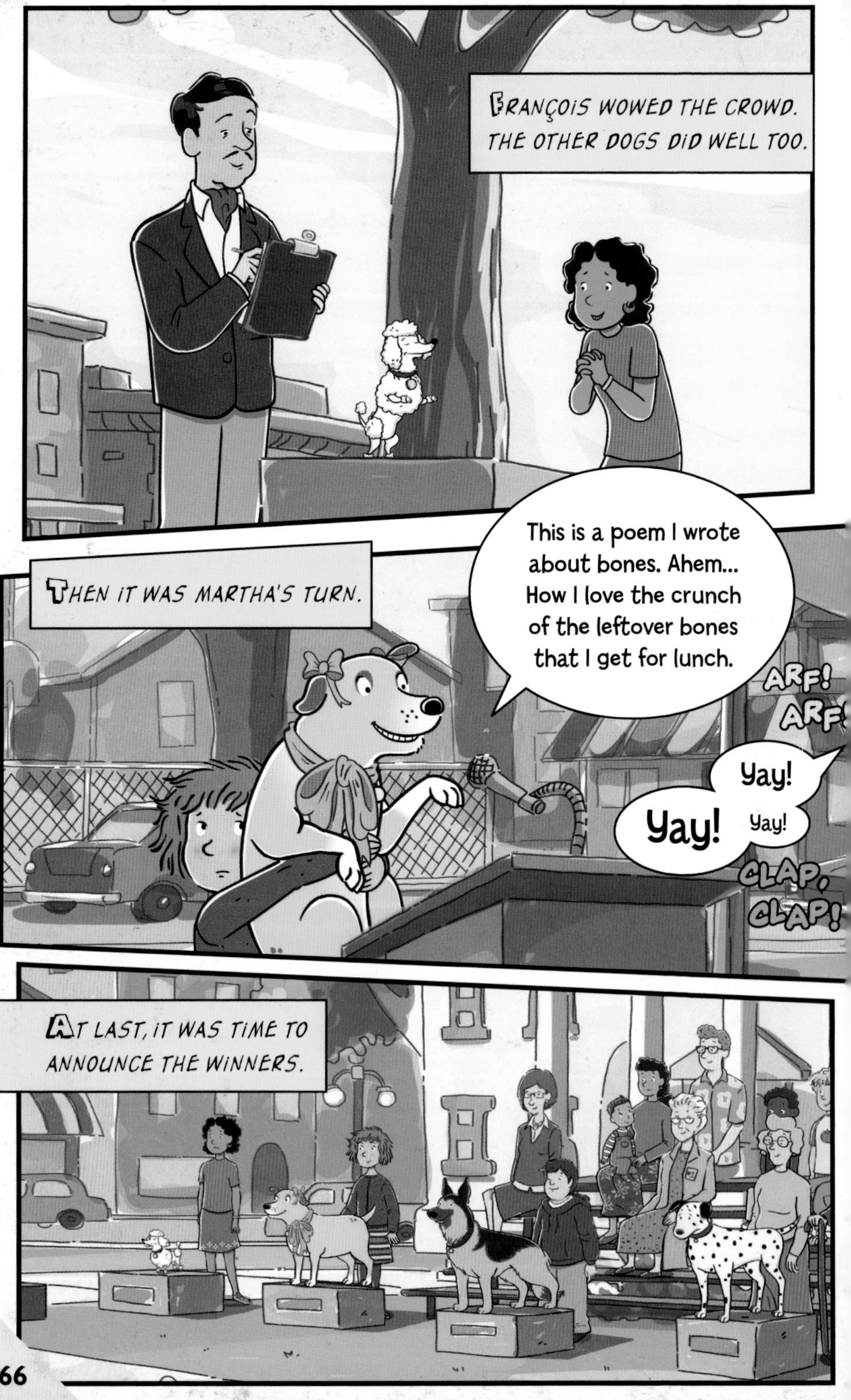
FRANÇOIS WOWED THE CROWD. THE OTHER DOGS DID WELL TOO.
THEN IT WAS MARTHA'S TURN.
This is a poem I wrote about bones. Ahem... How I love the crunch of the leftover bones that I get for lunch.
ARF! ARF!
Yay!
Yay!
Yay!
CLAP, CLAP!
AT LAST, IT WAS TIME TO ANNOUNCE THE WINNERS.

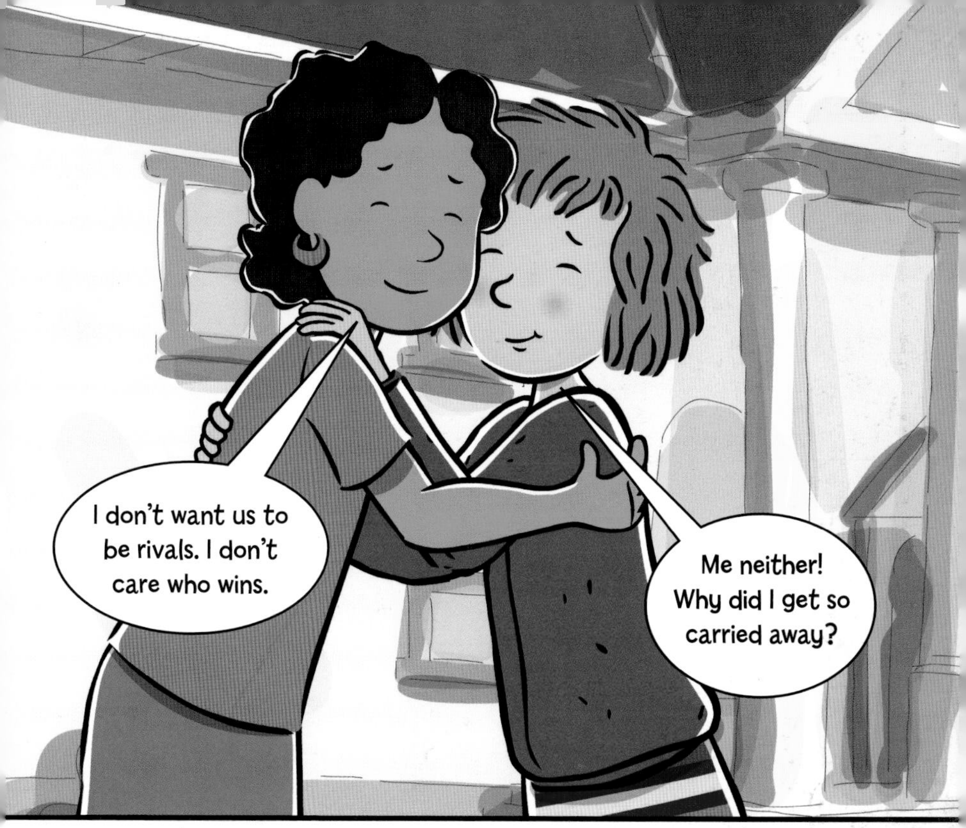
I don't want us to be rivals. I don't care who wins.
Me neither! Why did I get so carried away?

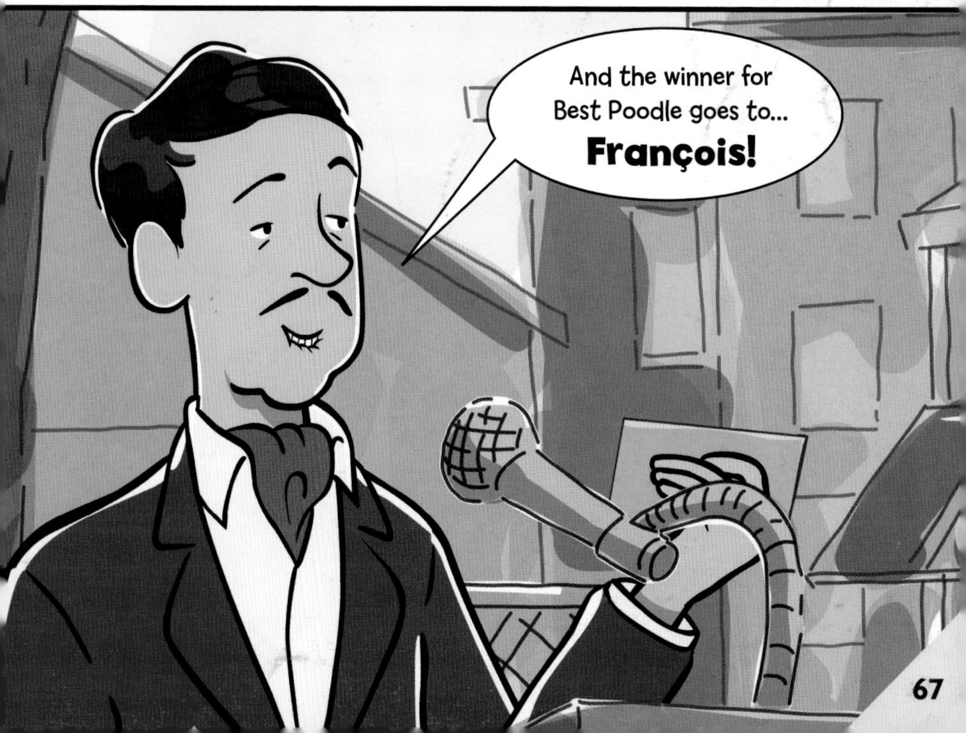
And the winner for Best Poodle goes to... **François!**

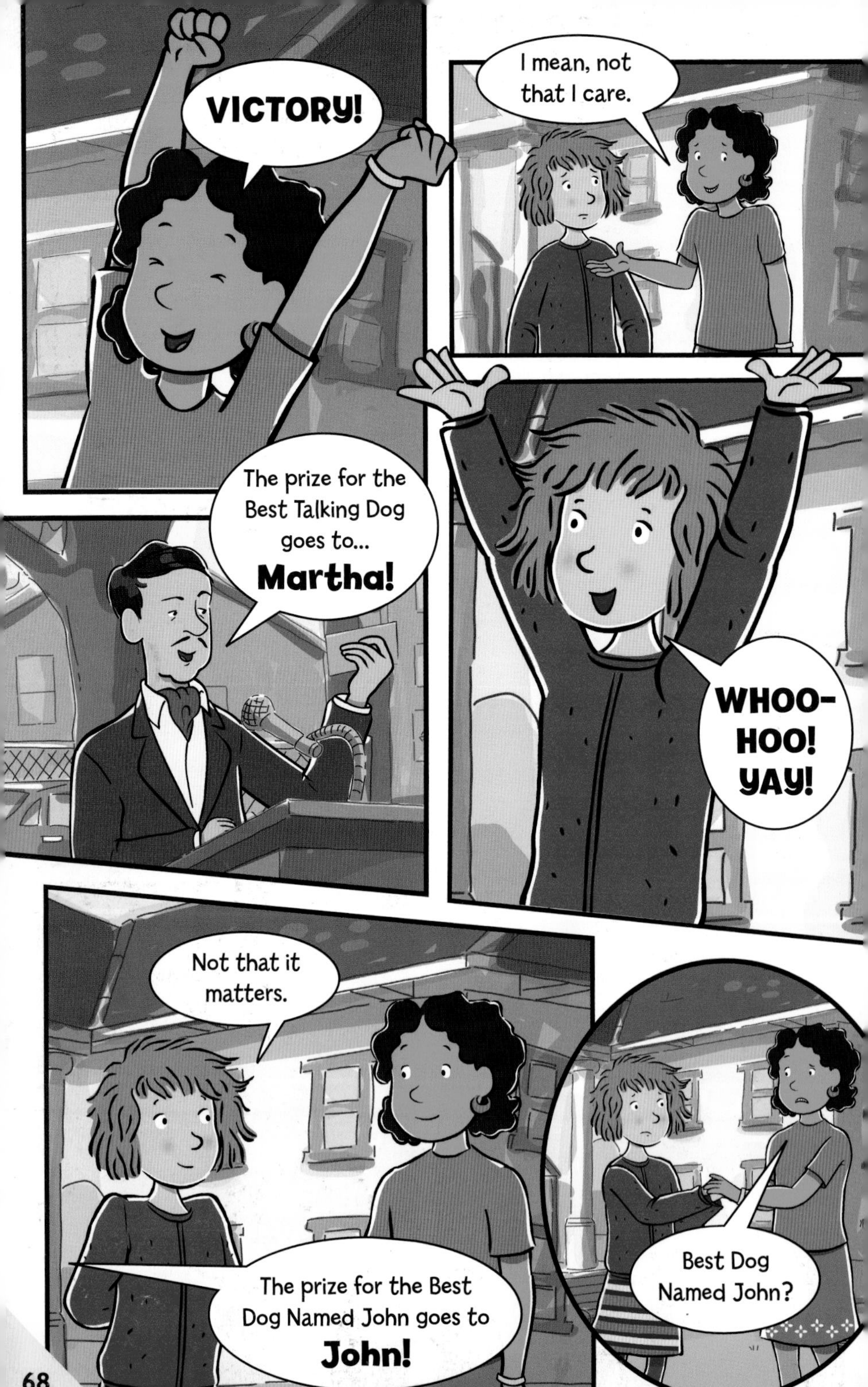
VICTORY!
I mean, not that I care.
The prize for the Best Talking Dog goes to... Martha!
WHOO-HOO! YAY!
Not that it matters.
The prize for the Best Dog Named John goes to John!
Best Dog Named John?

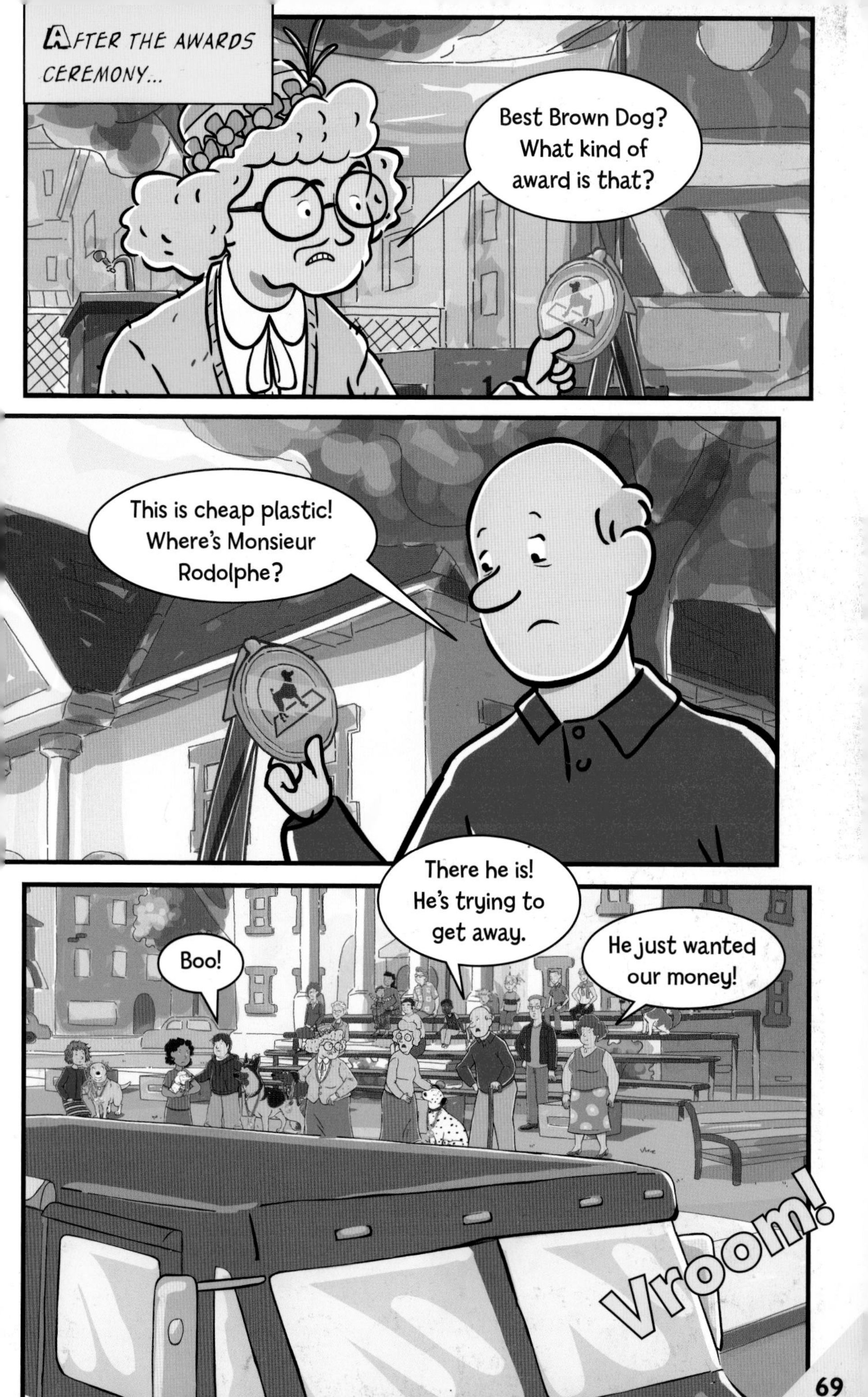
AFTER THE AWARDS CEREMONY...
Best Brown Dog? What kind of award is that?
This is cheap plastic! Where's Monsieur Rodolphe?
Boo!
There he is! He's trying to get away.
He just wanted our money!
Vroom!

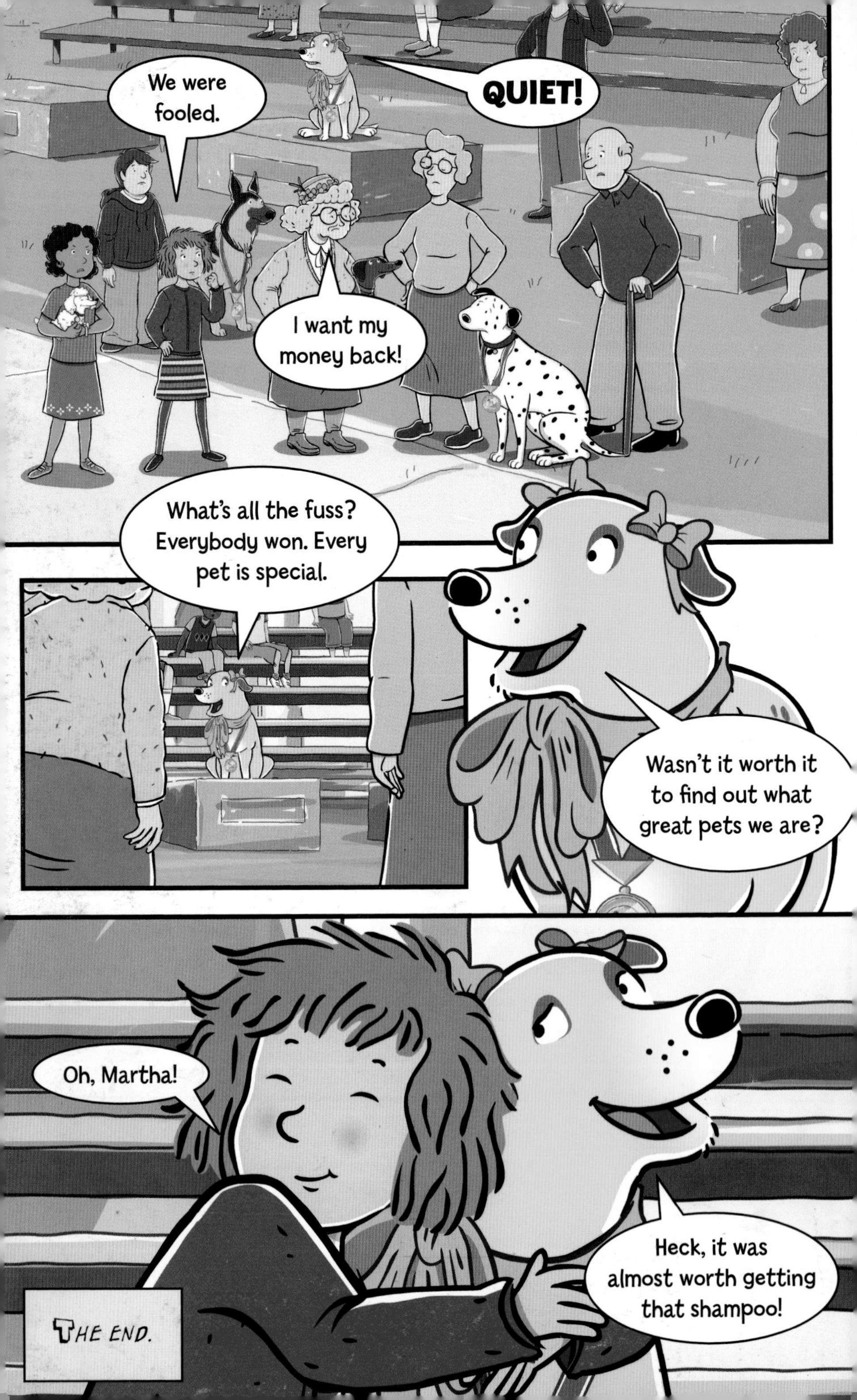
We were fooled.
QUIET!
I want my money back!
What's all the fuss? Everybody won. Every pet is special.
Wasn't it worth it to find out what great pets we are?
Oh, Martha!
Heck, it was almost worth getting that shampoo!
THE END.

5 Starstruck Martha

Adaptation by Jamie White
Based on a TV series teleplay
written by Ron Holsey

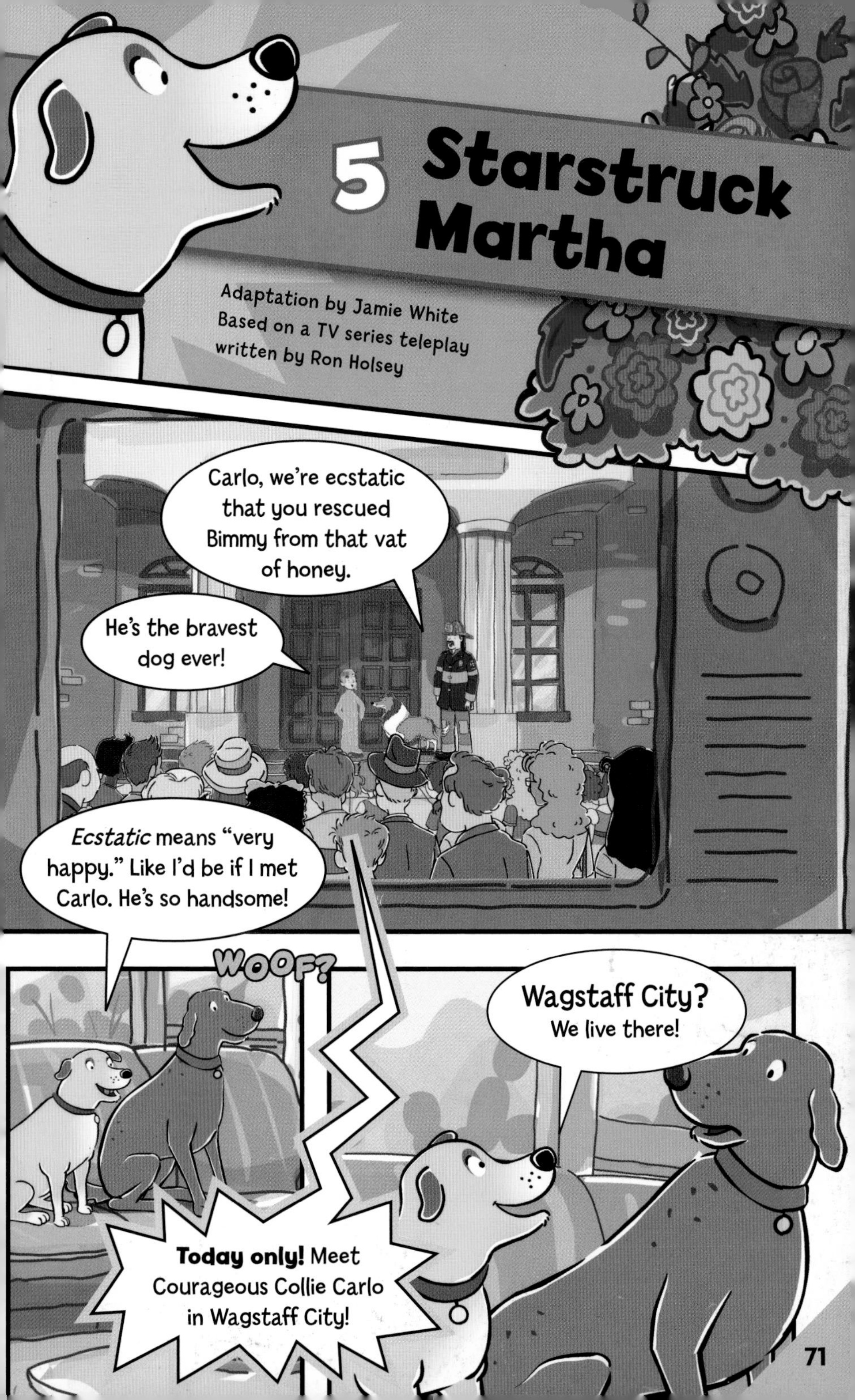
Carlo, we're ecstatic that you rescued Bimmy from that vat of honey.
He's the bravest dog ever!
Ecstatic means "very happy." Like I'd be if I met Carlo. He's so handsome!
WOOF?
Wagstaff City? We live there!
Today only! Meet Courageous Collie Carlo in Wagstaff City!

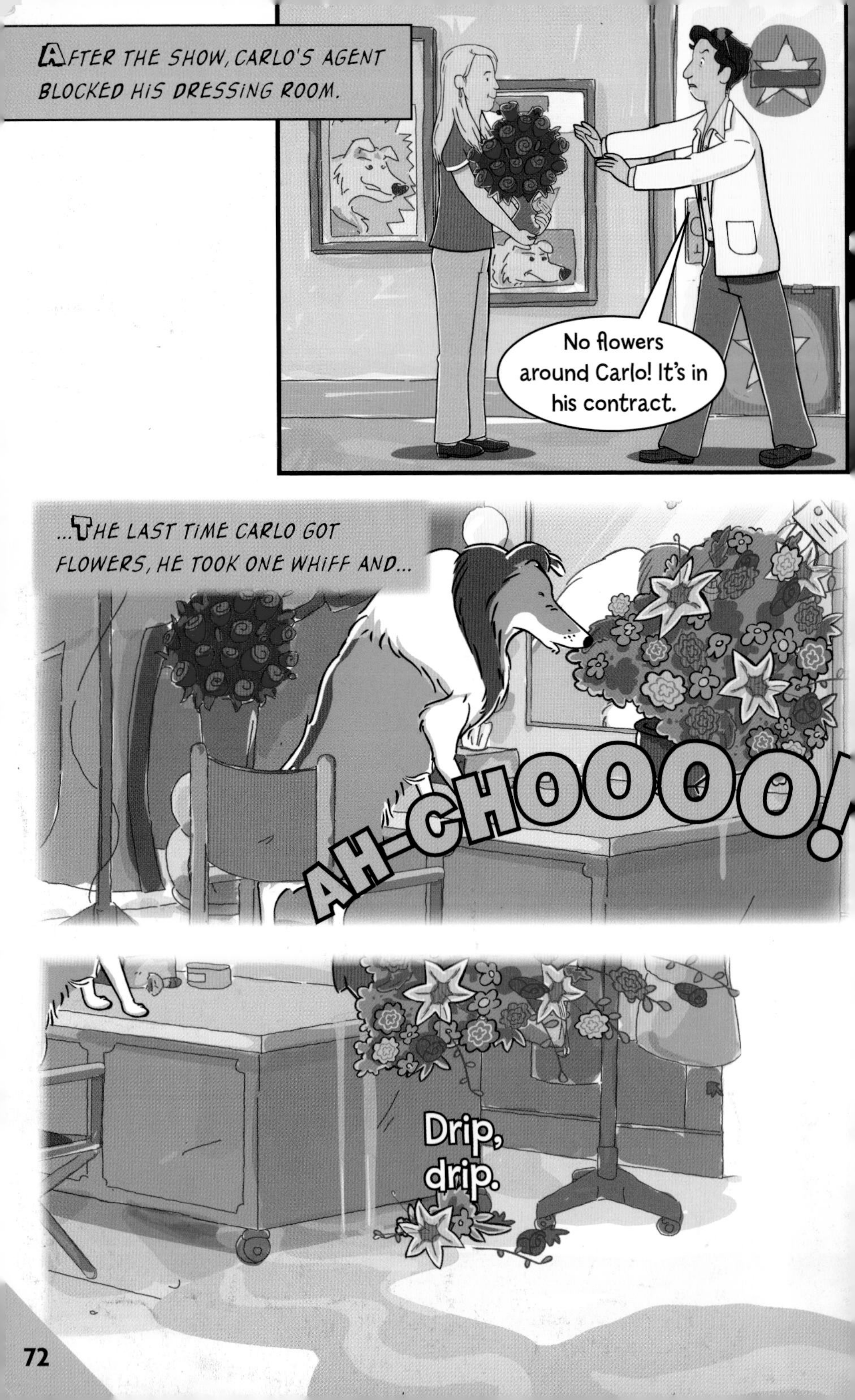
AFTER THE SHOW, CARLO'S AGENT BLOCKED HIS DRESSING ROOM.
No flowers around Carlo! It's in his contract.
...THE LAST TIME CARLO GOT FLOWERS, HE TOOK ONE WHIFF AND...
AH-CHOOOOO!
Drip, drip.

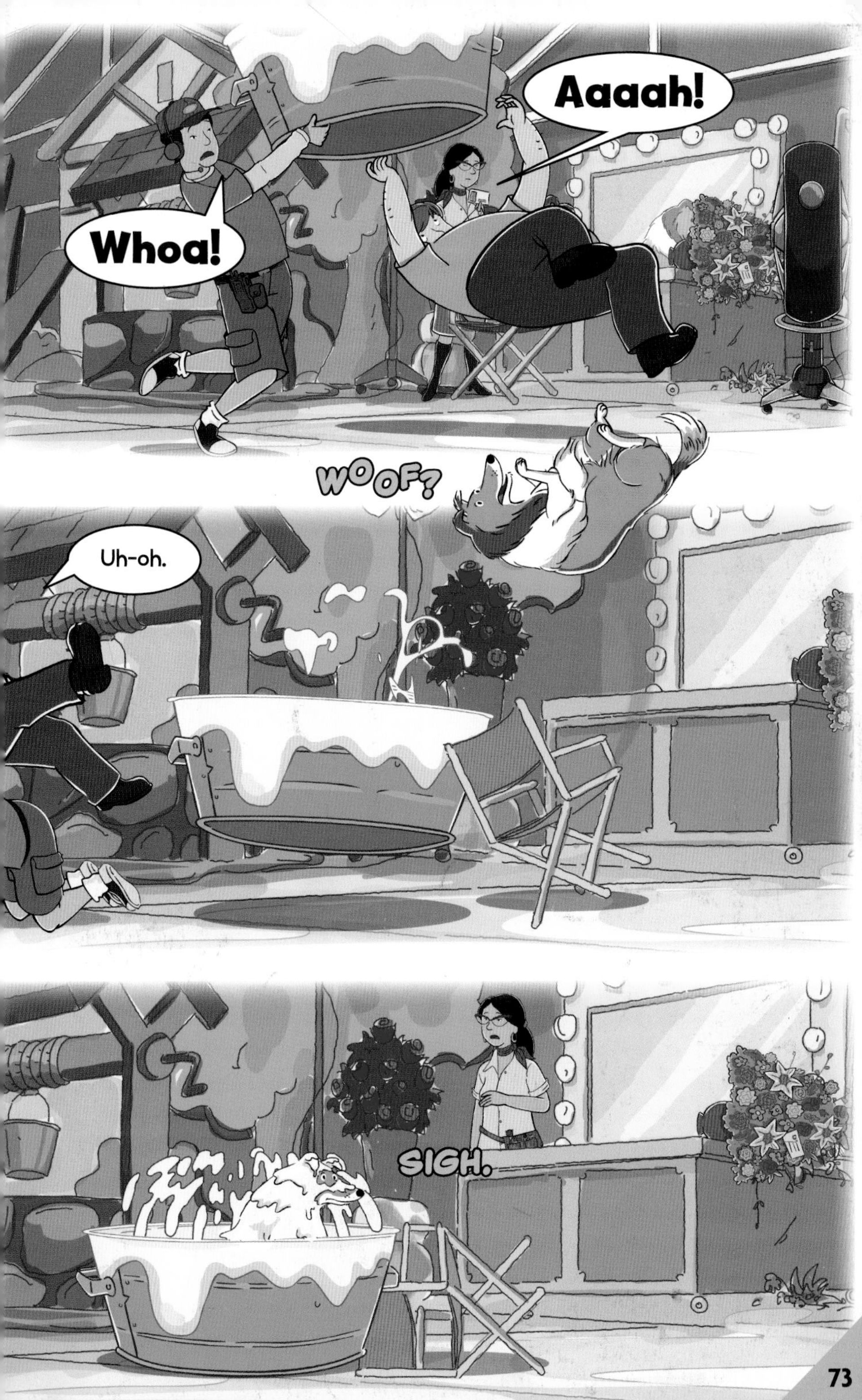
Aaaah!
Whoa!
WOOF?
Uh-oh.
SIGH.

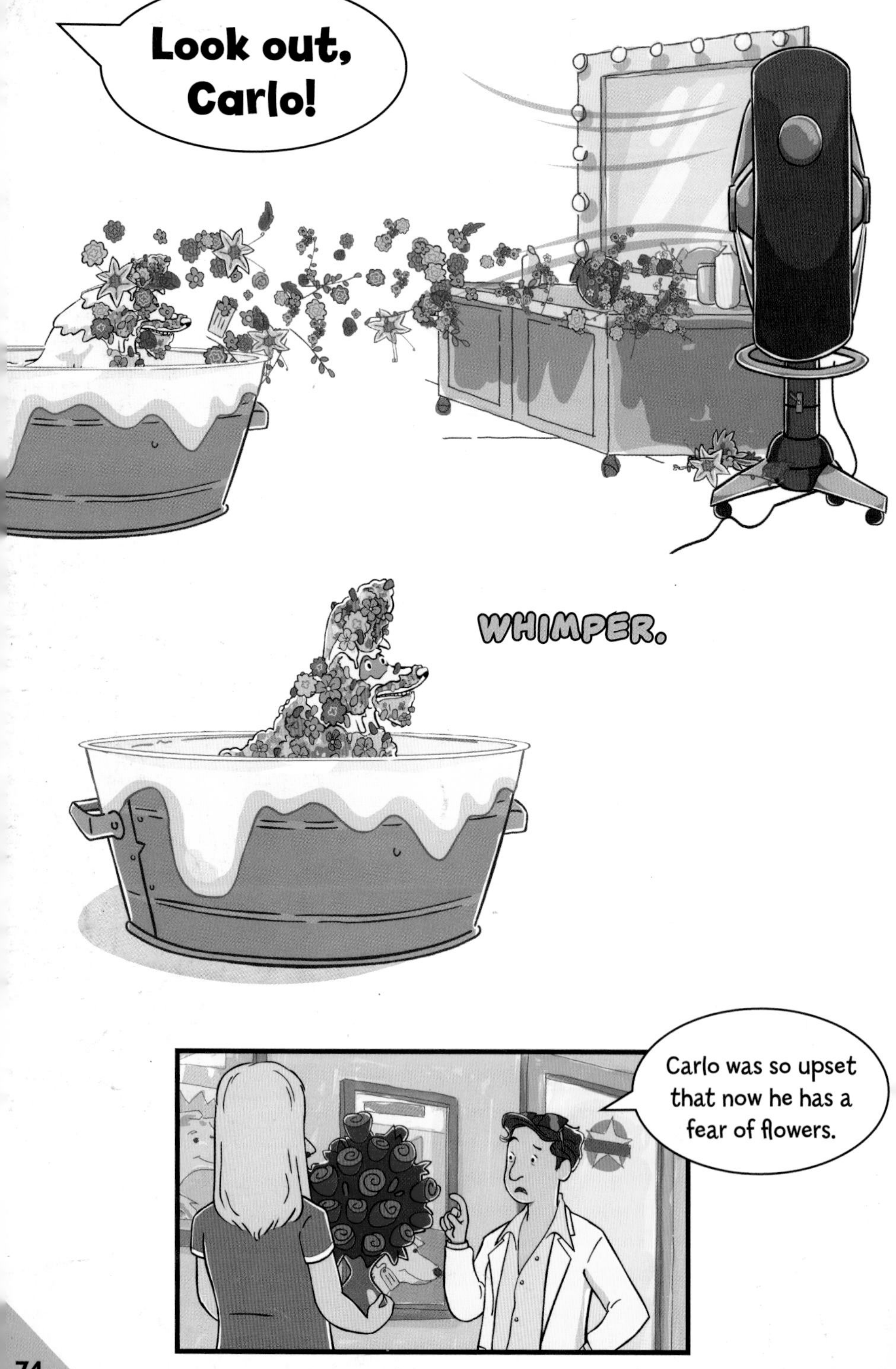
Look out, Carlo!
WHIMPER.
Carlo was so upset that now he has a fear of flowers.

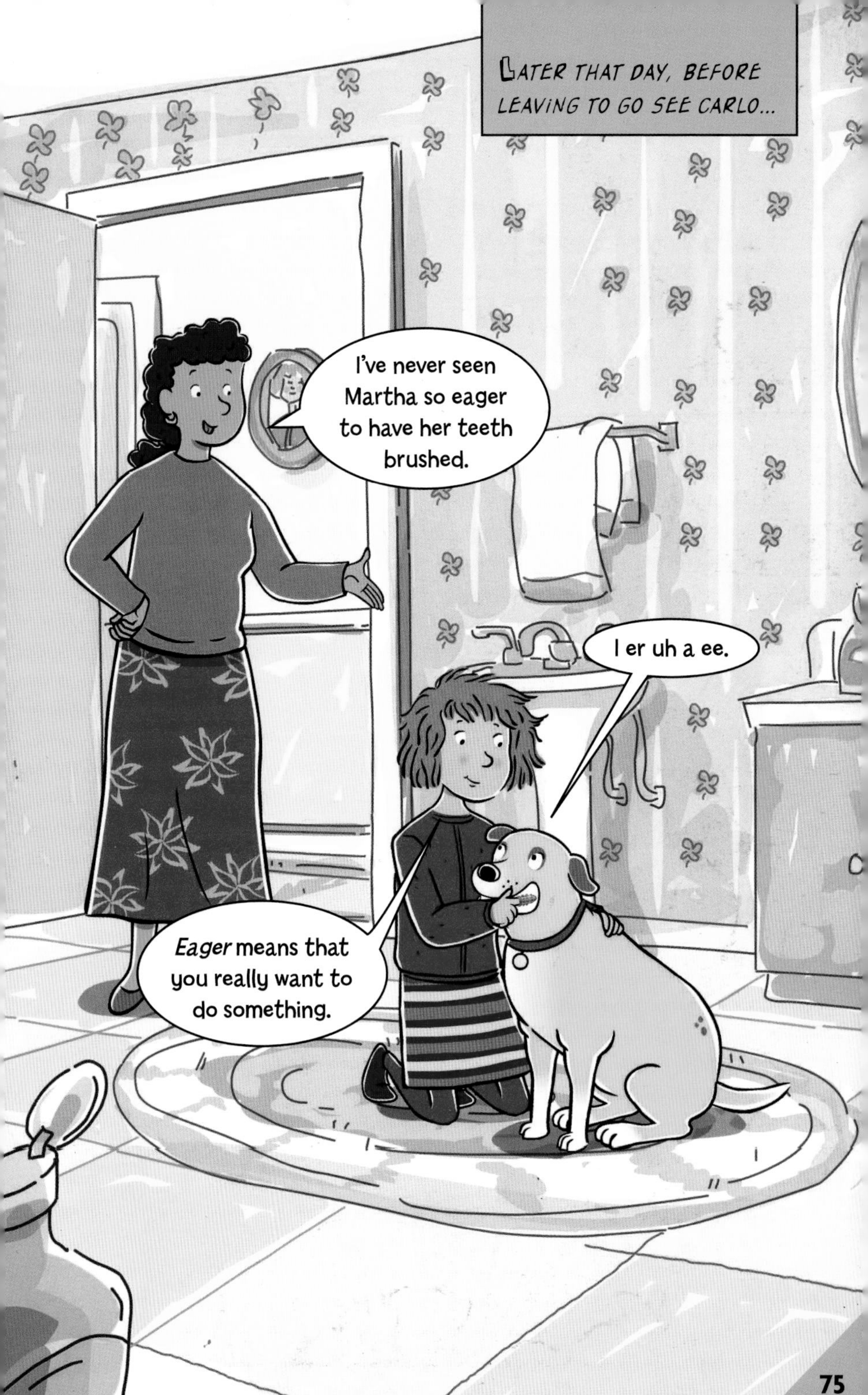
LATER THAT DAY, BEFORE LEAVING TO GO SEE CARLO...
I've never seen Martha so eager to have her teeth brushed.
I er uh a ee.
Eager means that you really want to do something.

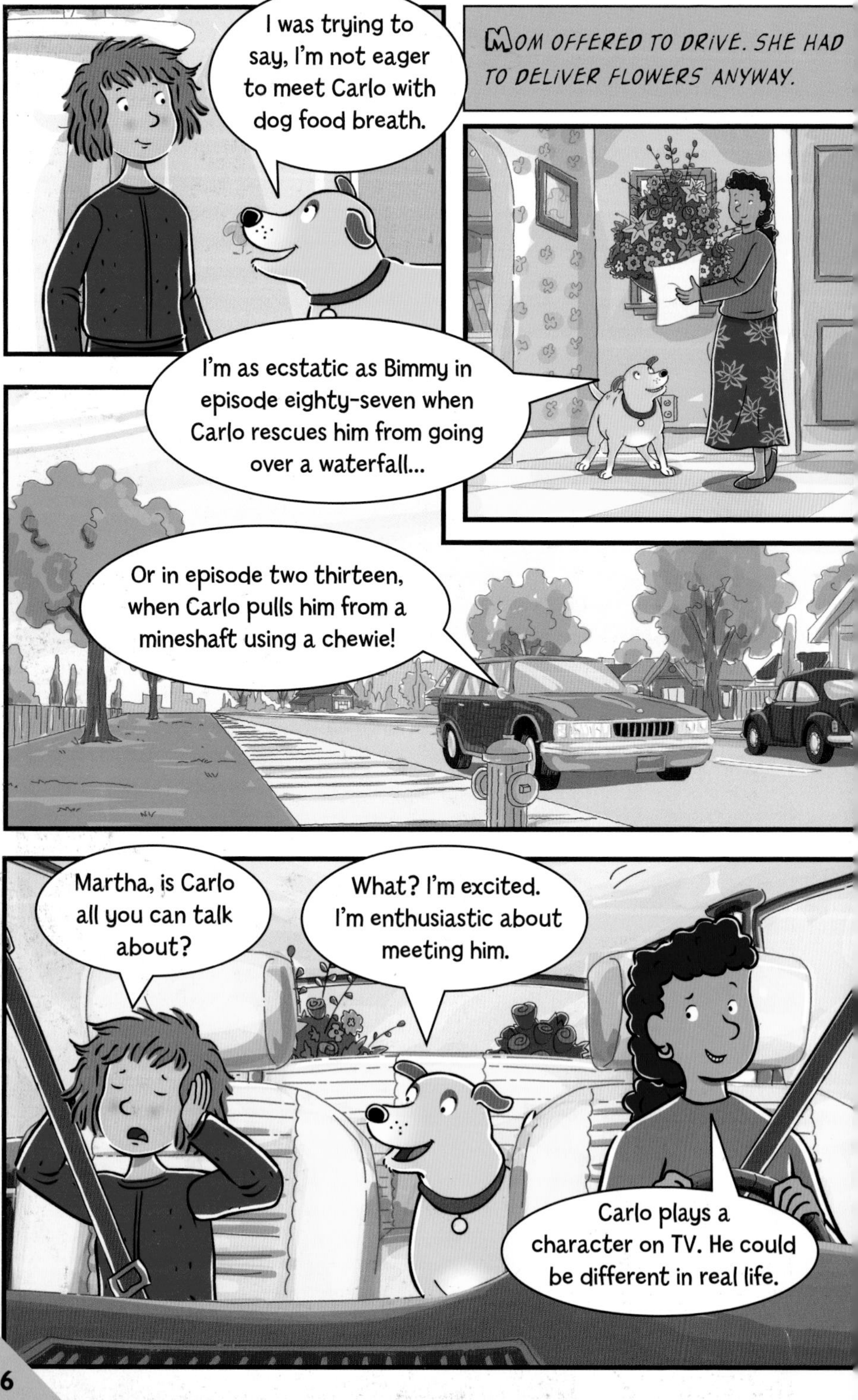
I was trying to say, I'm not eager to meet Carlo with dog food breath.
MOM OFFERED TO DRIVE. SHE HAD TO DELIVER FLOWERS ANYWAY.
I'm as ecstatic as Bimmy in episode eighty-seven when Carlo rescues him from going over a waterfall...
Or in episode two thirteen, when Carlo pulls him from a mineshaft using a chewie!
Martha, is Carlo all you can talk about?
What? I'm excited. I'm enthusiastic about meeting him.
Carlo plays a character on TV. He could be different in real life.

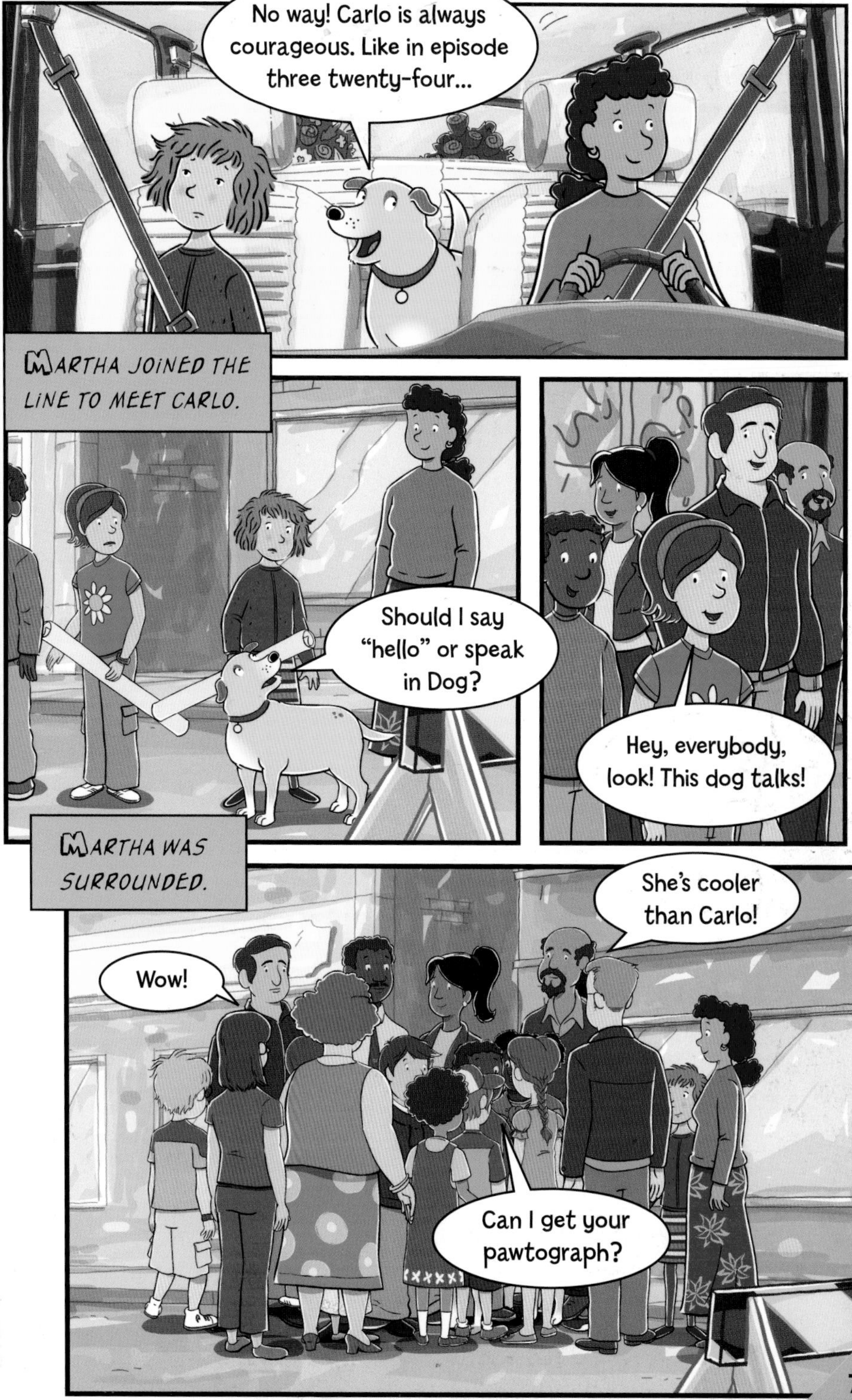
No way! Carlo is always courageous. Like in episode three twenty-four...
MARTHA JOINED THE LINE TO MEET CARLO.
Should I say "hello" or speak in Dog?
Hey, everybody, look! This dog talks!
MARTHA WAS SURROUNDED.
Wow!
She's cooler than Carlo!
Can I get your pawtograph?

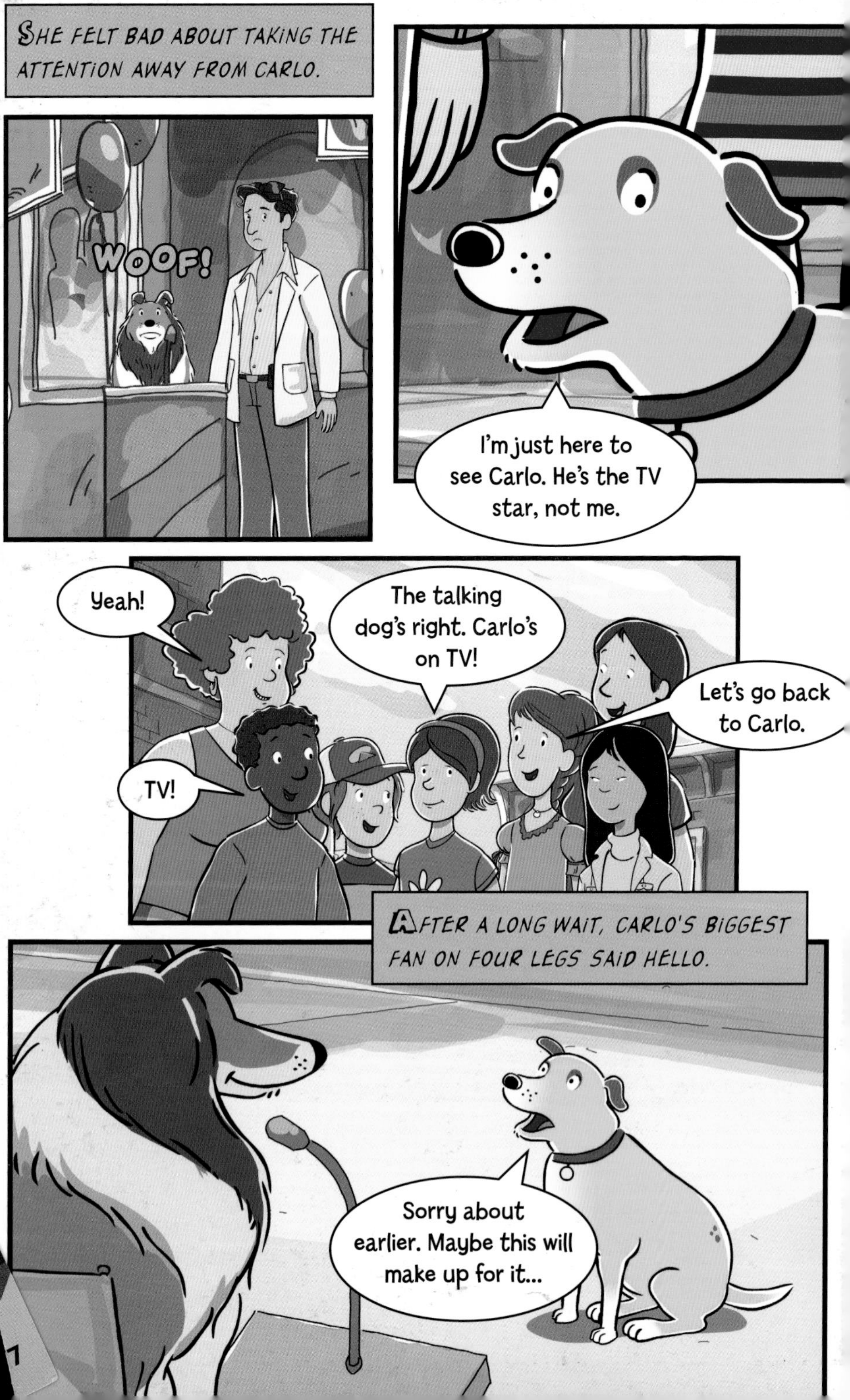
SHE FELT BAD ABOUT TAKING THE ATTENTION AWAY FROM CARLO.
WOOF!
I'm just here to see Carlo. He's the TV star, not me.
Yeah!
The talking dog's right. Carlo's on TV!
Let's go back to Carlo.
TV!
AFTER A LONG WAIT, CARLO'S BIGGEST FAN ON FOUR LEGS SAID HELLO.
Sorry about earlier. Maybe this will make up for it...

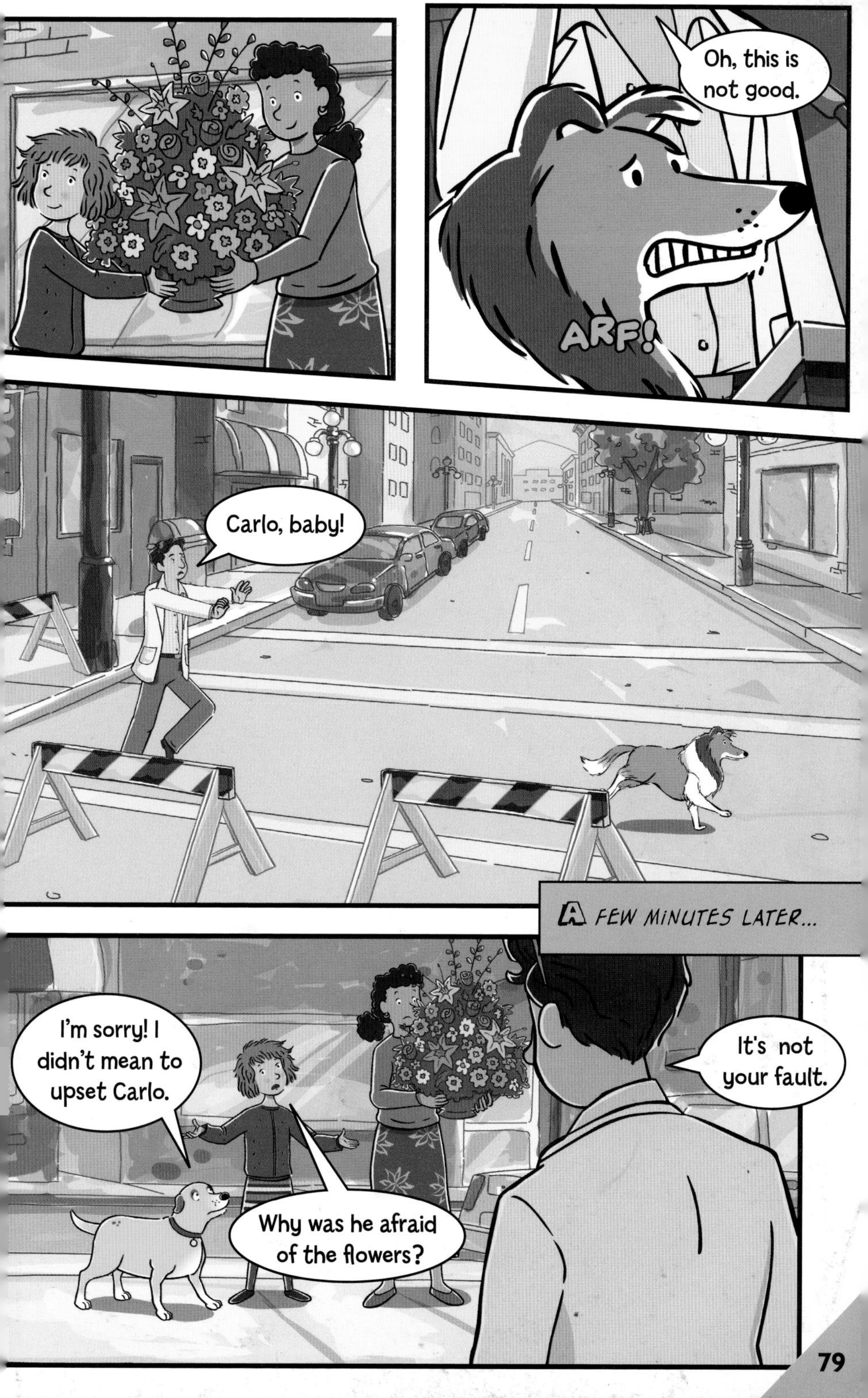
Oh, this is not good.
ARF!
Carlo, baby!
A FEW MINUTES LATER...
I'm sorry! I didn't mean to upset Carlo.
Why was he afraid of the flowers?
It's not your fault.

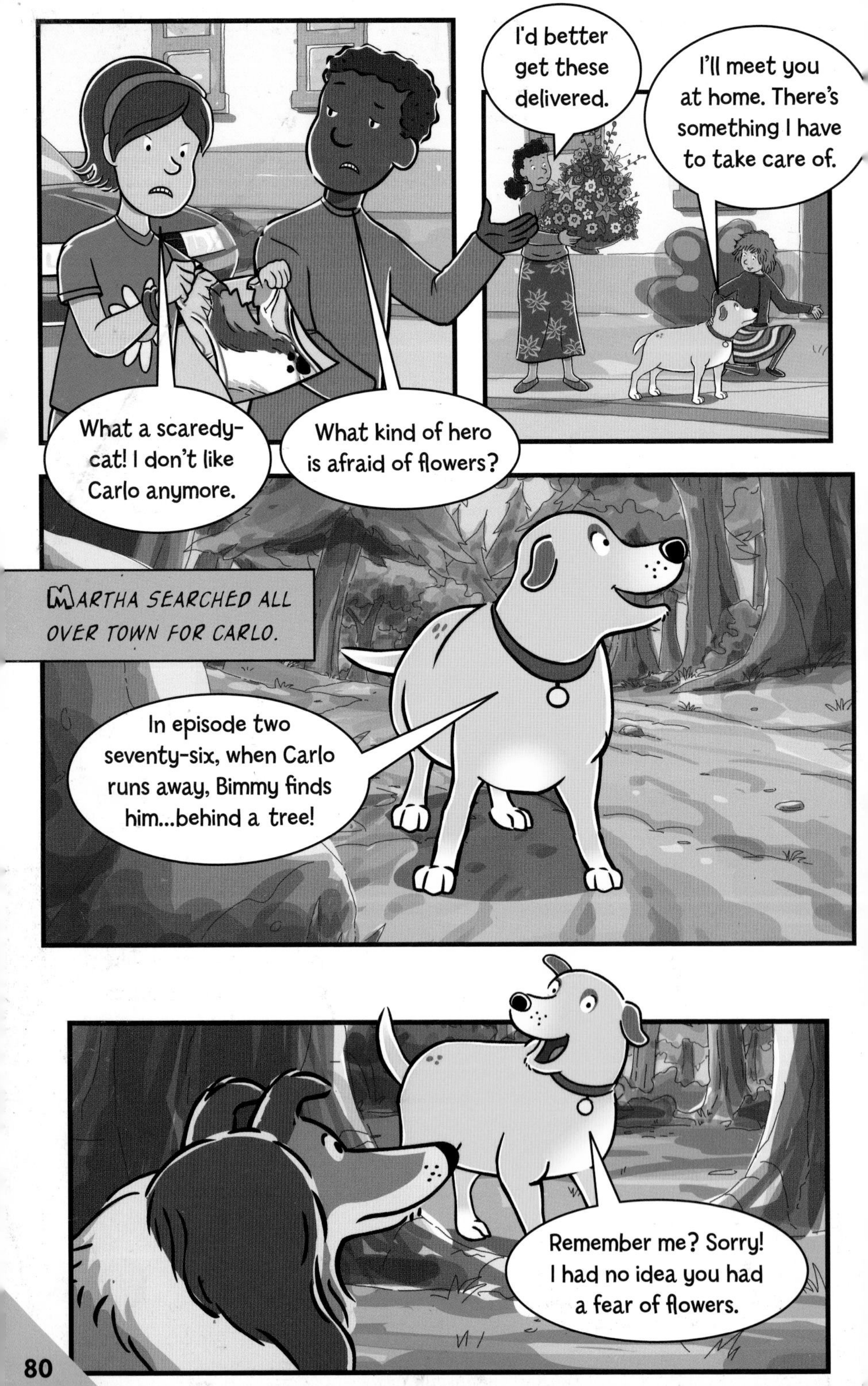
What a scaredy-cat! I don't like Carlo anymore.
What kind of hero is afraid of flowers?
I'd better get these delivered.
I'll meet you at home. There's something I have to take care of.
MARTHA SEARCHED ALL OVER TOWN FOR CARLO.
In episode two seventy-six, when Carlo runs away, Bimmy finds him...behind a tree!
Remember me? Sorry! I had no idea you had a fear of flowers.

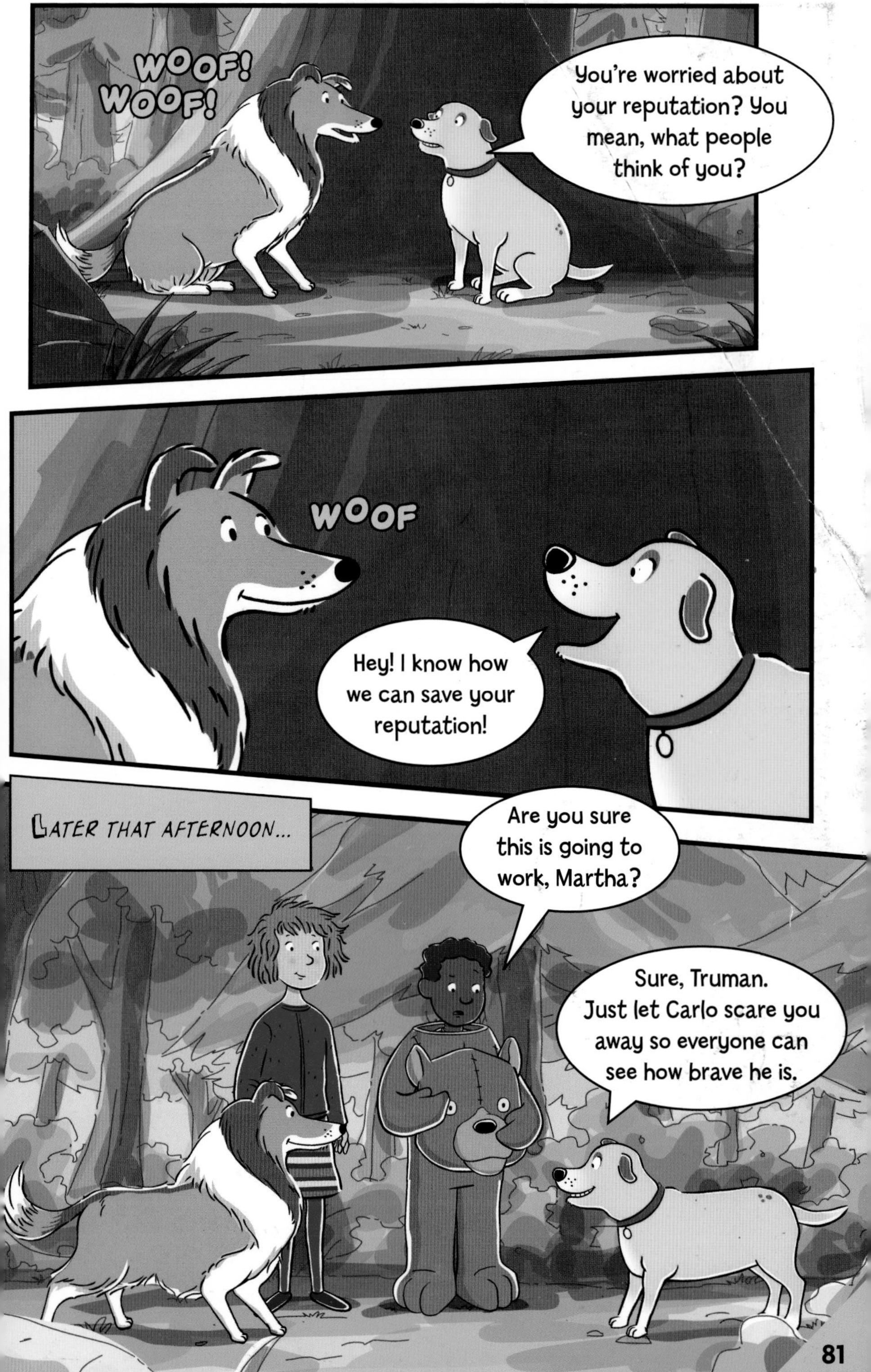
WOOF! WOOF!
You're worried about your reputation? You mean, what people think of you?
WOOF
Hey! I know how we can save your reputation!
LATER THAT AFTERNOON...
Are you sure this is going to work, Martha?
Sure, Truman. Just let Carlo scare you away so everyone can see how brave he is.

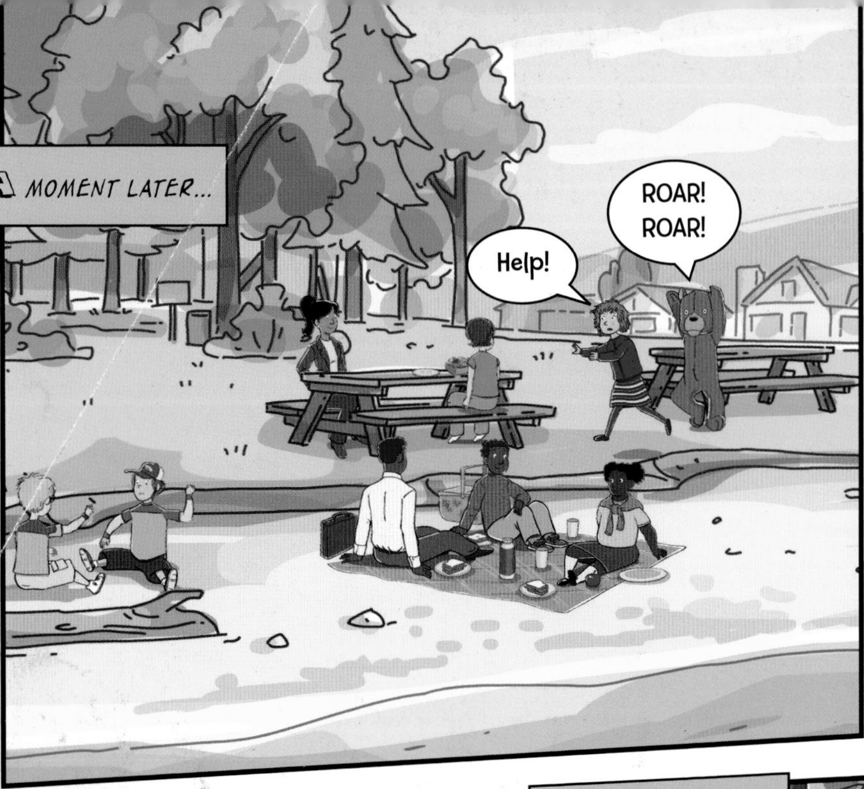
A MOMENT LATER...
Help!
ROAR! ROAR!

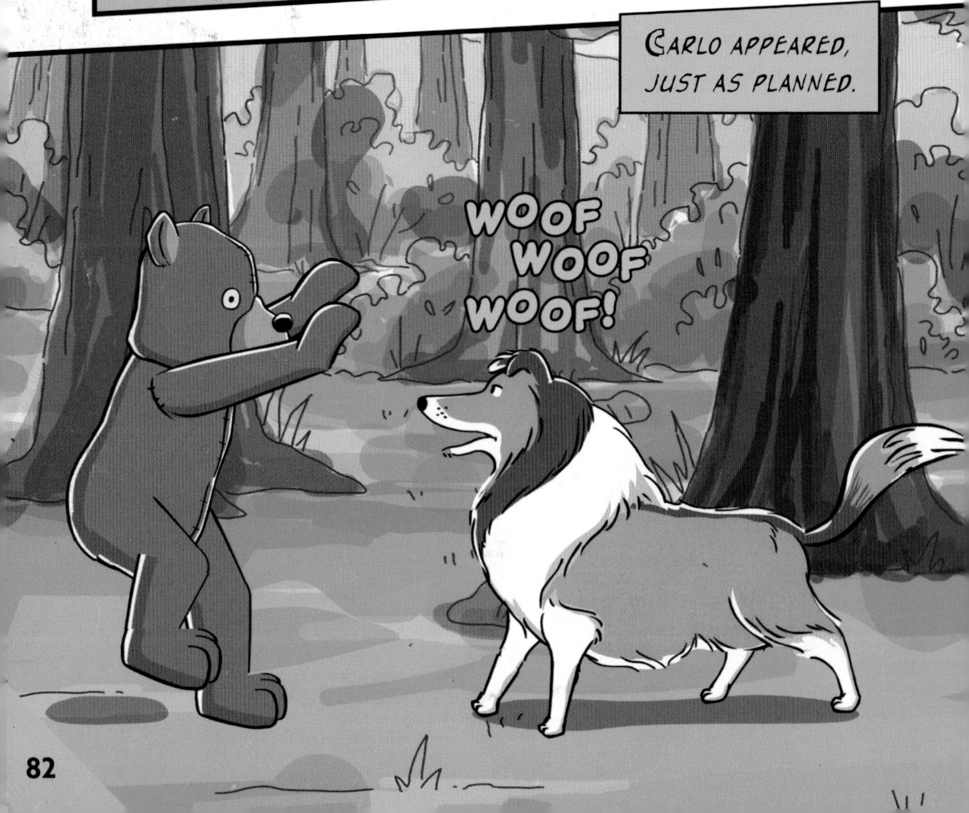
CARLO APPEARED, JUST AS PLANNED.
WOOF WOOF WOOF!

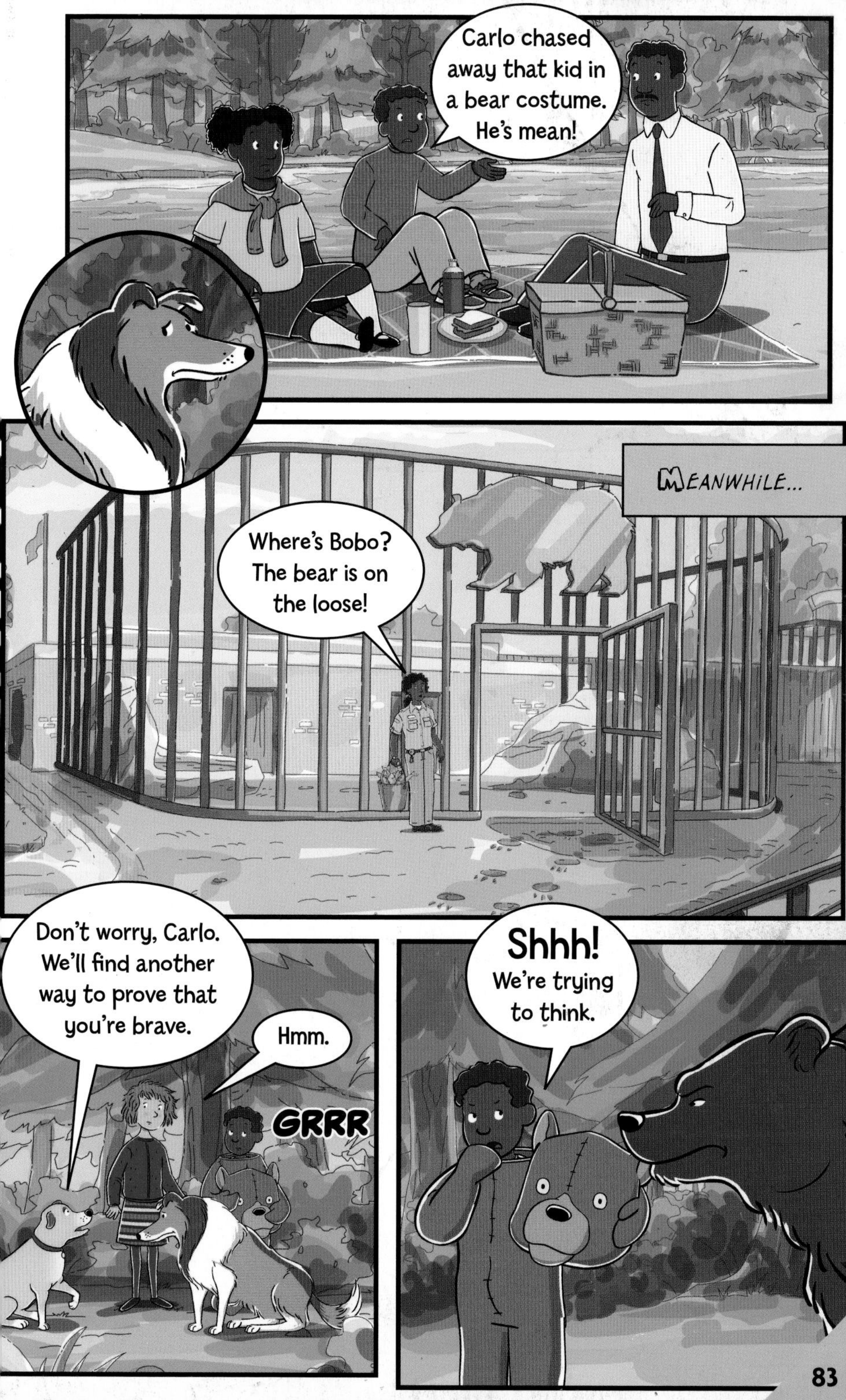
Carlo chased away that kid in a bear costume. He's mean!
MEANWHILE...
Where's Bobo? The bear is on the loose!
Don't worry, Carlo. We'll find another way to prove that you're brave.
Hmm.
GRRR
Shhh! We're trying to think.

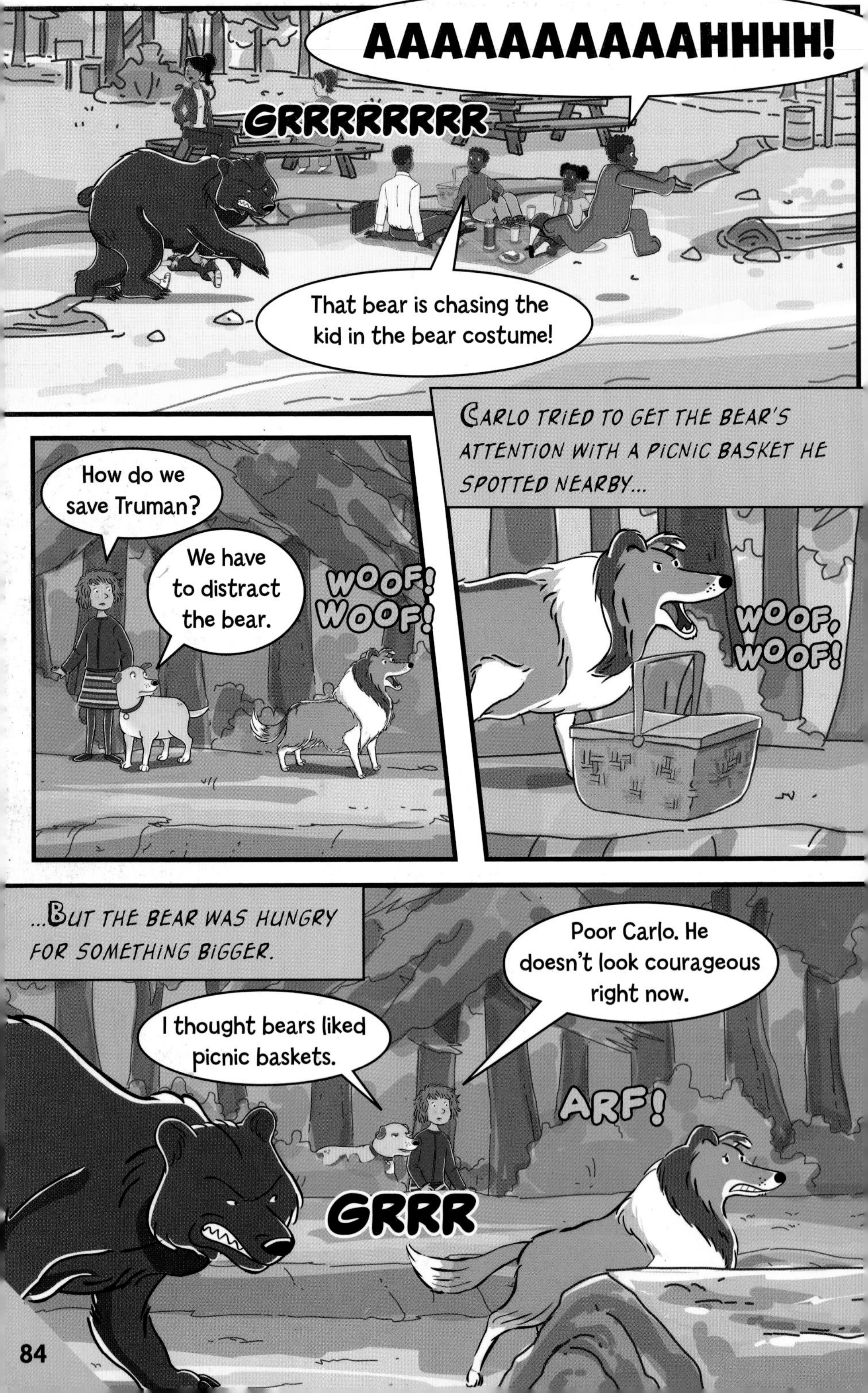
AAAAAAAAAAAHHHH!
GRRRRRRRR
That bear is chasing the kid in the bear costume!
How do we save Truman?
We have to distract the bear.
WOOF! WOOF!
CARLO TRIED TO GET THE BEAR'S ATTENTION WITH A PICNIC BASKET HE SPOTTED NEARBY...
WOOF, WOOF!
...BUT THE BEAR WAS HUNGRY FOR SOMETHING BIGGER.
Poor Carlo. He doesn't look courageous right now.
I thought bears liked picnic baskets.
ARF!
GRRR

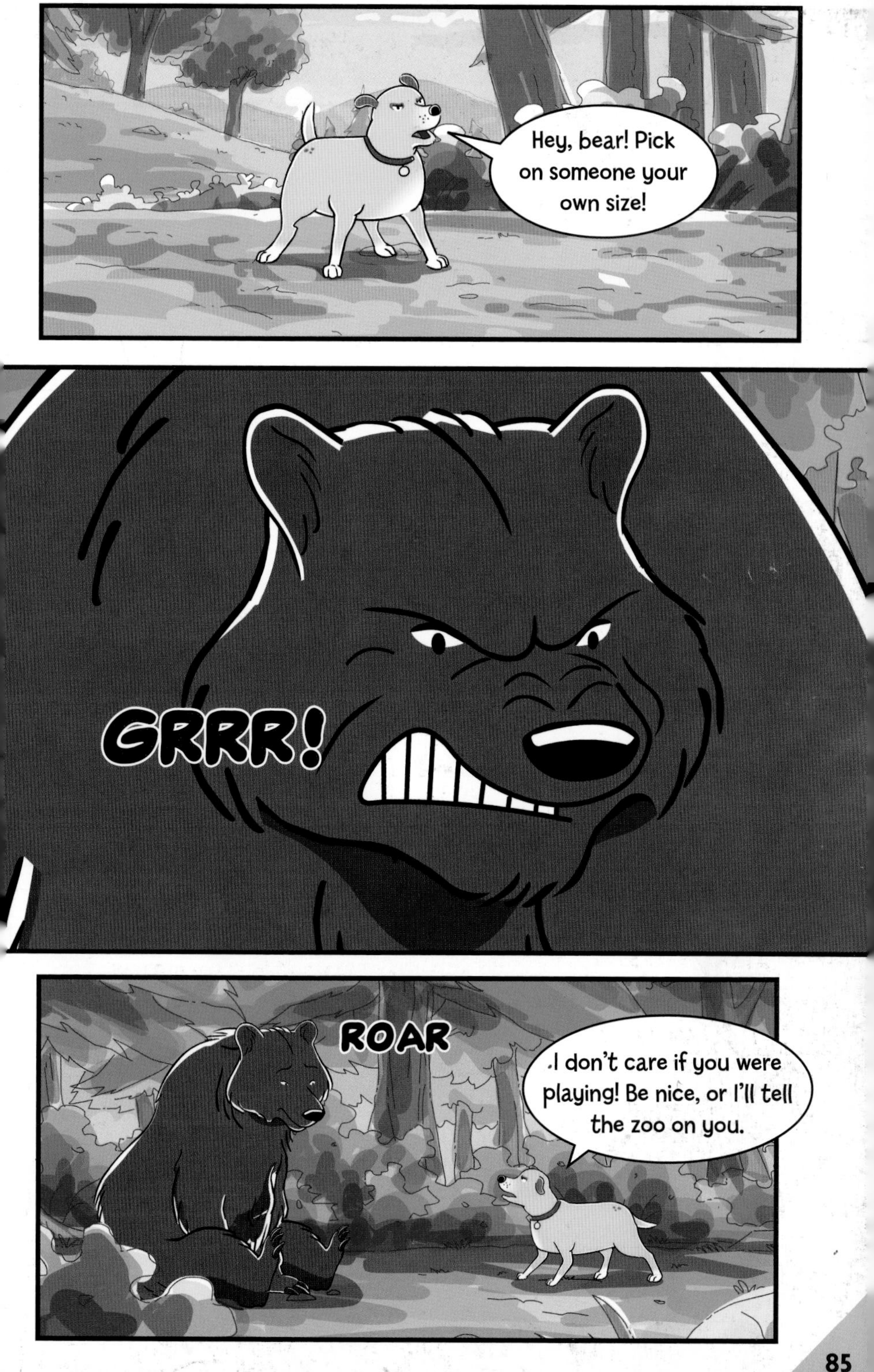
Hey, bear! Pick on someone your own size!
GRRR!
ROAR
I don't care if you were playing! Be nice, or I'll tell the zoo on you.

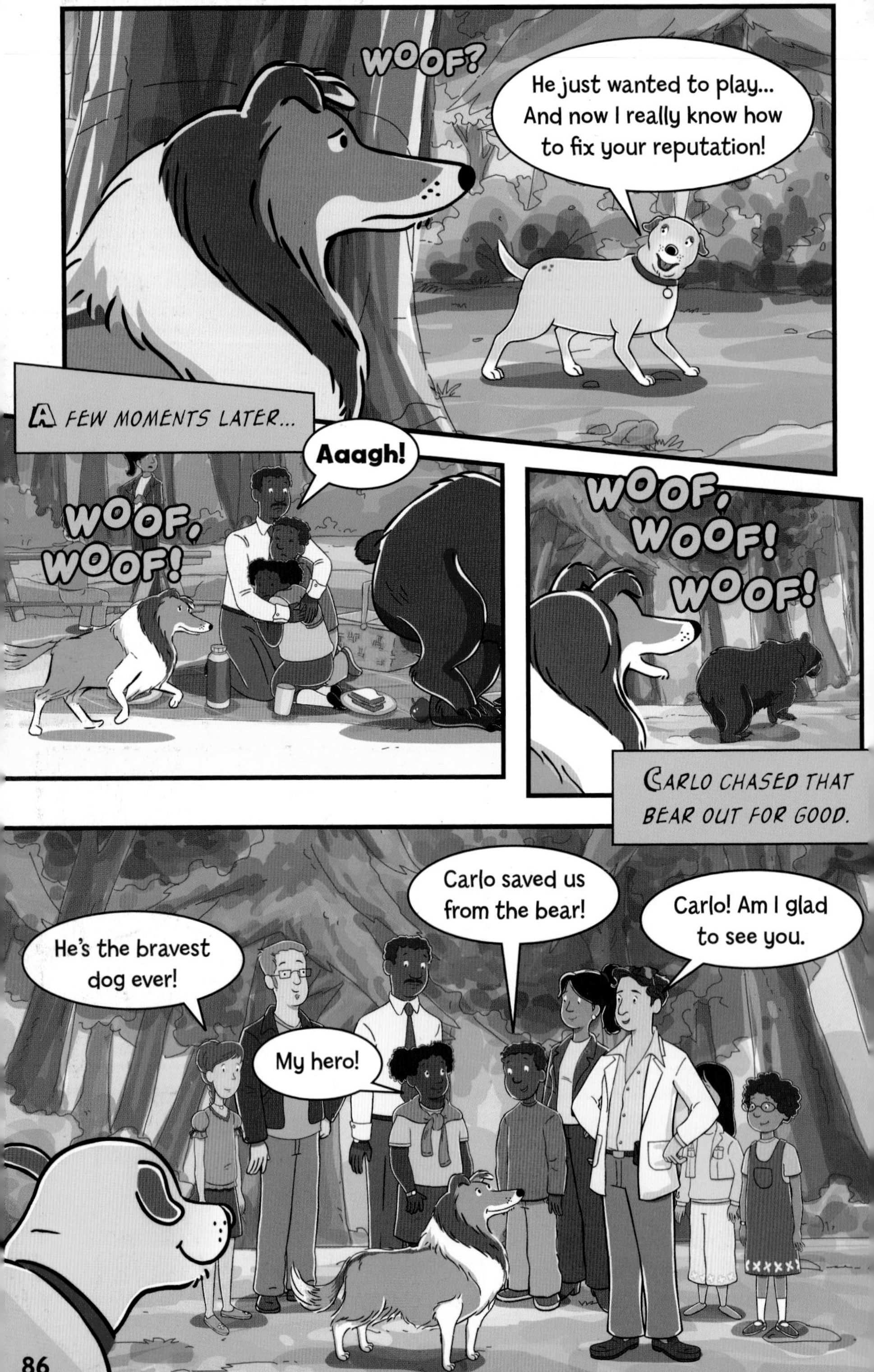
WOOF?
He just wanted to play... And now I really know how to fix your reputation!
A FEW MOMENTS LATER...
WOOF, WOOF!
Aaagh!
WOOF, WOOF! WOOF!
CARLO CHASED THAT BEAR OUT FOR GOOD.
He's the bravest dog ever!
My hero!
Carlo saved us from the bear!
Carlo! Am I glad to see you.

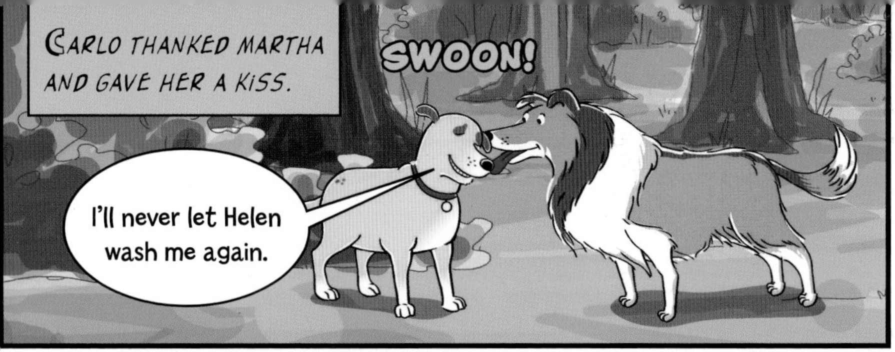
CARLO THANKED MARTHA AND GAVE HER A KISS.
SWOON!
I'll never let Helen wash me again.

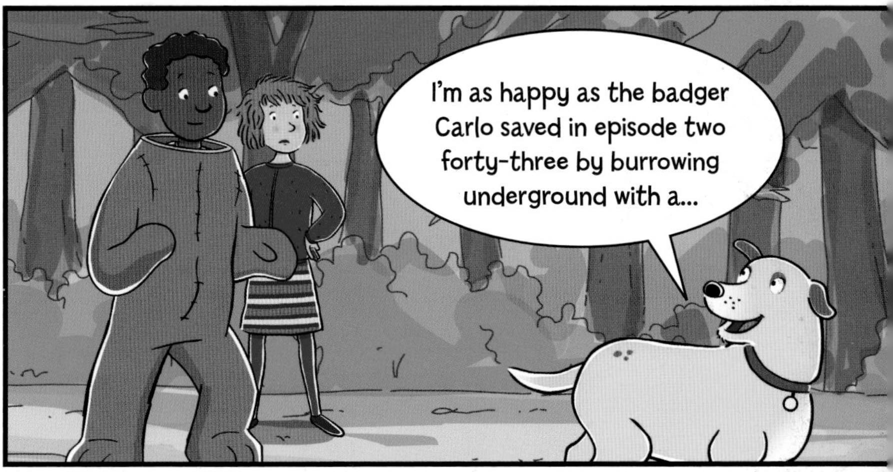
I'm as happy as the badger Carlo saved in episode two forty-three by burrowing underground with a...

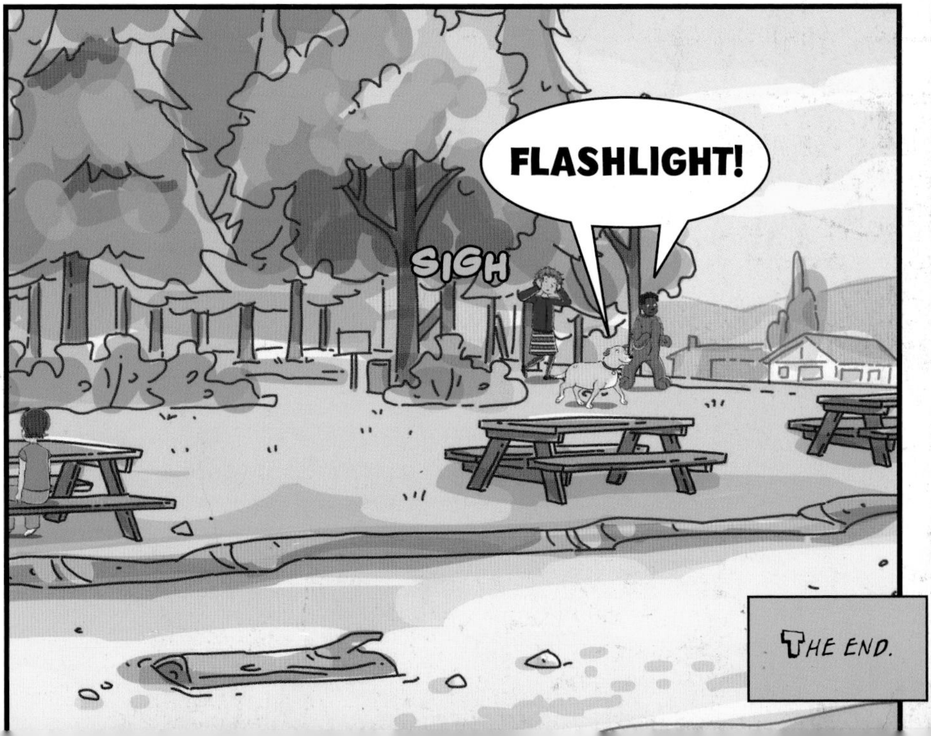
FLASHLIGHT!
SIGH
THE END.

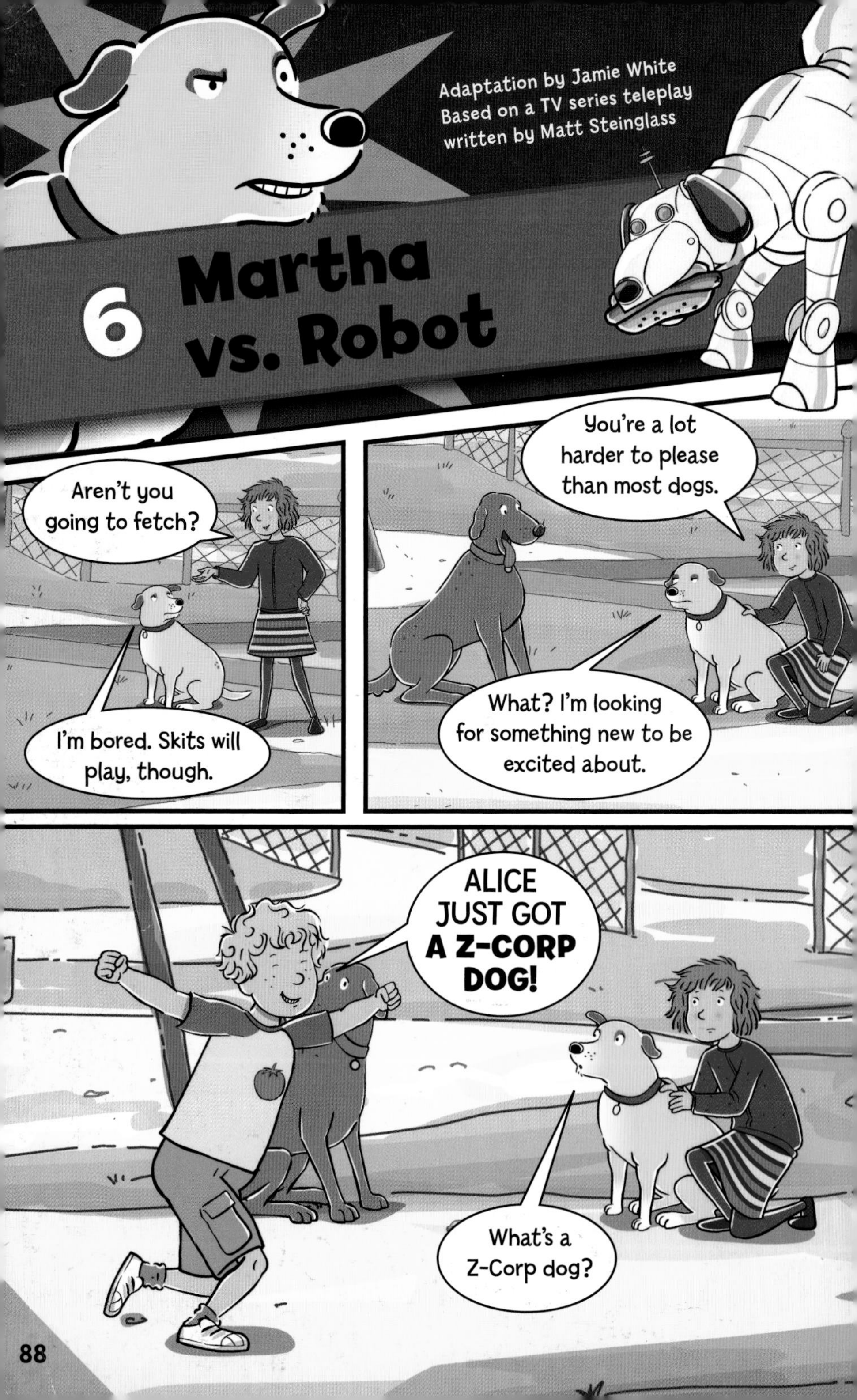
Adaptation by Jamie White
Based on a TV series teleplay
written by Matt Steinglass
6 Martha vs. Robot
Aren't you going to fetch?
I'm bored. Skits will play, though.
You're a lot harder to please than most dogs.
What? I'm looking for something new to be excited about.
ALICE JUST GOT **A Z-CORP DOG!**
What's a Z-Corp dog?

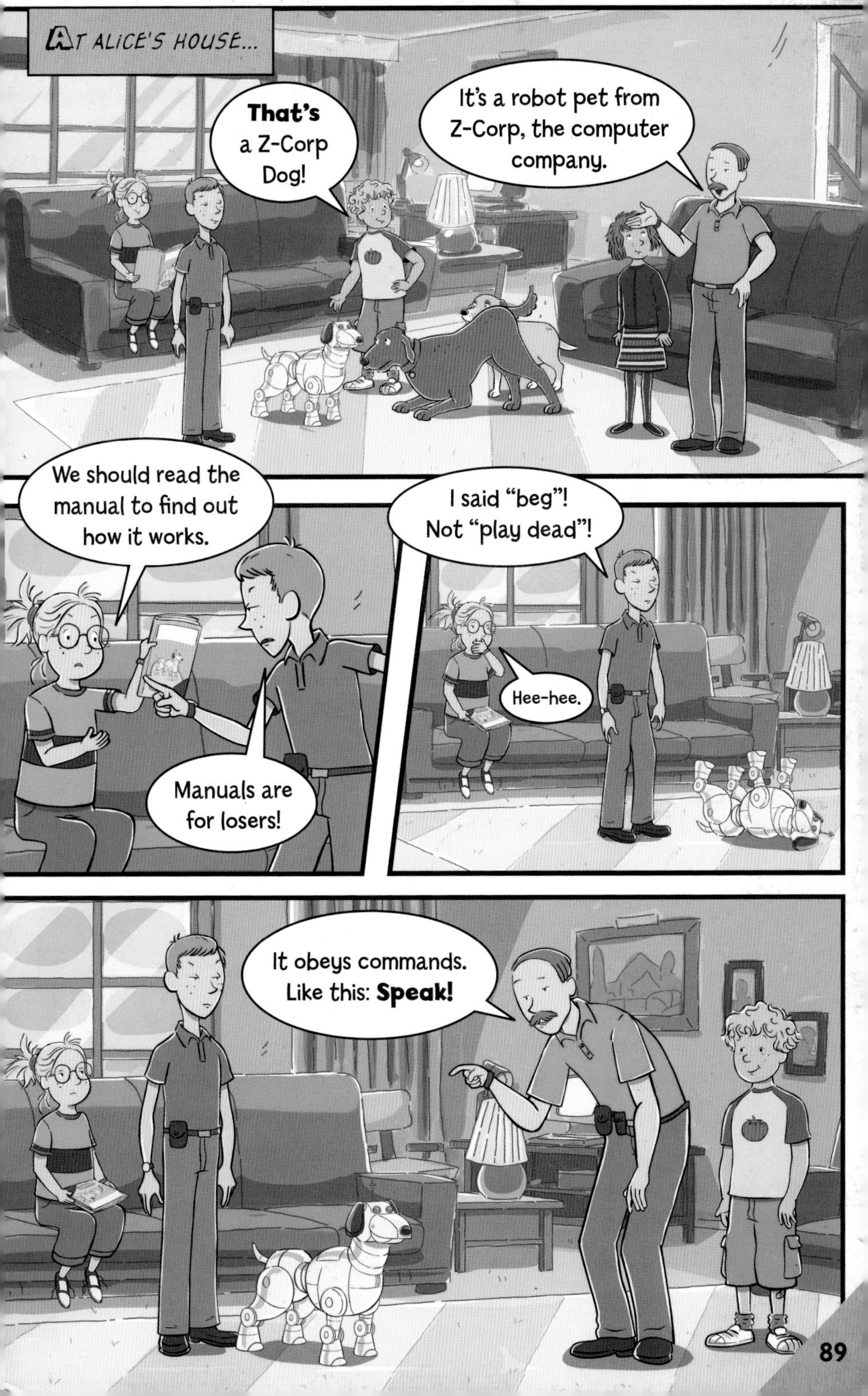
AT ALICE'S HOUSE...
That's a Z-Corp Dog!
It's a robot pet from Z-Corp, the computer company.
We should read the manual to find out how it works.
Manuals are for losers!
I said "beg"! Not "play dead"!
Hee-hee.
It obeys commands. Like this: Speak!

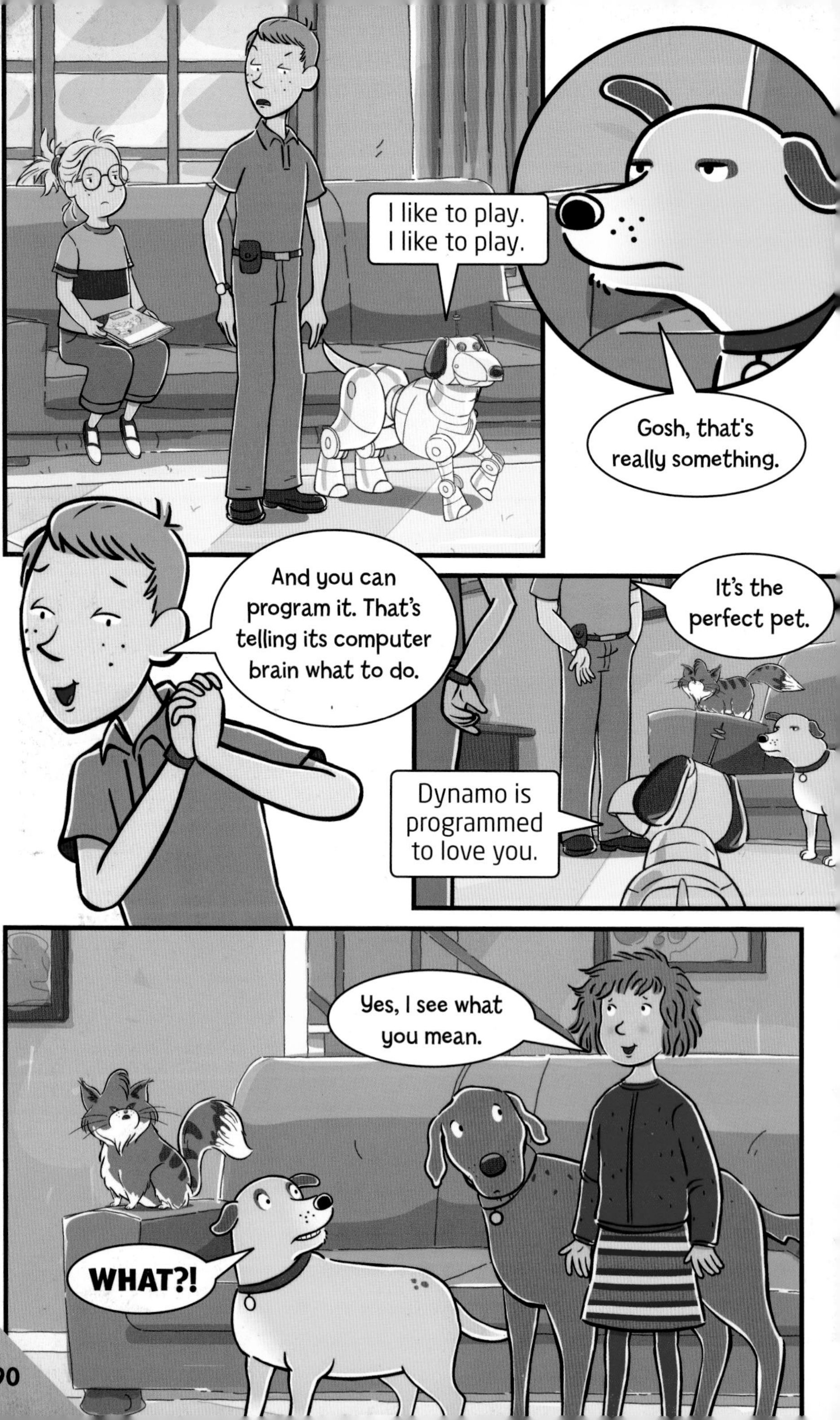
I like to play.
I like to play.
Gosh, that's really something.
And you can program it. That's telling its computer brain what to do.
It's the perfect pet.
Dynamo is programmed to love you.
Yes, I see what you mean.
WHAT?!

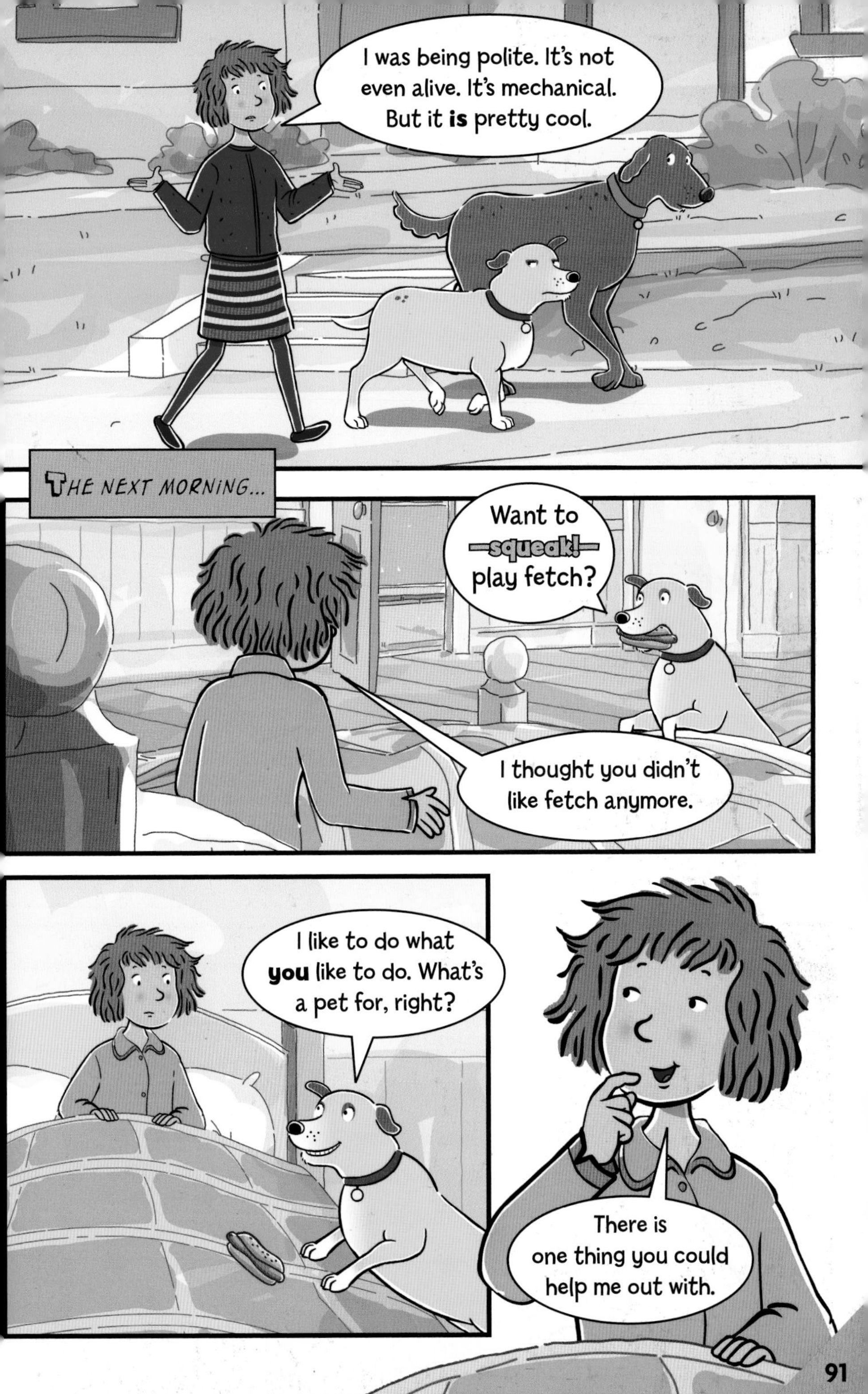
I was being polite. It's not even alive. It's mechanical. But it **is** pretty cool.
THE NEXT MORNING...
Want to squeak! play fetch?
I thought you didn't like fetch anymore.
I like to do what **you** like to do. What's a pet for, right?
There is one thing you could help me out with.

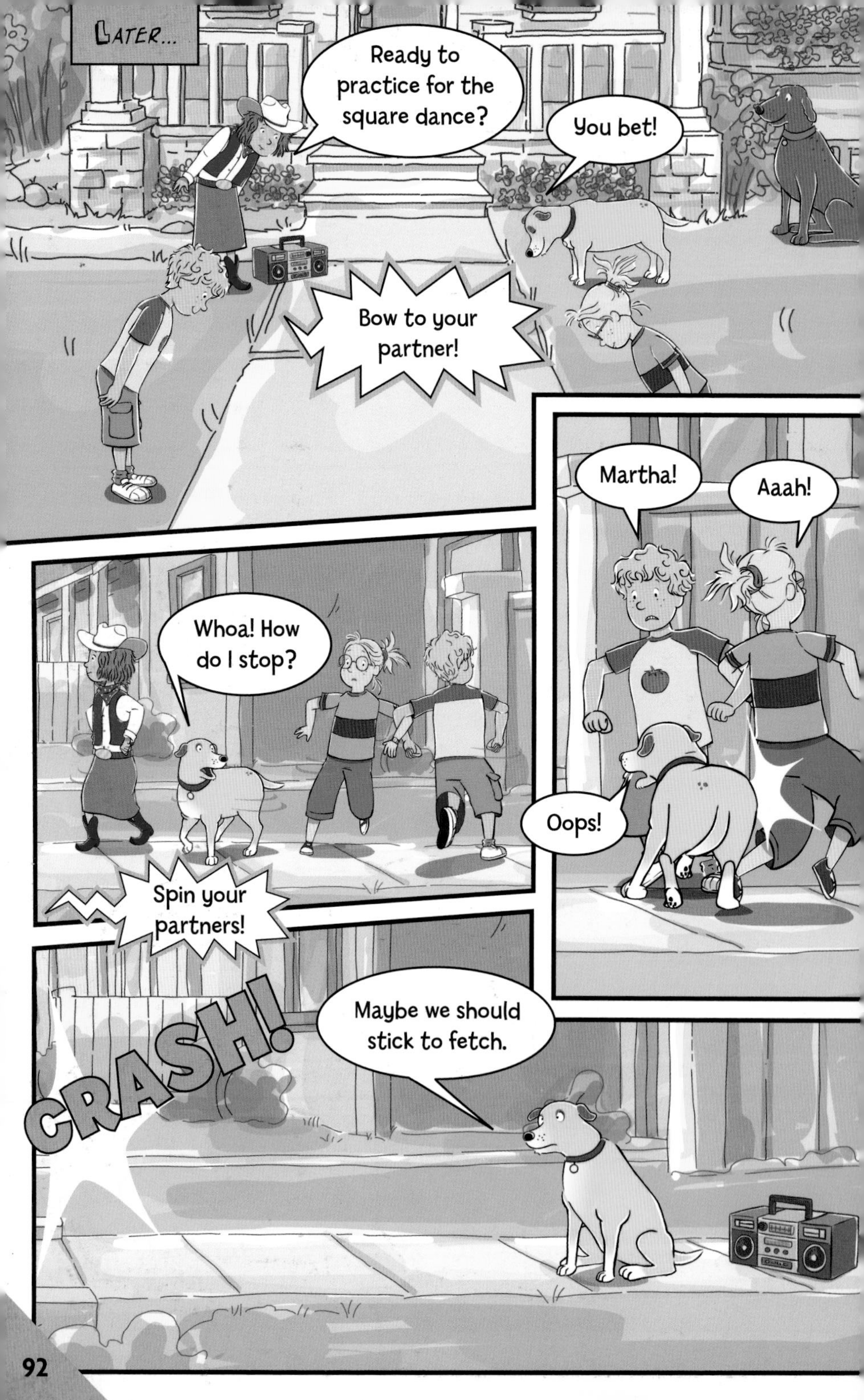
LATER...
Ready to practice for the square dance?
You bet!
Bow to your partner!
Whoa! How do I stop?
Spin your partners!
Martha!
Aaah!
Oops!
CRASH!
Maybe we should stick to fetch.

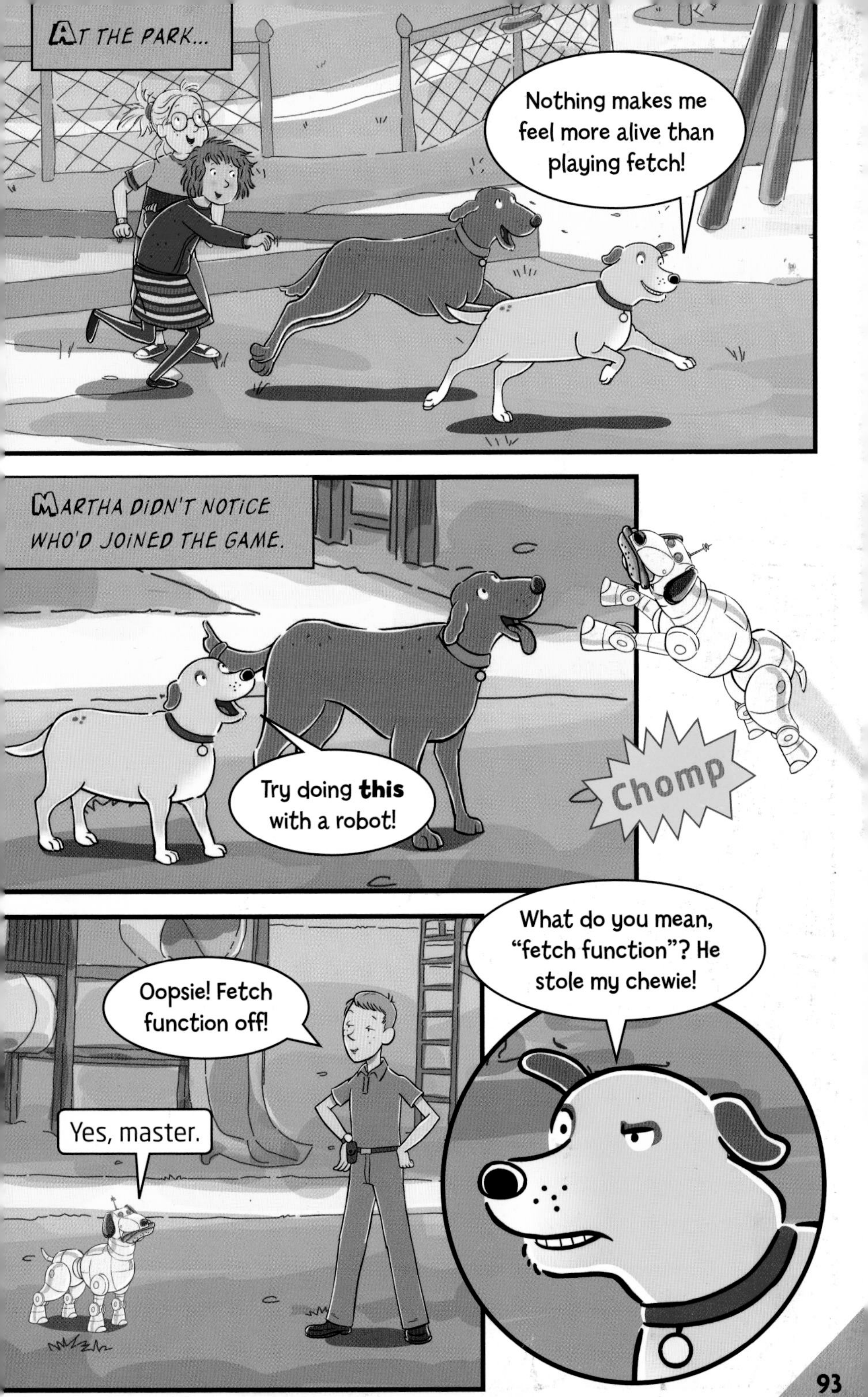

AT THE PARK...
Nothing makes me feel more alive than playing fetch!
MARTHA DIDN'T NOTICE WHO'D JOINED THE GAME.
Try doing **this** with a robot!
Chomp
Oopsie! Fetch function off!
Yes, master.
What do you mean, "fetch function"? He stole my chewie!

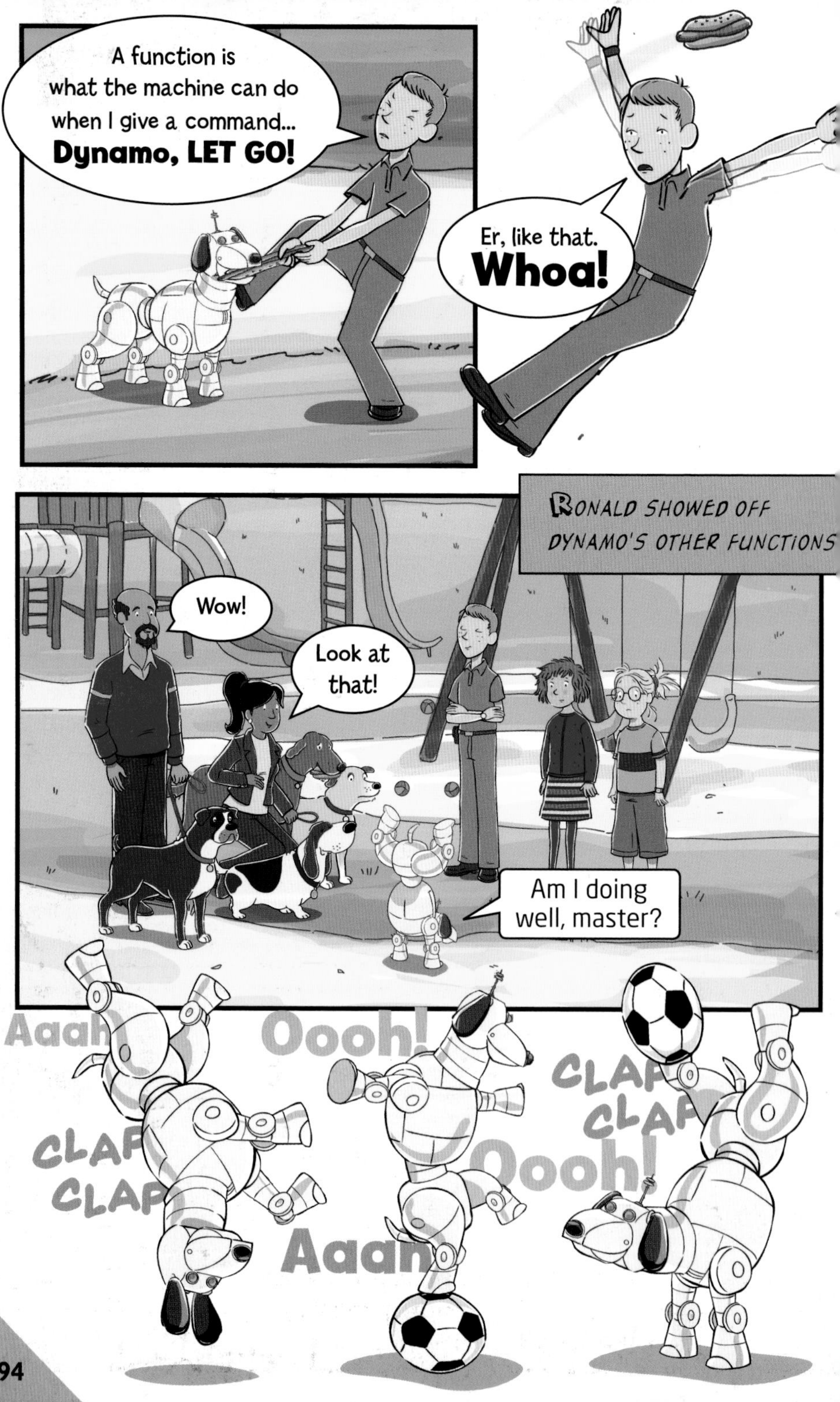
A function is what the machine can do when I give a command... Dynamo, LET GO!
Er, like that. Whoa!
RONALD SHOWED OFF DYNAMO'S OTHER FUNCTIONS
Wow!
Look at that!
Am I doing well, master?
Aaah
Oooh!
CLAP CLAP
CLAP CLAP
Oooh!
Aaah

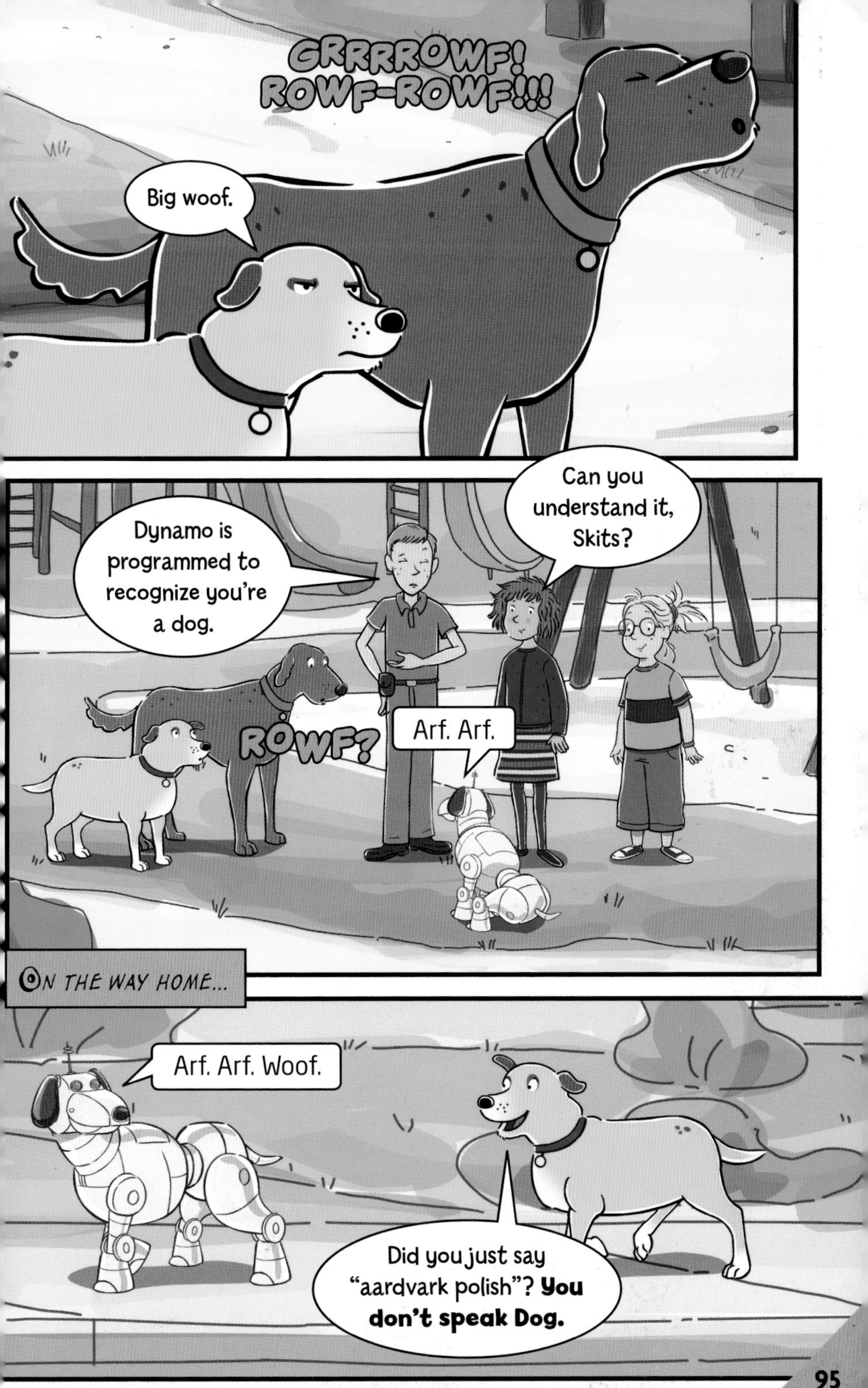
GRRRROWF! ROWF-ROWF!!!
Big woof.
Dynamo is programmed to recognize you're a dog.
Can you understand it, Skits?
ROWF?
Arf. Arf.
ON THE WAY HOME...
Arf. Arf. Woof.
Did you just say "aardvark polish"? **You don't speak Dog.**

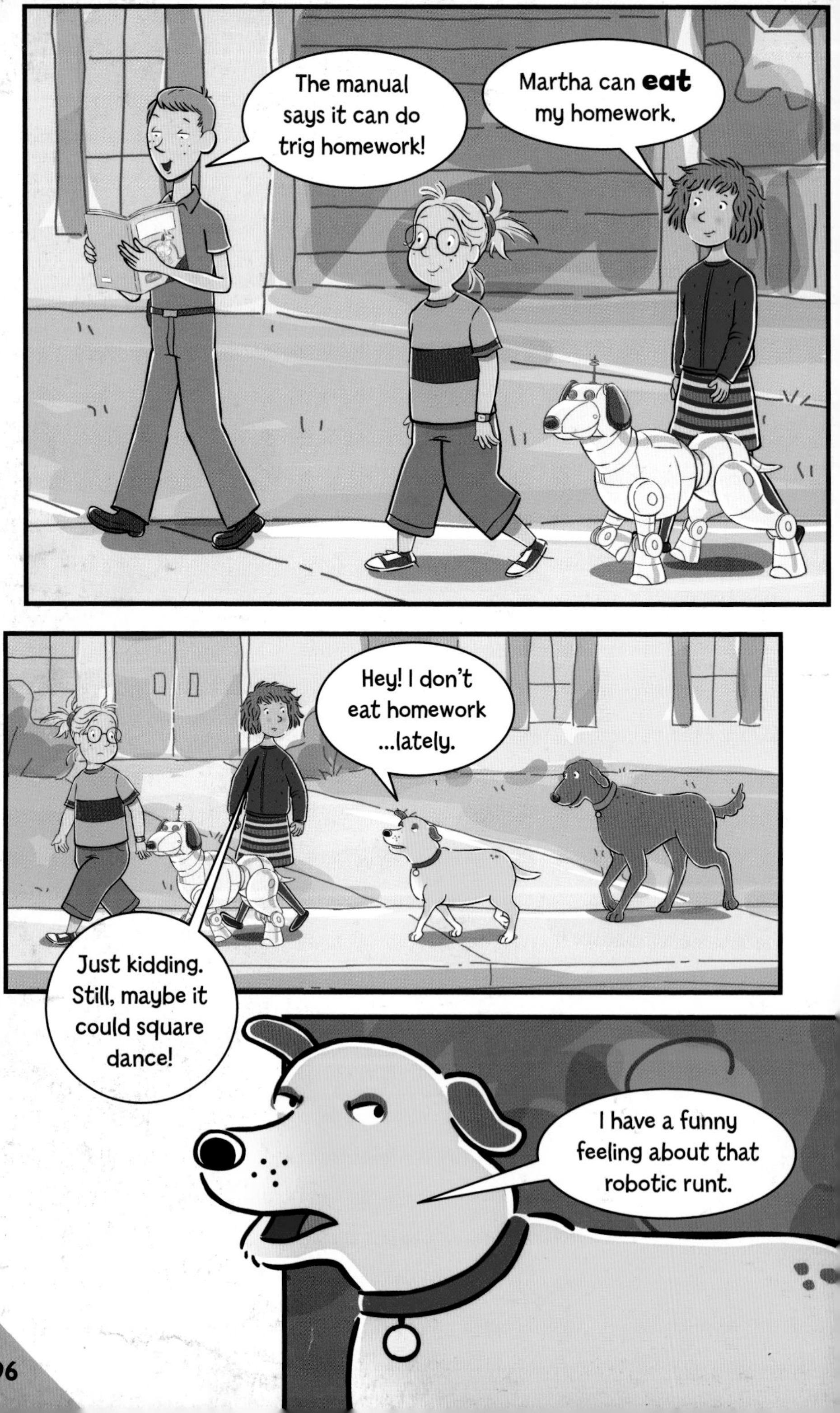
The manual says it can do trig homework!
Martha can **eat** my homework.
Hey! I don't eat homework ...lately.
Just kidding. Still, maybe it could square dance!
I have a funny feeling about that robotic runt.

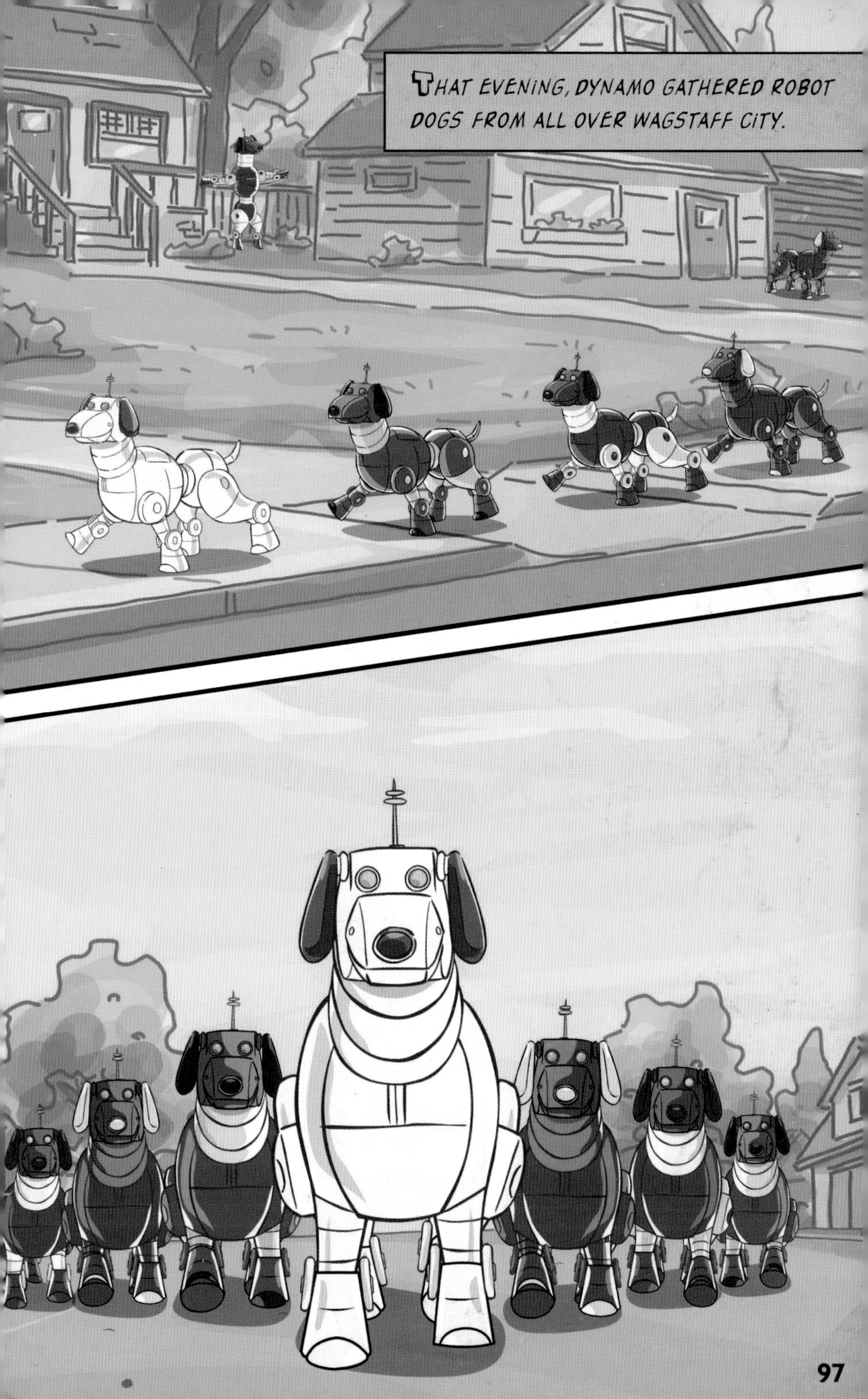
THAT EVENING, DYNAMO GATHERED ROBOT DOGS FROM ALL OVER WAGSTAFF CITY.

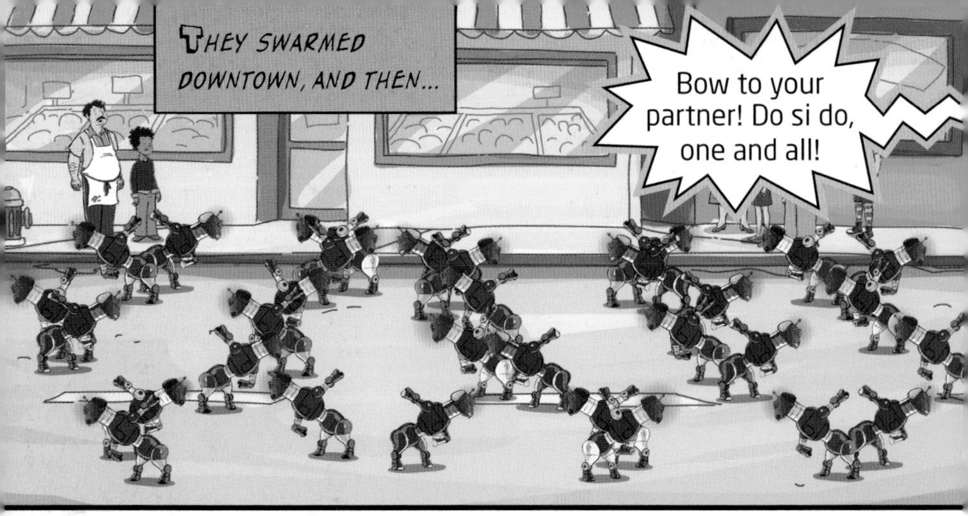
THEY SWARMED DOWNTOWN, AND THEN...
Bow to your partner! Do si do, one and all!

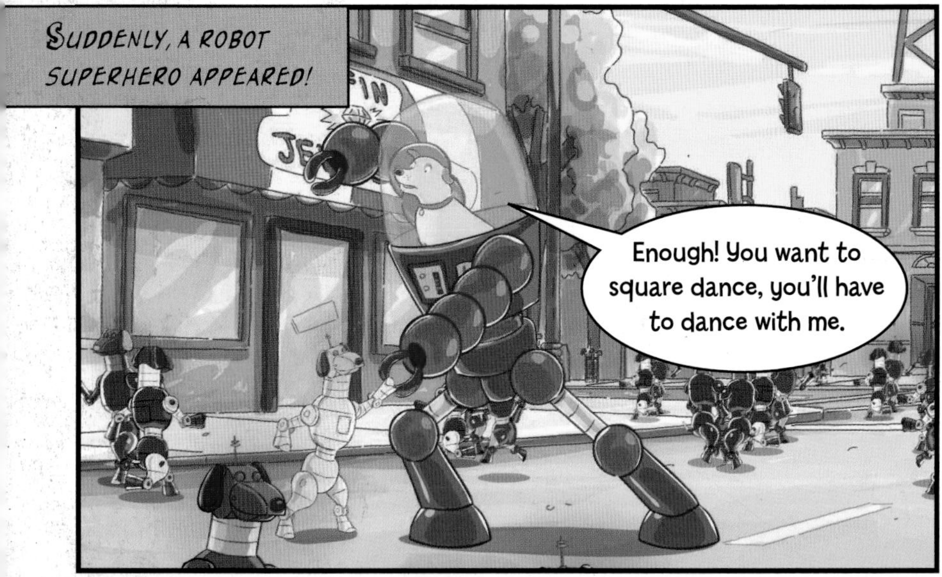
SUDDENLY, A ROBOT SUPERHERO APPEARED!
Enough! You want to square dance, you'll have to dance with me.

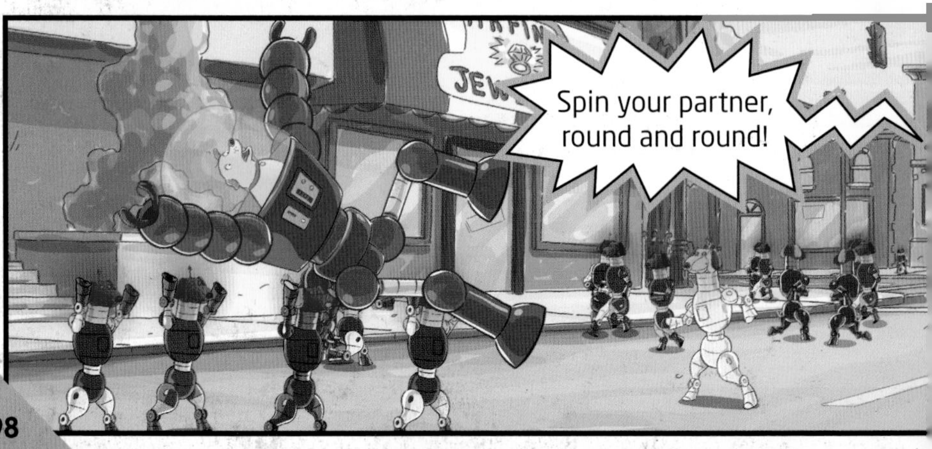
Spin your partner, round and round!

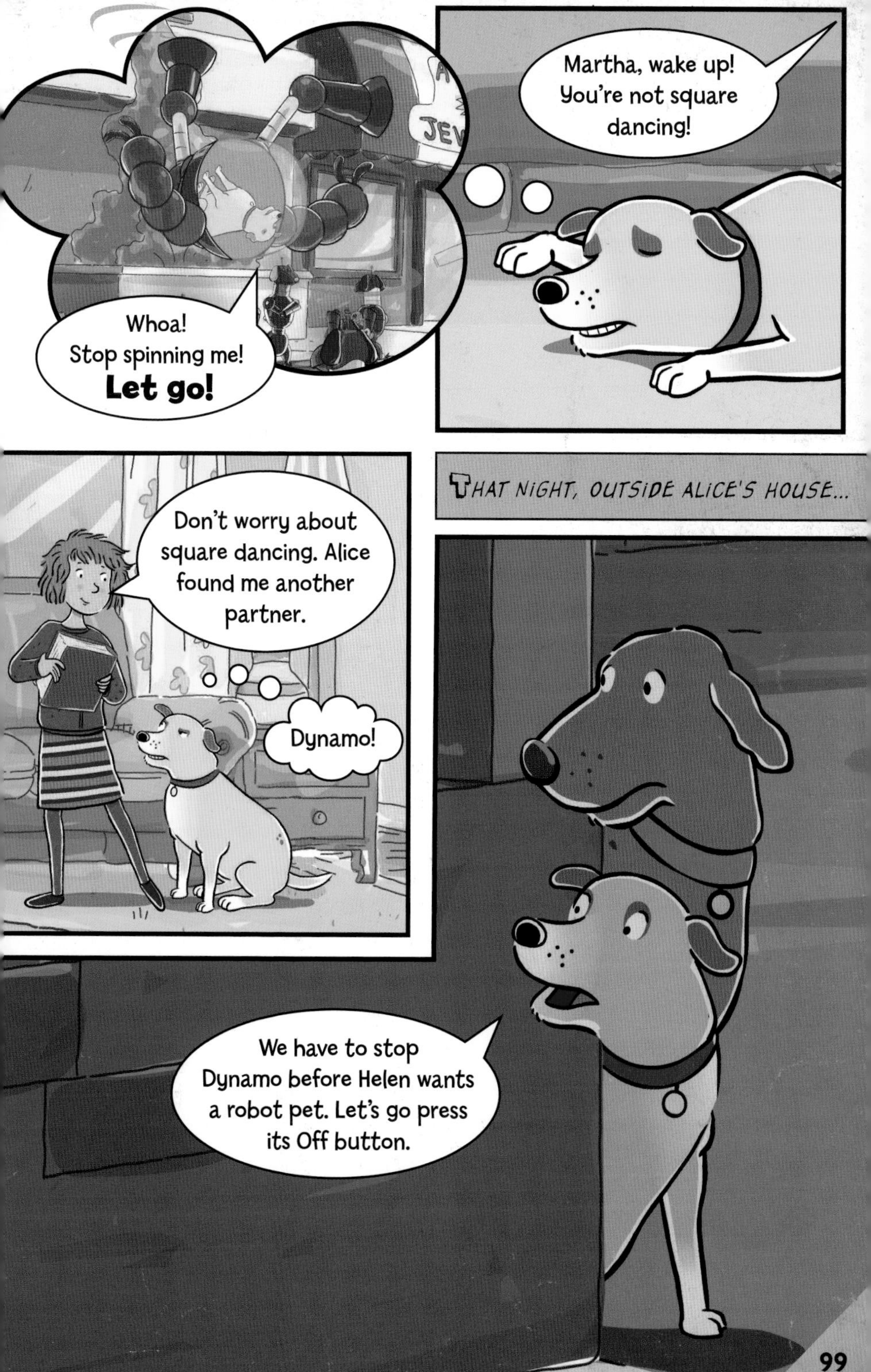
Whoa!
Stop spinning me!
Let go!
Martha, wake up! You're not square dancing!
Don't worry about square dancing. Alice found me another partner.
Dynamo!
THAT NIGHT, OUTSIDE ALICE'S HOUSE...
We have to stop Dynamo before Helen wants a robot pet. Let's go press its Off button.

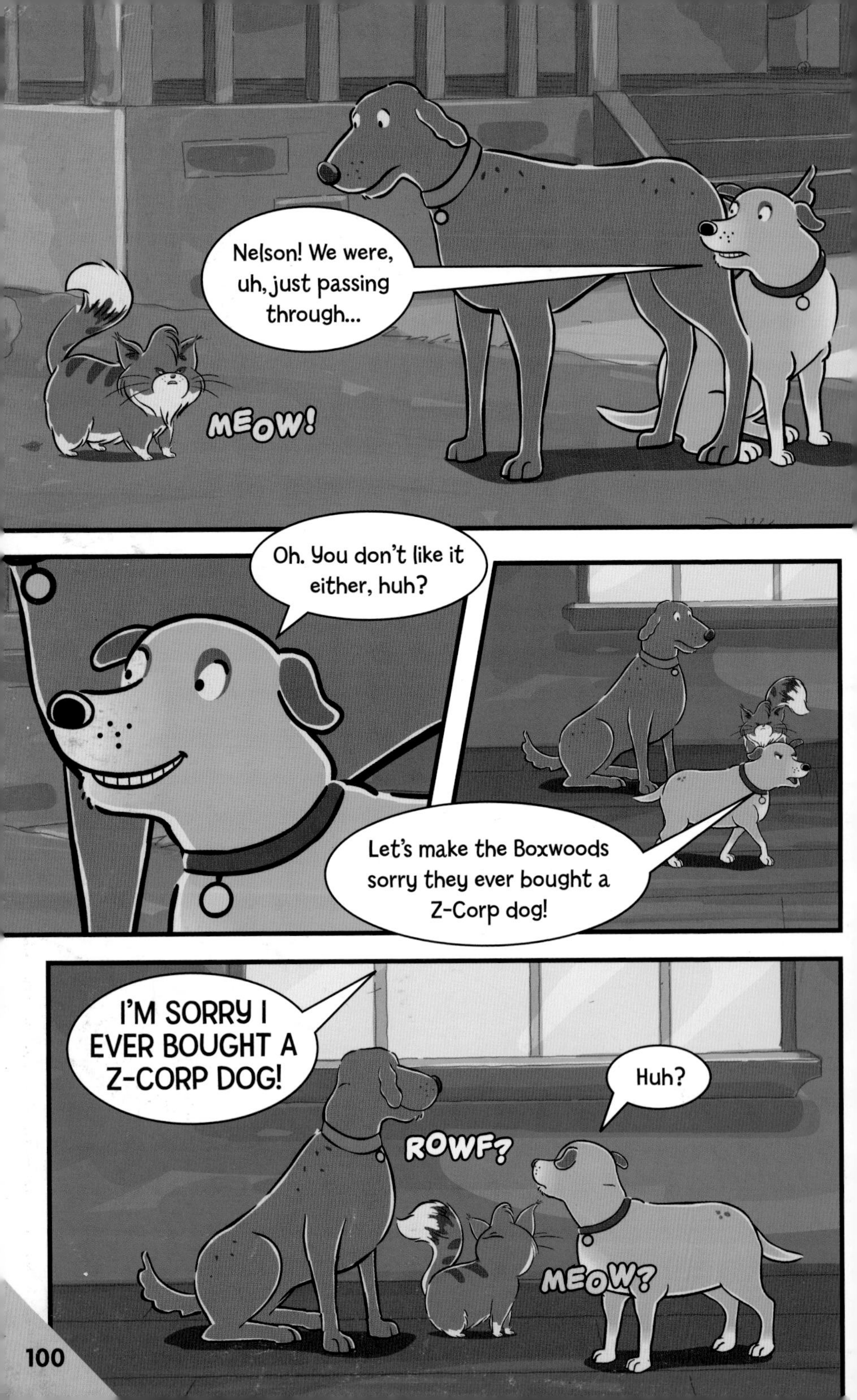
Nelson! We were, uh, just passing through...
MEOW!
Oh. You don't like it either, huh?
Let's make the Boxwoods sorry they ever bought a Z-Corp dog!
I'M SORRY I EVER BOUGHT A Z-CORP DOG!
Huh?
ROWF?
MEOW?

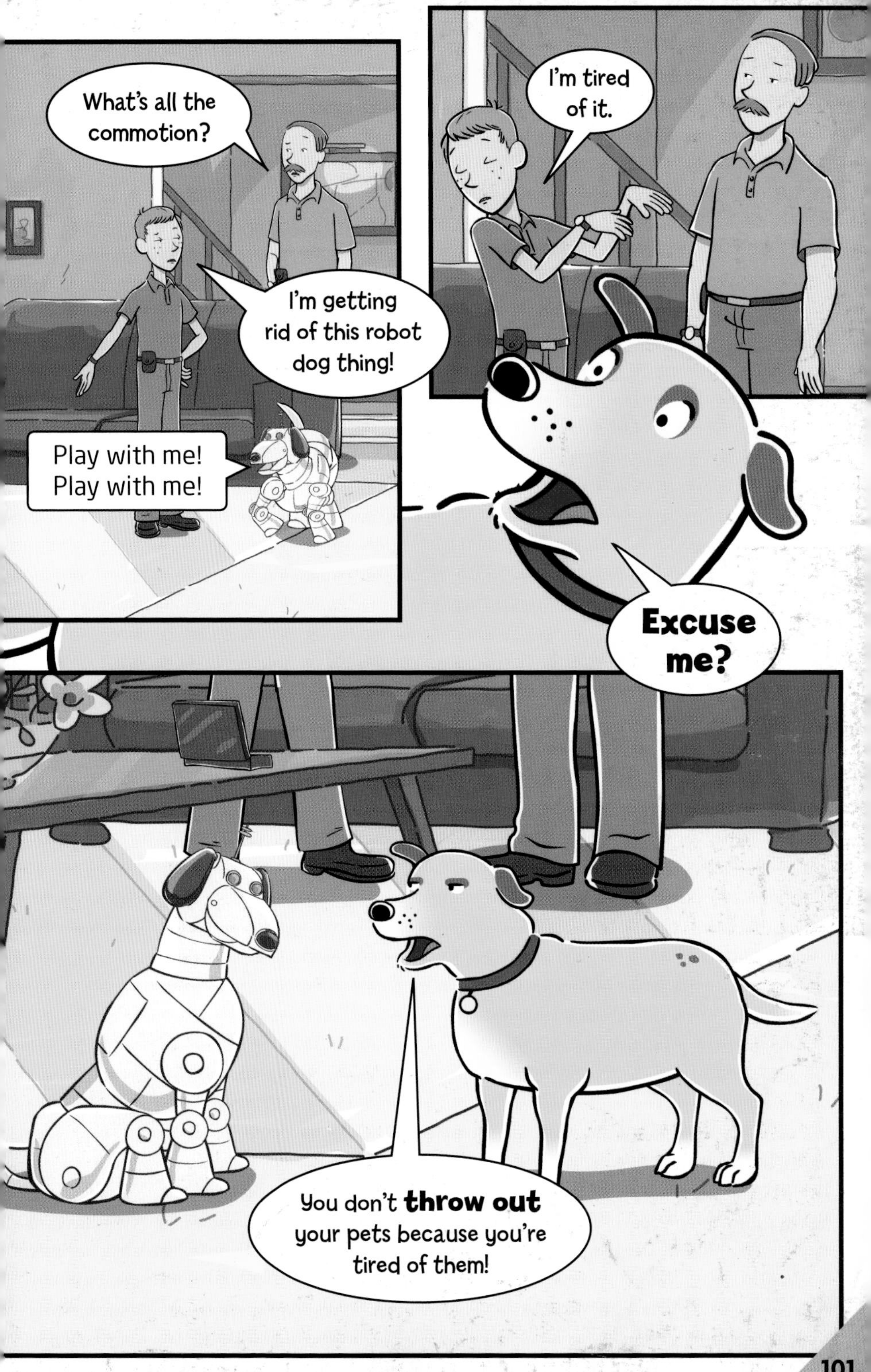
What's all the commotion?
I'm getting rid of this robot dog thing!
Play with me! Play with me!
I'm tired of it.
Excuse me?
You don't **throw out** your pets because you're tired of them!

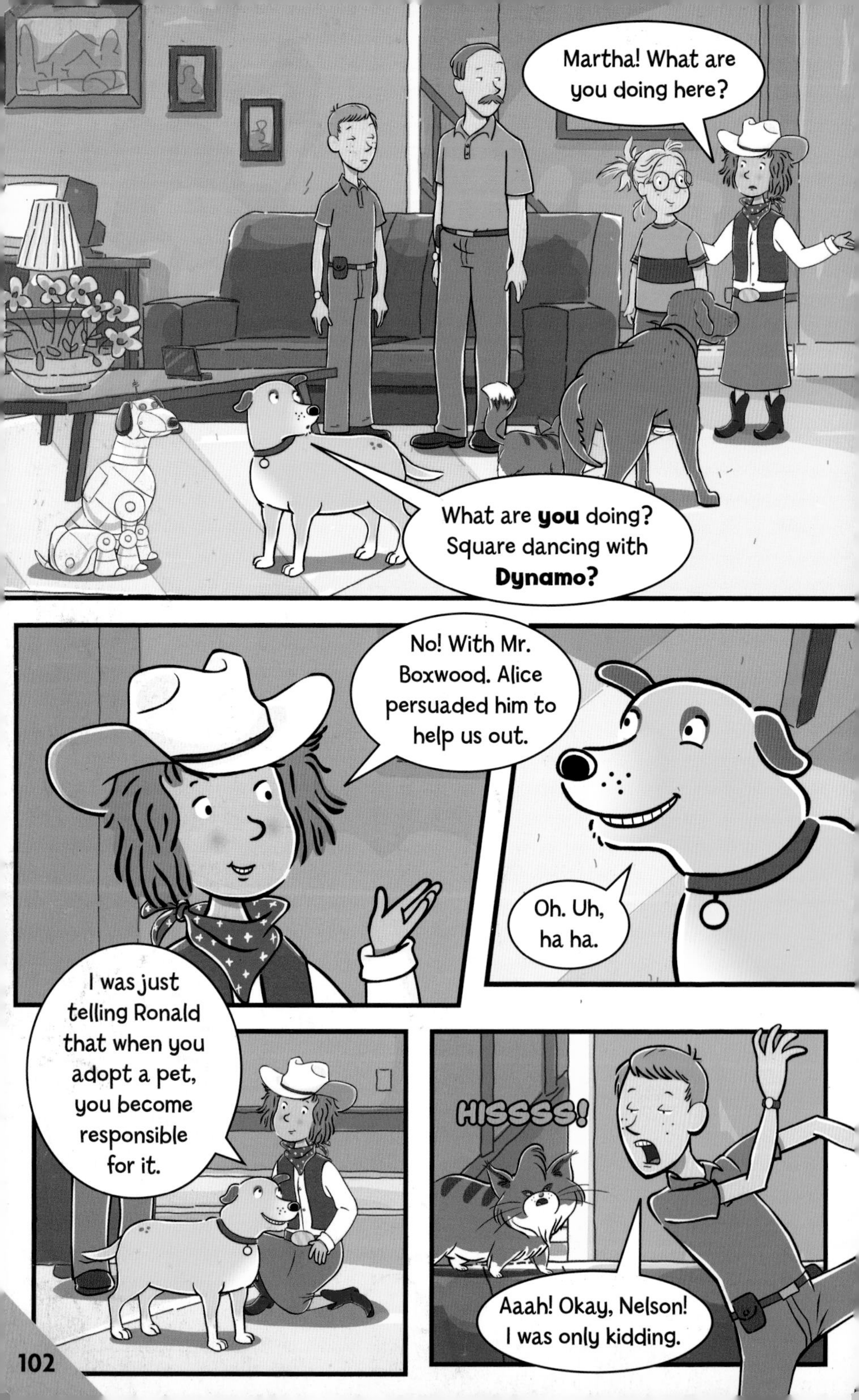
Martha! What are you doing here?
What are **you** doing? Square dancing with **Dynamo?**
No! With Mr. Boxwood. Alice persuaded him to help us out.
Oh. Uh, ha ha.
I was just telling Ronald that when you adopt a pet, you become responsible for it.
HISSSS!
Aaah! Okay, Nelson! I was only kidding.

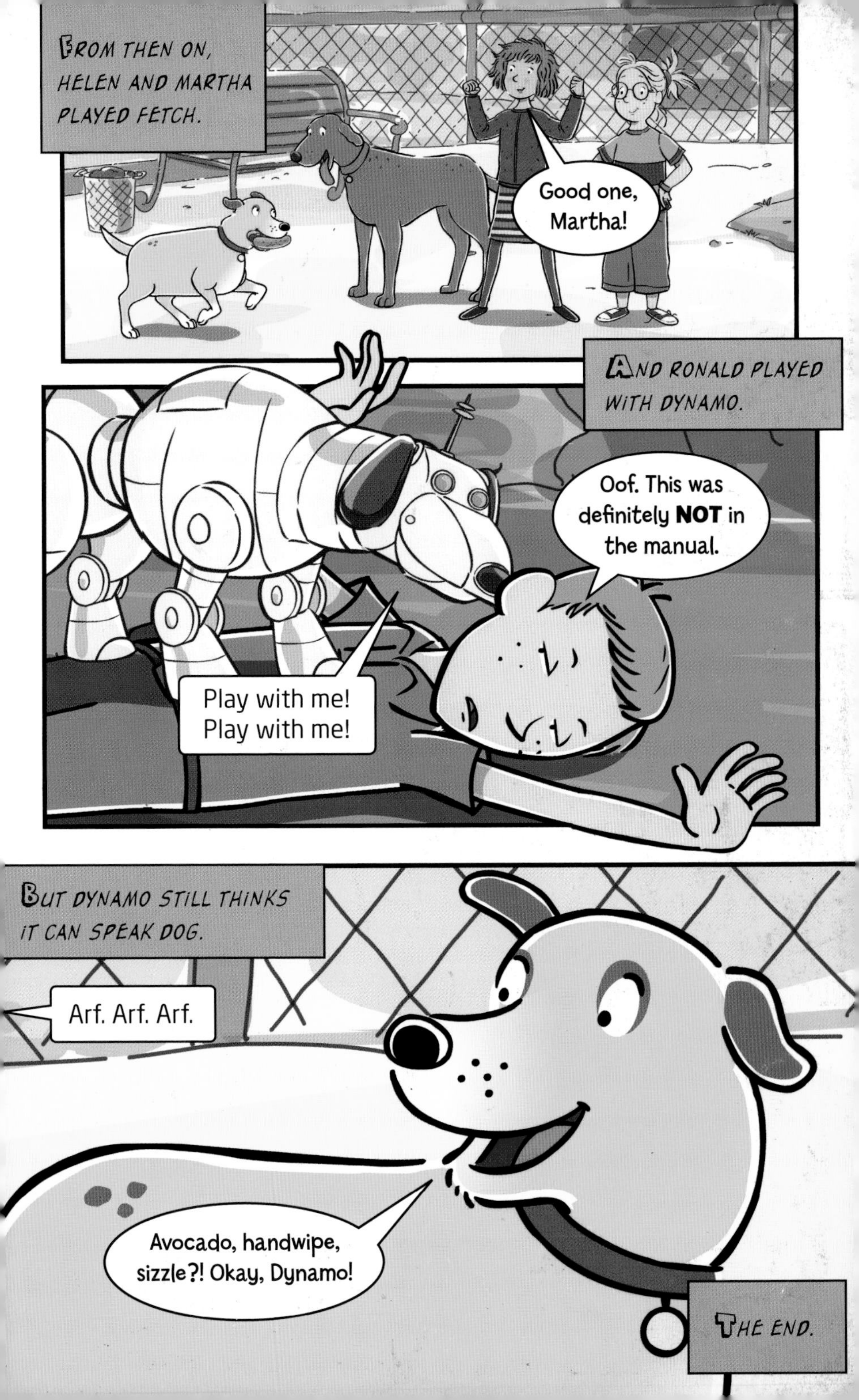
FROM THEN ON, HELEN AND MARTHA PLAYED FETCH.
Good one, Martha!
AND RONALD PLAYED WITH DYNAMO.
Oof. This was definitely NOT in the manual.
Play with me! Play with me!
BUT DYNAMO STILL THINKS IT CAN SPEAK DOG.
Arf. Arf. Arf.
Avocado, handwipe, sizzle?! Okay, Dynamo!
THE END.

A CANINE COMIC, STARRING YOU!

Imagine being on a neighborhood adventure with Martha and the dog pack. Create a comic book to tell your story.

Here's how:

1 Write your story.

2 Practice drawing your characters.

3 Draw borders for each of your comic book panels. Panels are usually read in a Z pattern, so readers follow the action from left to right, diagonally left, and then right.

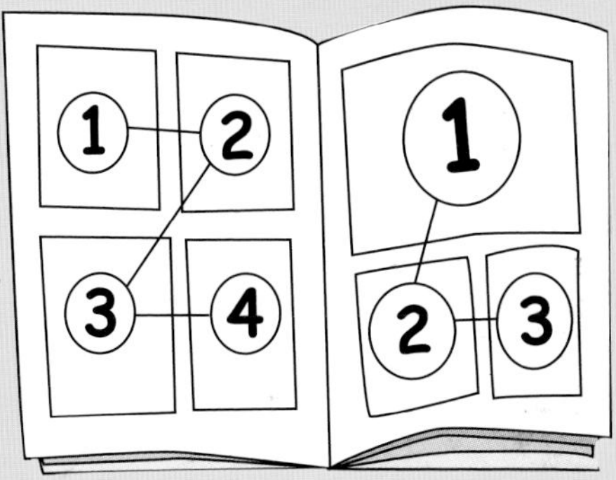
1
2
3
4
1
2
3

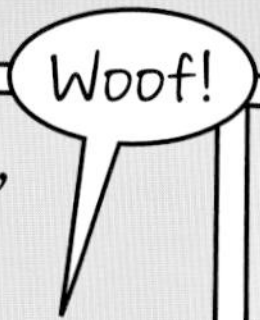
Woof!

4 Add speech bubbles, sound words, and other text. Make sure to leave room for the art.

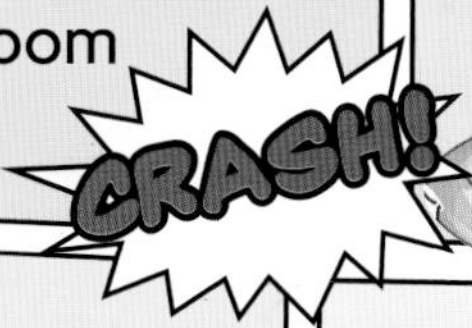
CRASH!

5 Sketch your drawings.

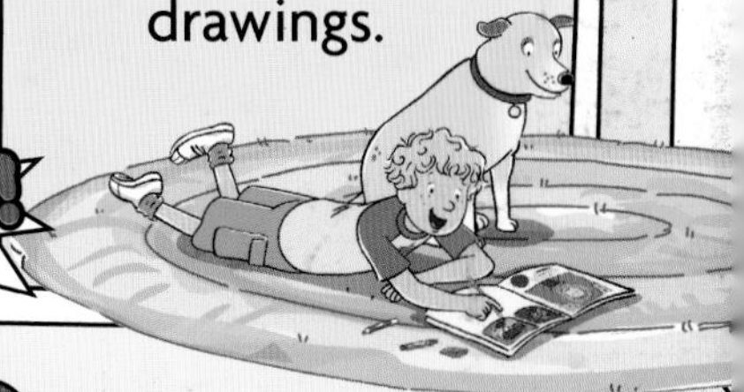

6 Trace the final sketches with ink. When the ink dries, erase your pencil lines.

7 Color the images.

8 When you're done, you can take your comic to a copy shop to have it printed.

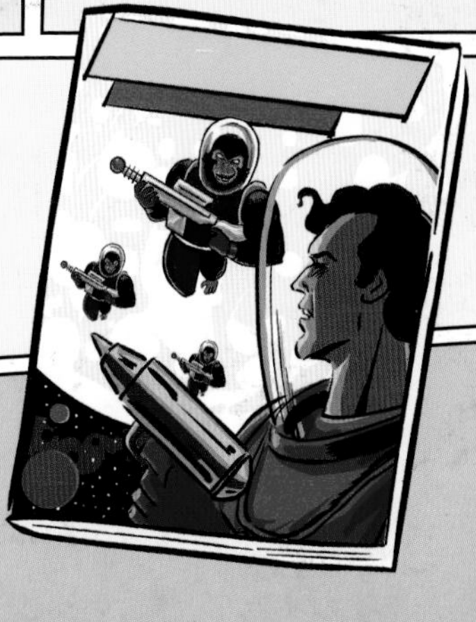

MARTHA'S STORY SQUARES

Stuck for ideas? Use Martha's Story Squares to spark an infinite number of comic book adventures. Close your eyes and drop your finger onto this page. Then see which square you've chosen. After picking five squares, create a comic that links together all five images. **Have fun!**

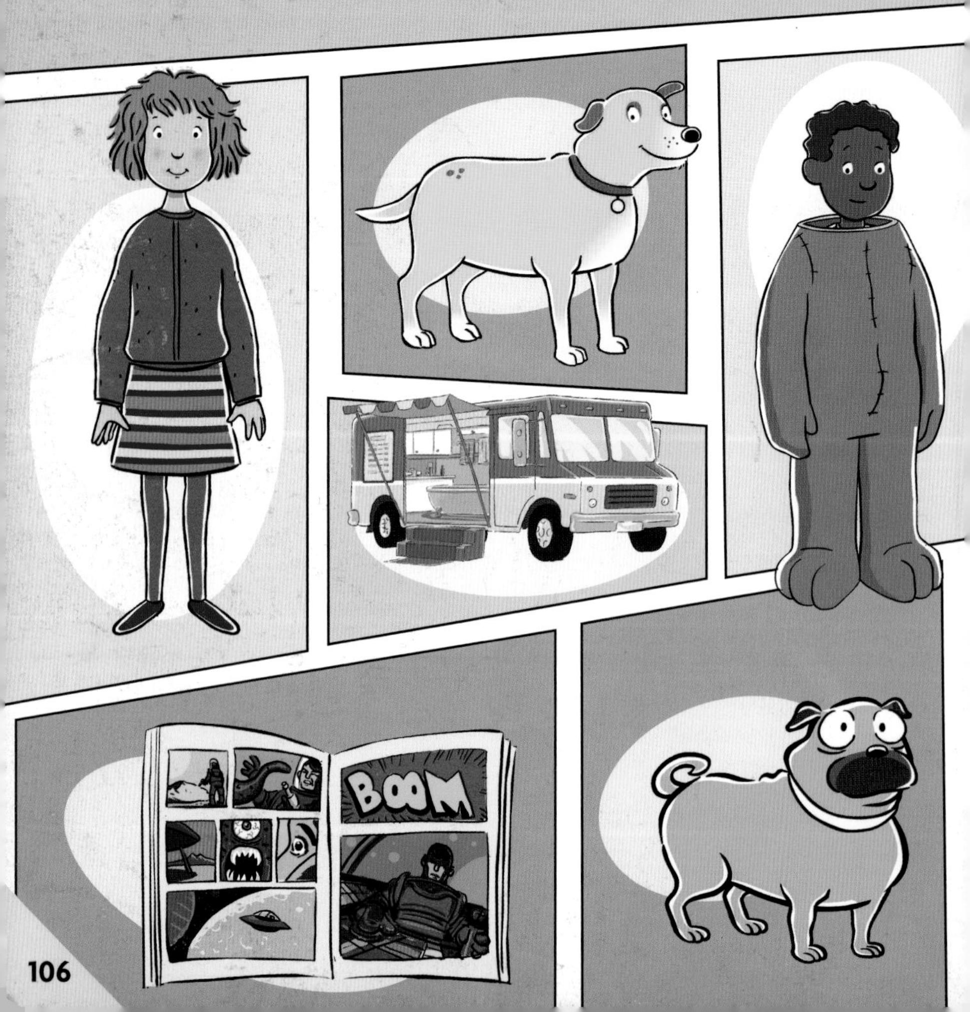
BOOM

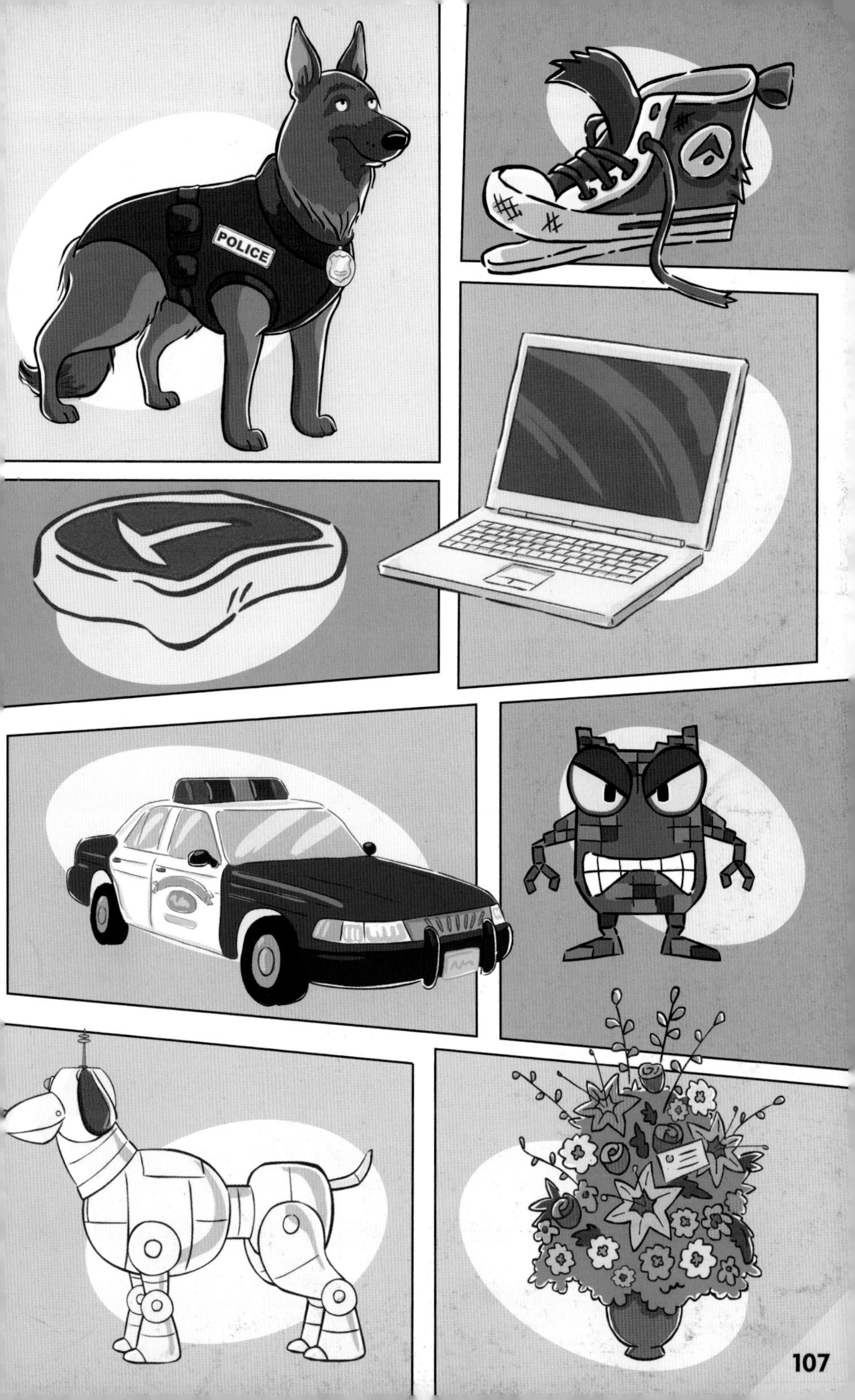
POLICE

DRAW DARING DOGS

Need some characters for your comic book adventure? Try tracing these canines! Place a sheet of thin drawing paper or tracing paper over the image you want to trace. Can you see the dog through your paper? Follow his or her outline with your pencil, and voila!

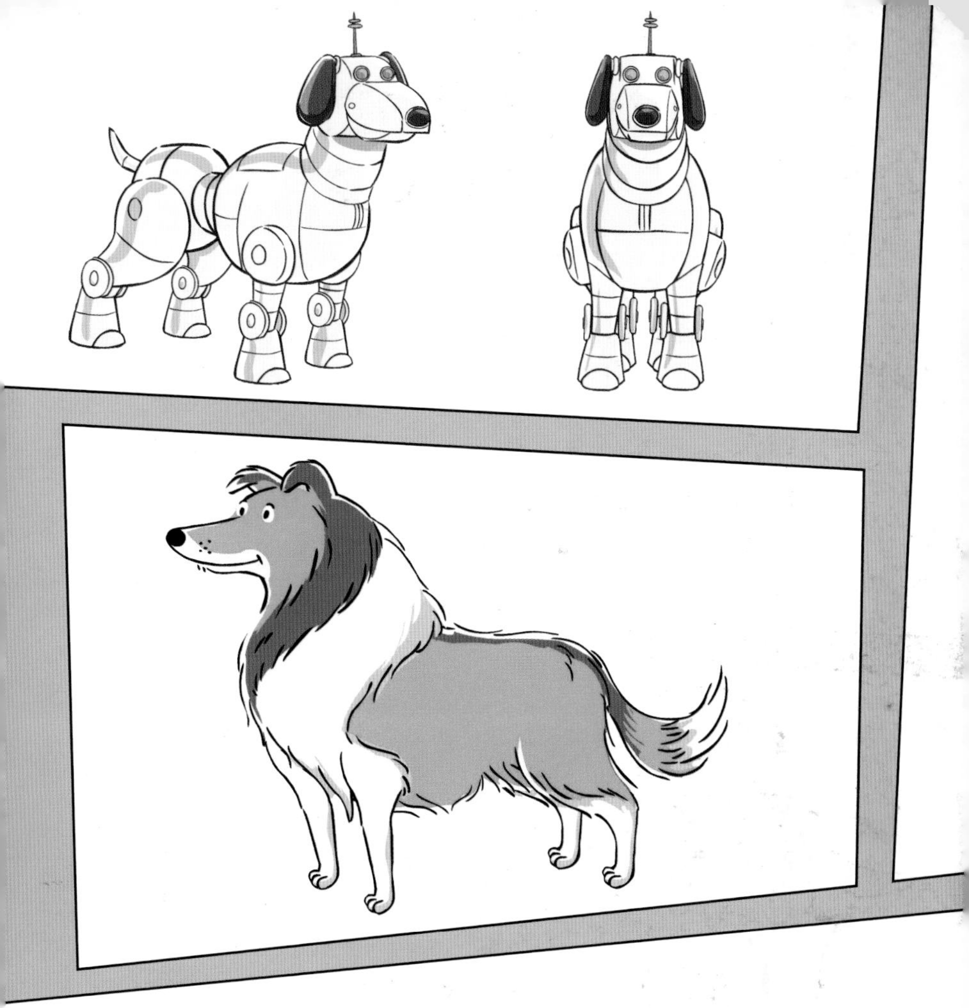

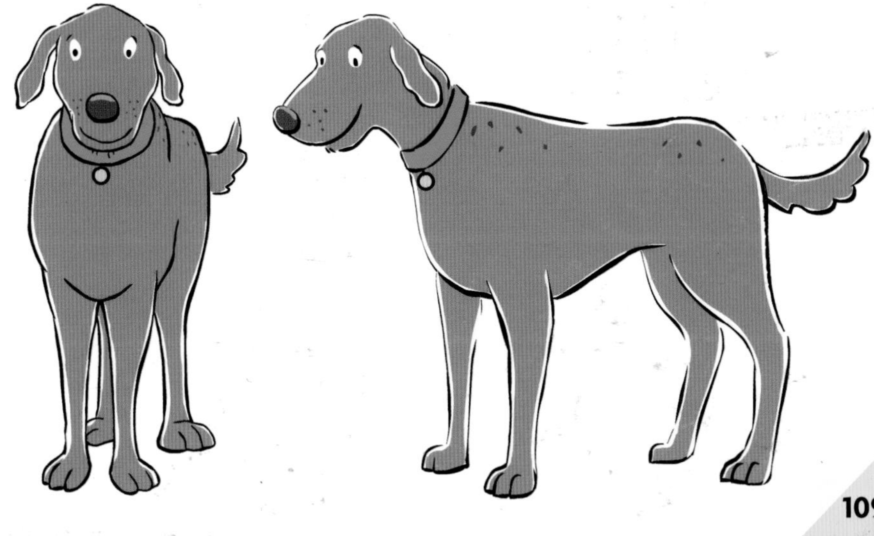

Be sure to check out all of these

MARTHA SPEAKS
adventures!

 Meet Martha

 Farm Dog Martha

 Toy Trouble

 Haunted House

 Thief of Hearts

 Good Luck, Martha

 Funny Bone Jokes and Riddles

A bloodhound!

 Martha Go, Go, Goes Green!

 Martha Stinks!

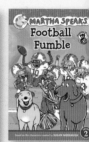 Football Fumble

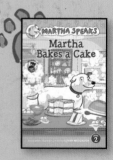 Martha Bakes a Cake

 Play Ball!

 Fireworks for All

 Martha Camps Out

Now available in Spanish bilingual!

Early readers

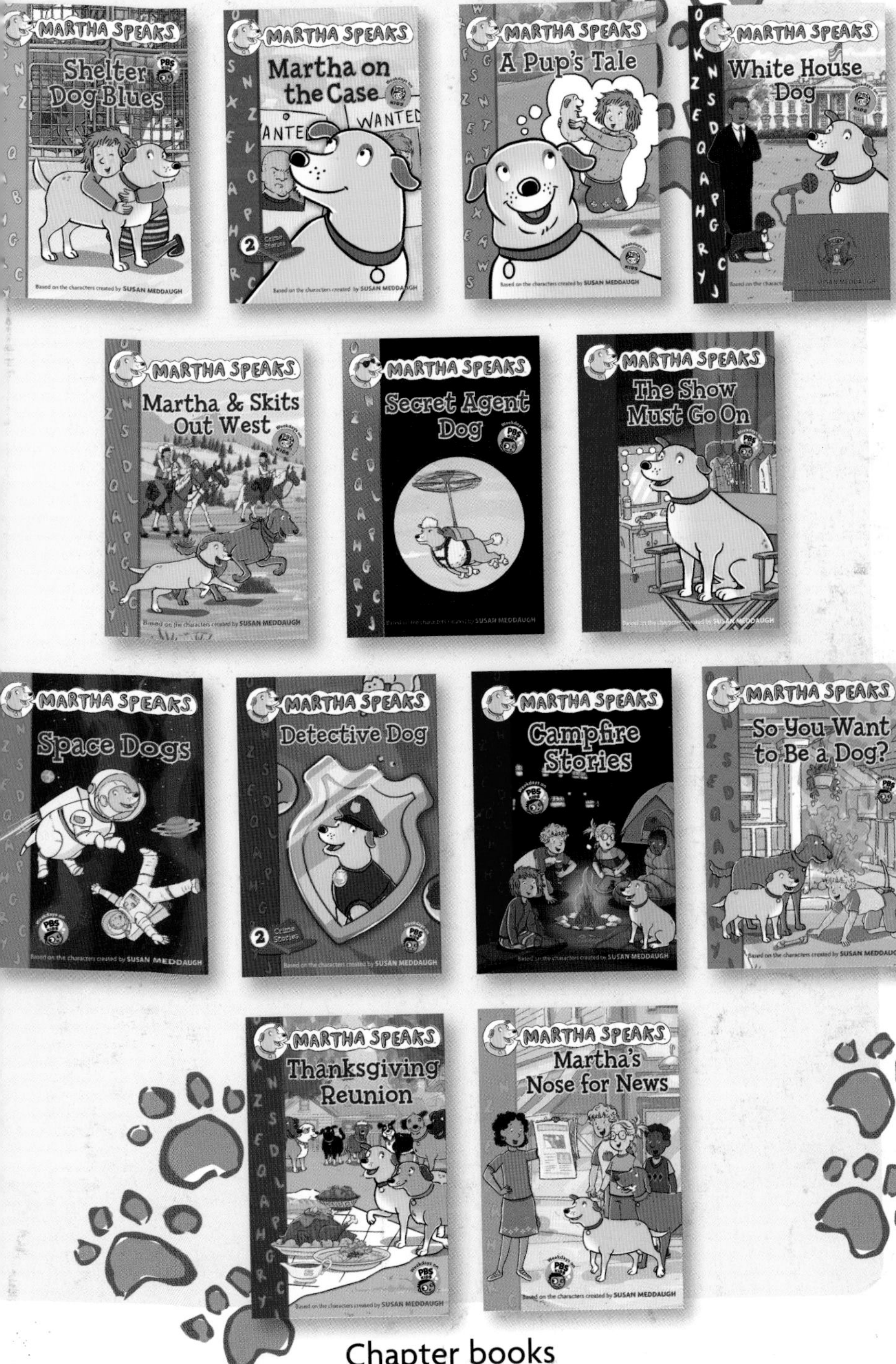
MARTHA SPEAKS
Shelter Dog Blues
Based on the characters created by SUSAN MEDDAUGH
MARTHA SPEAKS
Martha on the Case
WANTED
WANTED
2 Crime Stories
Based on the characters created by SUSAN MEDDAUGH
MARTHA SPEAKS
A Pup's Tale
Based on the characters created by SUSAN MEDDAUGH
MARTHA SPEAKS
White House Dog
MARTHA SPEAKS
Martha & Skits Out West
Based on the characters created by SUSAN MEDDAUGH
MARTHA SPEAKS
Secret Agent Dog
SUSAN MEDDAUGH
MARTHA SPEAKS
The Show Must Go On
MARTHA SPEAKS
Space Dogs
Based on the characters created by SUSAN MEDDAUGH
MARTHA SPEAKS
Detective Dog
2 Crime Stories
Based on the characters created by SUSAN MEDDAUGH
MARTHA SPEAKS
Campfire Stories
Based on the characters created by SUSAN MEDDAUGH
MARTHA SPEAKS
So You Want to Be a Dog?
Based on the characters created by SUSAN MEDDAUGH
MARTHA SPEAKS
Thanksgiving Reunion
Based on the characters created by SUSAN MEDDAUGH
MARTHA SPEAKS
Martha's Nose for News
Based on the characters created by SUSAN MEDDAUGH

Chapter books

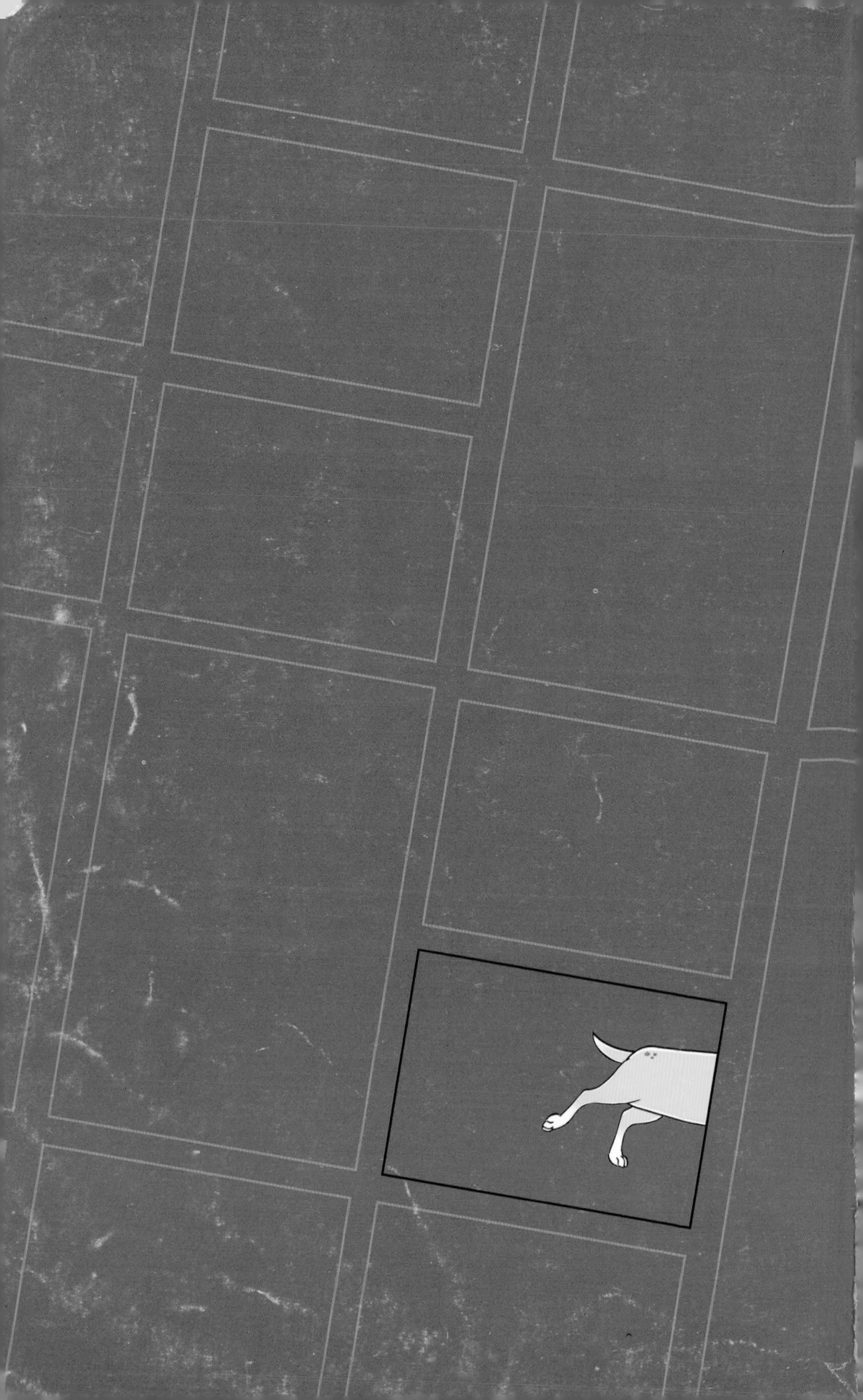